THE COLONEL'S MISTAKE

Published by Thomas & Mercer
P.O. Box 400818
Las Vegas, NV 89140

ISBN-13: 9781612183350
ISBN-10: 1612183352

THE
COLONEL'S
MISTAKE

DAN MAYLAND

f THOMAS & MERCER

To my mother, Nan
And to the memory of my father, Paul

Cursed are those who perform the prayer
unmindful of how they pray
who make of themselves a display
but hold back the small kindness.

—THE QUR'AN, SURA 107

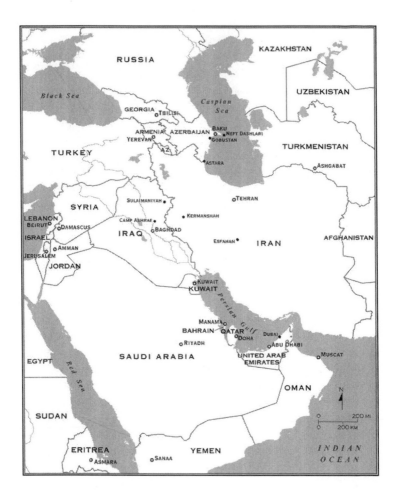

PART I

1

Baku, Azerbaijan

The first week of August was the hottest ever recorded in Baku. The stink of petroleum and sulfur fouled the stagnant air, grapevines wilted, and despite the halfhearted efforts of city employees who drove around in huge watering trucks, the leaves of the olive trees turned brown.

People looked to the sea and shook their heads, incredulous that there still was no sign of the *khazri*, the strong north wind that often blew down from Russia. It has to come soon, they said.

But this summer, what little wind there was drifted slowly up from the south, from the hell-furnaces of Iran's Kavir and Lut Deserts. The second week of August delivered no relief, nor the third. The children ran through the warm waters of Fountains Square each morning, but by noon the broiling city streets were empty except for air-conditioned cars and wild cats sleeping under sidewalk benches.

The *khazri* finally did come, but not until in the middle of the fourth week.

When it did, the cool wind brought back crowds and carnival music to the long promenade that ran along the Bay of Baku. And at night it brought people out onto their balconies.

⊠

Former CIA station chief Mark Sava had never known a city more in love with its balconies than Baku. Even the Soviets, when they'd defaced the city with their concrete housing developments, had been civilized enough to provide a private balcony for every apartment above the first floor. So it was a given that Sava's own apartment, part of a brand-new twenty-story complex, had one as well.

On the first night the wind started to blow, he was asleep outside on it. Asleep, that is, until someone started knocking on his door.

"Did you hear that?"

The woman who lay next to him slowly opened her eyes. "Hear what?"

"Someone at the door."

"No." The woman, whose name was Nika, lifted her head off his chest and stretched her bare, olive-skinned arms. "What time is it?"

A half-moon hung in the sky. Mark picked his wristwatch up off the ground and turned it so that it faced the bleak moonlight, but he didn't have his reading glasses on, and even squinting he couldn't distinguish between the hour and minute hands.

Nika took the watch from him and read it herself. "It's nearly midnight. I should call a taxi."

Mark figured maybe the knocking had been coming from a neighbor's apartment. "I'll drive you."

Nika smiled and settled her head back on Mark's shoulder. "OK."

They were pressed up tight next to each other, sharing a single cushioned lounge chair and surrounded by potted tomato plants. The feel of Nika's moist breath on his chest, and the heavy weight of her leg atop his own, annoyed him a little.

Eight stories below, the streets of Baku were silent except for the sound of an old Russian delivery truck rumbling over potholes. Even with the breeze, the air remained thick and hot, and it still stank of petroleum.

Mark kissed the top of Nika's head and closed his eyes, still groggy from the liter bottle of Georgian wine they'd finished earlier that evening. Her hair smelled of sand and saltwater and it reminded him of the day they'd spent together with her son.

But then the knocking started up again, this time with more authority. Nika stiffened. "It's late," she said.

"I'll see who it is."

Mark lifted himself out of the lounge chair and searched unsuccessfully for his underwear. Another series of rapid-fire knocks broke the silence. Screw it, he thought, giving up. He threw on his shirt and slacks and slipped his bare feet into a pair of black dress shoes. As he stepped inside his apartment, he heard a blunt object being hammered against his front door.

He put his eye to the peephole just in time to see a thickset man in a gray uniform holster his gun. Mark wondered how badly his door had been dented and how much it was going to cost him to fix it.

Ignorant fucker, he thought.

Behind him, Nika flipped on the light and began pulling up her skirt. Mark blinked as his eyes adjusted to the glare. The empty bottle of wine still sat on his kitchen counter. Nika's black hair was disheveled. He wanted to shut the light off and return to the quiet peace of the balcony.

Instead he put his eye back to the peephole and saw that several more uniformed men had appeared behind the guy with the gun. Mark turned to Nika.

"It's state security."

"What are they doing here?"

"I don't know."

"Have you done anything wrong?"

That was a considerably more complicated question than Nika intended it to be. "Not that I'm aware of," he said, by which he meant not lately.

The banging started up again. With each blow the wooden door flexed. Mark was afraid they were going to break it down.

"Get back," he said. "Hide in the bedroom."

"I'm not hiding."

Mark looked at Nika as she finished buttoning her blouse. She was roughly his height, with a full chest and hips that could appear either matronly or sexy depending on what she was wearing. And she was a true Azeri, born and raised in Azerbaijan, which meant she could be stubborn as hell. Mark saw that she was determined to stay put, decided maybe it was for the better, and opened the door.

Five men stood in front of him. Four were young guys, barely eighteen, he figured, whose uniforms were a little too big for them.

The fifth—the one holding the gun—was shorter, fatter, and older than the others. A brass star was affixed to the center of his cap.

"What can I do for you, officers?"

"Mark Sava?"

"Yes."

The brass-star Azeri glanced behind him, prompting two of his young recruits to step forward and grab Mark by the elbows.

"Get your fucking hands off me."

"You can't do this!" yelled Nika as Mark was being pushed out the door.

"Call the American embassy," he said. "Tell them what's happened."

Nika followed them down the hall, calling out for help. When the security officers got to the elevator, the brass-star guy turned around and pointed a pistol at her head.

"Get back."

"*Pokhuvu ye*," she said. *Eat your shit.*

The elevator doors closed and the men descended to the ground floor. Mark was escorted out of the building and shoved into the back of a prisoner transport van. Before closing the van doors, the Azeris handcuffed him and locked the chain connecting his handcuffs to a bolt on the floor.

"Where are you taking me?"

They ignored him.

"I have friends," said Mark as the doors were closing. "Orkhan Gambar, even Aliyev. Don't do something you'll regret."

2

After an hour the van came to an abrupt stop, and the back doors were yanked open. He looked out at an enormous stone building, lit by powerful xenon arc lights and encircled by a rusted ten-foot-tall chain-link fence. Beyond the fence lay only darkness and barren desert.

With a stifling feeling of dread, Mark realized he knew exactly where he was.

Two men unshackled his hands from the floor, grabbed him by the elbows, and frog-marched him to the entrance of the building.

"What am I being charged with?"

"You're not being charged with anything." Someone gave him a sharp push. "It's your friend you have to worry about."

"What friend?"

Daria Buckingham sat huddled on the concrete floor of an unbearably hot cell, her arms wrapped around her knees. Stone walls, grimy and black from the hands of previous prisoners, enclosed her on three sides. Boyishly slender, she looked much younger than her thirty-two years.

Mark approached to within a few inches of the metal bars that formed the fourth side of the cell. The only light came from a single bulb, which dangled from a thin electric wire. The nearby cells were empty and the guards had disappeared, although Mark assumed they were close. A small video camera sat on a tripod right outside the cell. The recording light was on.

Daria stood up, wobbling a bit because the heel from one of her black leather pumps had broken off. She wore a pleated black skirt and a frilly short-sleeved silk blouse. Her face was smudged with dirt.

"Jesus, Daria."

"It's a long story." She held her head high and tried to smile, but her attempt at bravado wasn't convincing.

"You OK?"

"I'm fine."

Her face—ordinarily striking, marked by high cheekbones and a wide, pretty smile—was distorted with lines of worry.

"What are you doing here? What am I doing here?"

Gobustan Prison was a strict regime prison that housed many of Azerbaijan's criminals and political prisoners. Mark knew Daria was neither. She was a CIA operative, and a privileged one at that—the daughter of wealthy Washington diplomats, a product of Duke University and Georgetown Law.

"They're holding me as a suspect."

"For what?" Mark took a step closer to her and lightly gripped the metal bars of the cell.

"You didn't hear?"

He slowly shook his head.

"Wasn't it on TV?"

"I got rid of my TV."

She approached the bars of the cell and placed her hands over his own. "Jack Campbell was assassinated," she whispered urgently.

Mark remembered a competent, uncontroversial deputy secretary of defense who had served for two years and retired over a decade ago.

"Where?"

"Here! In Baku, at the oil convention. Shot in the head."

In years past Mark had always attended the big annual international oil and gas convention in downtown Baku. But this year he'd forgotten that it was even taking place.

"It happened this afternoon, around four."

At four Mark had still been at the beach with Nika and her nine-year-old son, helping to build an enormous sand castle. When they'd finally left, Nika's son had asked to listen to a Russian pop music station on the car radio. After knocking back four beers on the beach, Mark had been game for anything. No one had bothered with the news.

"He was here for the convention. Somebody killed him a couple minutes before he was supposed to give his speech." Daria paused. "I was alone with him when he was shot, Mark. Standing right next to him, in one of the back rooms off the stage. It was awful."

Mark stared at her for a moment. "Why were you alone with him?"

"I was assigned to be his translator." She relayed the details of the shooting, adding that she'd had her gun on her and had tried to shoot back. "The Azeris found me next to Campbell. I was trying to help him, trying to keep his head together, but it was just me and it all kept coming and coming...When the Azeris showed up, they pulled me off him and now they think I had something to do with it."

Mark looked at the smudges on Daria's face. They weren't dirt, he realized.

She gripped his hands tighter—which made Mark uneasy. Despite Daria's petite size, of all the CIA operations officers who'd worked under him she'd been the most capable of taking care of herself. For her to be this rattled, he suspected things were even worse than she was letting on.

He tried to read in her eyes the things that she might not want to say aloud, in front of the video camera. And he wondered why she'd felt the need to be carrying a gun at the convention.

"The embassy know you've been taken?"

"The Iranian embassy does."

"Great."

Daria must have had her fake Iranian passport on her when she'd been arrested, Mark realized. Which meant the Azeris would feel free to treat her like shit.

"The guards messing with you?"

She shrugged.

"What happened?"

3

Daria felt a sharp push from behind.

"Sürðtlð!" Faster!

Although she was blindfolded, the chorus of fuck-me suck-me catcalls and din of inmates banging on metal bars told her she was inside some kind of prison.

She was led down one hall, and then another. The banging stopped. A key turned in a door lock. Someone pushed her forward and removed her blindfold, revealing a metal cot and a filthy toilet hole.

One of her three guards kicked her inside the prison cell with a foot to her backside. As she rose to her knees, she felt a prickly beard on the nape of her neck, then wet lips, then a nose.

Instinctively she snapped her head straight back as hard as she could.

The guard behind her reacted by clubbing the side of her head with his fist. She scurried across the floor, quickly zeroed in on another guard—the one wearing a wedding ring, the one looking ashamed—made eye contact with him, and held it.

"Buyurun! Please!" she called out as she tried to fend off the guard with the bleeding nose.

"Get off her!" said the ashamed-looking guard. "She's evidence! I'm not losing this job because of your dick."

The guards had backed off. The cell door had clanged shut.

But she had made an enemy.

"How bad was it?"

Daria looked at Mark, trying to gauge whether it was worth telling him. He had a sharp, square jaw and dark, heavy-lidded, wide-set brown eyes that made him look a little mean. But he'd never been mean to her. He was only average height, his hands were smallish, his palms smooth, and his hair was beginning to gray. Prior to serving as chief of station/Azerbaijan, he'd been an analyst.

She thought of the guards and found it easy to imagine one of them grabbing Mark by the collar of his dress shirt and beating the piss out of him.

"Just words," she said.

"How'd your shirt get ripped?"

"Listen, I told the guards that you knew me and that you could help put things right. They already had my ATM card. I said I'd give them my PIN if they would just let me contact you."

"I severed all my contacts with the Agency six months ago, Daria. For real, I don't even consult."

She could tell he was speaking carefully, for the benefit of the video camera. And she suspected he was stretching the truth. But he was no longer running the Azeri station, and that was what counted.

"I didn't have anyone else I could turn to."

Which wasn't true. But she was hoping Mark would understand that she couldn't risk contacting any active CIA officers who were stationed in Baku—that she'd contacted him, a former CIA station chief who'd worked closely with the Azeri intelligence service over the years, in order to hint at her relationship to the CIA, so the Azeris wouldn't think she was an Iranian assassin, without completely blowing her cover.

Mark stared at her until she dropped her hands from his, turned her head, and said, "I'm sorry for dragging you into this. I thought maybe they'd just call you and—"

"What do you need, Daria? If I can help I will."

"Make sure the right people know I'm here," she said. "And do it as quickly as you can. That's all."

4
=

Mark was dumped just outside the prison gates, which meant that he had to walk three kilometers back to the dusty town of Gobustan—an indignity that someone of his former stature should not have been made to suffer, he thought. It was still dark out and he was tired and irritated that he wasn't wearing socks or underwear. His feet started to blister and little pebbles kept getting stuck in his shoes.

You've got to be kidding me, he thought.

He wondered how alarmed Nika would be by this whole incident. As far as she knew, he was a former foreign service officer who'd decided on a midlife career change. Seeing him get carted off like a common criminal by the Azeri security forces would make her scared. And curious. He hoped she'd taken a cab back to her parents' place, where she lived with her son.

In Gobustan he managed to convince a young guy who was helping his father open an AzPetrol station to drive him back to Baku for ten Shirvans, payable upon arrival. They careened up the two-lane highway that hugged the coast of the Caspian Sea, driving through a blasted desert wasteland in a wretched old Russian Volga that had dirty blankets for seat covers. The windows of the Volga were closed and the vent fan was going full blast, emitting a piercing whine and blowing in air that smelled like car exhaust.

To the right, across an expanse of calm sea, massive offshore oil rigs appeared to float above the water in the serene orange light of dawn.

※

Nika had left his apartment, but when he called her on her cell phone she picked up after the first ring.

"Where are you?"

Her worried tone made him wonder whether she'd slept at all. It also surprised him a bit. They'd only been dating for a couple months. Neither of them had mentioned love or anything like that.

"Back at my apartment."

"Are you in trouble?"

"Not really."

"I called the US embassy. They said they couldn't do anything about it until morning."

"This was all just about some foreign service guy I know. He got picked up drunk on the street and thought maybe I could help him get out of trouble, so he started throwing my name around."

"And that is why they have to cart you off like that in the middle of the night?"

"Yeah, I'm thinking of registering a complaint with my elected representative."

"What?"

Although Nika was pretty fluent in English, sarcasm sometimes went over her head.

"I'm just kidding," said Mark, thinking how all it took was a little brush with his old life to bring back the old habits. While working for the CIA, there had been a lot to be sarcastic about. But after quitting he'd resolved not to spend the rest of his life looking at everything with a jaded eye. "Listen," he said, in as pleasant a voice as he could muster. "I'm sorry about what happened last night. It was a little crazy, I know, but nothing we need to worry about now. Thanks for calling the embassy."

He thought about how she'd held her ground in front of the security goons and it made him like her even more than he already did.

"I'm just glad you're OK," she sighed. "Sometimes when these things happen people don't come back."

Mark agreed to tell her all about it over dinner at her place that evening.

After hanging up, he put on a pair of underwear and socks—which at this point felt like a luxury—and retrieved his silver-rimmed reading glasses and black diplomatic passport.

Finally, before leaving for the embassy, he gave his apartment a cursory inspection. The place almost looked as though it had been searched, although he didn't think it had. An orange beach towel lay on the floor outside the bathroom. An unwashed plate from his breakfast yesterday sat on the tile counter near the sink. In the spare bedroom, his computer was surrounded by hand-written notes related to the book he was working on, tentatively titled *Soviet Intelligence Operations in the Azerbaijan Democratic Republic, 1918–1922*.

Six months ago, Mark would have never let his apartment get so cluttered because it would have made it too difficult to assess whether anything had been moved in his absence. When he was with the CIA, everything had been assigned a precise space. Now there was chaos.

It was only six thirty in the morning and traffic was light. A few soot-covered minibuses rumbled down the streets. The sidewalk sweepers were out, mostly old women pushing oversized brooms that resembled bundles of kindling. The sight of them sweeping between mulberry trees reminded Mark of why he liked Baku, of why staying on to teach at Western University—to burnish his slender academic credentials before applying for a better teaching job in the US or Europe—hadn't been such a bad option.

He'd get this matter with Daria settled quickly, he thought. The death of Campbell was a huge deal, but once the US embassy crew figured out a way to convince the Azeris that Daria didn't have anything to do with it, she'd be fine. He figured he could get back to his apartment by seven thirty, sleep until noon, and then work on his book for most of the afternoon until it was time for dinner with Nika.

The embassy was on Azadlyq Avenue, a major thoroughfare that ran north out of the city. Four marines, instead of the usual two, were standing guard outside. All carried M-16 rifles. Since the embassy marines were never posted in Baku for very long, Mark didn't recognize any of them.

"*Qapali*," said the one manning the guardhouse. "Understand? Closed. Come back nine o'clock."

He eyed Mark suspiciously.

Mark hadn't shaved in two days and was dressed like a typical Azeri guy—black dress shoes, gray polyester-blend dress slacks, and a rumpled black dress shirt with extra wide lapels. It was the same outfit he'd worn to the beach.

He took out his diplomatic passport, thankful that he'd ignored the order from Langley to trade it in for a regular one.

"I'm an American. And I know the embassy doesn't open until nine, but I need to talk to George Logan right now."

The marine examined Mark's passport.

"He's the counselor for political affairs," said Mark.

"I know who he is."

No you don't, thought Mark. The marines weren't in the loop when it came to knowing who worked for the Agency and who didn't. "Just tell him I'm here to see him. He'll grant the access."

The marine picked up the guardhouse phone and asked whether Logan had arrived at work yet. He hadn't.

On an ordinary day, Mark wouldn't have expected George Logan, his successor as chief of station, to be at work so early. But this was no ordinary day. A former deputy secretary of defense had been shot in downtown Baku. Logan should have been in his office at the embassy, working the phones and the cables all night, acting as a liaison between his in-country operations officers, Washington, and the Azeris, trying to figure out who'd killed Campbell.

Maybe Logan was meeting with the Azeris now, thought Mark. But if that were the case, someone still had to be manning the phones.

"Then let me talk to his secretary, or the foreign-service officer assigned to him."

The marine studied Mark's passport again.

"This is important," said Mark. "It has to do with Campbell's assassination. You know about that, don't you?"

The marine didn't respond to Mark's patronizing tone but he picked up the phone again.

A few minutes later a heavyset, plain-faced woman emerged from the embassy. They met in the courtyard in front of the building.

DAN MAYLAND

"Thanks for coming down, Vicky," he said to her. "I know it must be chaos up there."

"What do you need?" She sounded frustrated. And dead tired.

"For you to put me in touch with Logan."

"I can't."

Mark knew that Logan carried a beeper twenty-four hours a day. A chief of station was always accessible, which was a part of the reason why Mark had left. In the old days, he might have had contact with Washington once a day or so, sometimes even once a week. But now, with e-mail and videoconferencing, it was like Washington practically ran the station.

Mark figured Vicky was just giving him the brush-off because she and Logan were busy beyond belief trying to deal with Washington and didn't want him complicating matters.

"Listen, I don't care how you do it, or who you wake up, or what Logan told you to tell me. I've got to talk to him. I have information about one of his officers that he needs to know. It's important. It has to do with Campbell."

"You don't understand, Mark. I've been trying to reach him all night. He's not calling in. The whole seventh floor is pissed to hell," she said, referring to senior management in Washington, DC.

"You've tried the direct line to his apartment?"

"Of course."

Mark studied her face again. Maybe it wasn't fatigue that was getting to her. Maybe it was worry. "Is there any reason he'd be AWOL?"

"Sometimes he forgets to turn on his beeper. He might not even know what happened."

"You try the Trudeau House?"

"Four times. No one's answering."

- 18 -

"The main crew usually doesn't get there until seven thirty."

"I know. That's when I'm planning on calling for the fifth time."

Mark envisioned Daria sitting out in Gobustan Prison. He didn't think the Azeris would be too rough with her, especially if his visit made them think she had ties to the CIA. But still, there was that wide, pretty mouth and damn-near-perfect skin...Her American mutt genes had mixed with Iranian genes in a way that was undeniably attractive. It was one of the reasons, in addition to being bright and too driven for her own good, that she'd been able to recruit so many male agents.

She would be a temptation. The sooner Logan started working her case, the better.

"I'll go by," said Mark. "One of the morning crew might know where he is."

5

Washington, DC

The colonel lowered his head and began to speak the Lord's Prayer.
Pater noster, qui es in caelis, sanctificetur nomen tuum...

After finishing, he looked up at the candles flickering near the empty white-marble altar, hoping for a sign. Eventually his knees began to ache.

The moral law prohibits exposing someone to mortal danger without grave reason, as well as refusing assistance to a person in danger.

He mumbled the words from the catechism in the dim light.

Grave reason, grave reason...that was the crux of it. There had been no grave reason for Daria to be exposed to mortal danger. To refuse to assist her now would be a mortal sin.

But he had already tried, and failed, to assist her. He'd sent Campbell.

There were other options. But if those options meant prolonging the life of the Iranian regime, would he not be committing another mortal sin of sorts?

The defense of the common good requires that an unjust aggressor be rendered unable to cause harm.

The colonel made the sign of the cross and touched his forehead to the back of the wooden pew in front of him.

He wished it were Sunday morning. The sound of the priest at the altar, facing away from the congregation as he spoke the same words in Latin that had been intoned for centuries—words that were uncorrupted by modern, watered-down notions of good and evil—was always a comfort to him. He only attended the old Latin masses now, the Tridentine ceremonies that reminded him of when he used to sit in the pews between his mother and father, all three of them hungry from skipping breakfast so that when they knelt to receive communion they could do so with a clear conscience.

The colonel looked at his watch. In an hour he would need to be at the White House. In the meantime, he would keep praying for guidance.

6

Mark hailed a cab and got dropped off near the crenellated walls of medieval Baku. At a street-level Turkish breakfast buffet, he bought a round piece of *simit* bread and black tea to go.

A short walk brought him to a 125-year-old limestone mansion. Covered in gnarled grapevines and topped with gargoyles, it was a relic of Baku's first oil-boom years, when rich Europeans like the Nobels and the Rothschilds had developed the oil fields in and around the city. Following the Cold War, the mansion had proved attractive to the CIA because after seventy years of vodka-swilling Russians using it as an overcrowded tenement house, no one had questioned the need to completely gut the place—making it easy for the Agency to install all the surveillance and security equipment that was needed.

Mark pushed the button on the intercom to the left of the brass plate that read *Trudeau House International, Inc.*, allegedly a financial services company run by expatriate Canadians.

He'd get in and get out, he thought as he tapped his foot impatiently, taking a swig of tea and looking up at one of the gargoyles, a smiling chimera.

It was seven thirty. By eight thirty, he figured, he could be back at his apartment. He wouldn't get much sleep, but if he pounded enough Turkish coffee this afternoon he'd be able to get some work done.

As he waited for a response, he wondered if the place had changed much since he'd left. He remembered a large oak receptionist's desk in the entrance hall and well-appointed offices where the Trudeau House's clients—mainly Azeris with newfound oil wealth and connections to the upper echelons of government—were wooed with excellent CIA-subsidized investment returns. The upper levels housed five additional offices that had sat vacant, waiting for operations officers who had been expected but had never arrived.

Mark felt a spike in his anxiety level until he reminded himself that he'd left all that political crap behind. He'd changed since quitting the Agency, he thought, and for the better. Teaching college kids about international relations, building a sand castle on the beach with a kid and his mom—those were the kinds of things that were important to him now.

No one responded to the intercom. He pushed the button again and waited, for longer this time. Again, nothing. Someone should have been there by now, asking politely what the hell he wanted. Unless standards had really slipped under Logan, which Mark thought probable.

He rang one more time and then walked to the end of the block. He turned right, then right again, down an alley that ran behind the Trudeau House and a series of adjacent buildings. He stopped at a steel door that had a small keypad above the knob. The security codes were changed on a weekly basis, but he'd helped implement the system and knew an override code that had worked in the past.

He typed in the code, opened the door, and descended a flight of stairs into a bare basement with a low ceiling and a stained but clean concrete floor. At the far end of the room stood another steel door. He typed in a second override code and this door opened as well.

"Hello?"

He ascended a staircase that led into a narrow back hallway on the first floor. He called out again, more loudly this time.

Still no answer. When he opened the door to the interior of the Trudeau House, no one greeted him, a lapse he found deeply unsettling. By now security should have been there. The entrance to the room where all the exterior camera feeds were monitored was a few feet ahead. The door was cracked open a few inches, another anomaly.

He knocked briefly before pushing the door open. Everything was in its place—the security monitors, a black swivel chair, a metal desk, and the central computer, which was used to set all the security codes. Only the guard was missing. Then Mark noticed that all the security monitor disks—which normally lined the shelves on the back wall—had disappeared.

He backed out of the room and slowly made his way, via another narrow hallway, to the formal entrance hall in the front of the building. Before opening the door, he paused for a moment, listening for sounds of people on the other side. All he could hear was the hum of the central air conditioner and the muted rumble of cars on the street.

He turned the doorknob. As he stepped into the entrance hall, he noticed that the beige carpet and the cream-colored wall behind the oak desk were stained dark brown with...he squinted, trying to make it out...

His eyesight was going. He really should get contacts, he thought.

Mark looked down at his feet and saw that he'd inadvertently stepped on a piece of human tissue, from what body part he couldn't begin to guess. The brown on the wall was dried blood. Three feet to his left, a body lay facedown, perfectly still, arms at his sides, palms up. A puddle of light from a street-facing window illuminated the man's head, a portion of which was missing. Beyond him, Mark could see more bodies.

He pivoted, and the thought of running back the same way he'd come crossed his mind. But if the killers were still in the building, they most certainly already knew he was there. If they wanted to take him out, then he was already dead. He didn't have a weapon. His heart was going like crazy.

Mark turned his gaze back to the main room. Once he really started looking, he couldn't stop himself from staring, struck by the fact that he'd been alive for as long as he had, that he hadn't just accidentally cut himself and bled to death. Because the people in front of him reminded him that bleeding to death was a terribly easy thing to do.

He approached the bodies so that he could see who they were. One was the security guard. He'd died with his gun drawn in front of a tiled fireplace. The body Mark had first noticed he now identified as a twenty-five-year-old operations officer, a man who'd been posing as a Canadian financial wizard. He'd been a top recruit from MIT and Mark had been his mentor. The third was a matronly Canadian woman who'd served as the administrator of the Trudeau House without ever knowing it was a CIA front company. She was slumped against the wall behind her desk, beneath an elongated brass sconce. Her chair had fallen over, likely pushed away, Mark thought, as she'd scrambled to try to save herself. All the bodies were riddled with bullet holes; Mark counted twenty, even thirty in each of them.

He breathed slowly, gaping at the scene sprawled out before him, searing the visual image into his memory. He wondered what could have led to such a brazen, unprecedented attack. The CIA had been operating in Baku ever since the Soviet Union had fallen apart, and no one had ever been killed. It was considered a friendly posting. The fact that the CIA had let him stay in Baku after resigning stood as a testament to that.

But it was a friendly posting in a bad neighborhood, with Iran to the south, Russia and Chechnya to the north, and a simmering civil war with the Armenians to the west. Somehow, Mark thought, his mind racing, some of that violence must have spilled over. A levee had broken.

He searched the first-floor offices. They were empty and undisturbed. On the second floor, near the top of the carpeted steps, he found another dead operations officer and chief of station George Logan. Logan's chest had a big hole where his heart should have been. The way the blood had seeped out made it look as though he had little wings growing out of his back.

Logan had been a Washington desk jockey with little experience abroad, Mark recalled. He bent down to pick up one of the spent bullet cartridges, his hand shaking a bit despite his admonitions to himself to stay centered. The kind of guy that, when Mark was feeling cynical, made him think that maybe the CIA's overreliance on technology wasn't such a bad thing after all.

Mark hadn't thought Logan deserved his own station. But the man sure as hell hadn't deserved this.

PART II

Port of Jebel Ali, United Arab Emirates

The soldier lay hidden beneath a canvas tarp, on top of a battered red shipping container that rested on three others and was surrounded by thousands more. Beyond this vast field of containers stood a row of yellow rust-stained cranes. Beyond the cranes, across an expanse of calm water, loomed the USS Ronald Reagan.

The soldier's digital camera made steady clicking sounds as he zoomed in on each section of the massive aircraft carrier.

Over a thousand feet long, the Reagan *was one of eleven nuclear-powered Nimitz-class aircraft carriers in existence. As the weak light of dawn grew stronger, the soldier grew bored and started imagining all the riveters and welders and electricians and nuclear technicians who must have been needed to put the thing together. But the more he thought about it, the harder it was for him to conceive that something so colossal could have been created by human hands.*

7

Mark called Ted Kaufman, his former division chief, from a secure line in the Trudeau House.

"*How many bodies?*" demanded Kaufman.

"Five." Mark listed their names.

"Christ."

The line went silent except for Kaufman's breathing. Mark imagined the panic that was setting in. He'd heard that Kaufman had been a decent operations officer decades ago, but as a division chief he'd proved to be much better at avoiding crises than managing them when they hit. Between Campbell's assassination and now the slaughter at the Trudeau House, Mark figured Kaufman was now facing the biggest crisis of his career. The Baku station was under siege.

"I think you have to assume all of your Azeri assets are in danger," said Mark. "Daria in particular. Gobustan is anything but secure. And I would not want to be a woman around some of those guards."

"Dammit all." The line went silent again. Then, recovering himself, Kaufman said, "We'll get a forensic team to the Trudeau House within twenty-four hours. In the meantime, get the hell out of there. And don't, I repeat, don't let the Azeris know what happened. I don't want them screwing up the scene before our guys get there."

"What are you going to do about Daria?"

"I'll handle it."

Mark wondered how Kaufman intended to "handle it," given that Kaufman's knowledge of the intricacies of Azerbaijan and Azeri politics was limited at best. Kaufman, although responsible for the whole Central Eurasian Division, was a Russia specialist. Azerbaijan was an afterthought for him.

Which meant that, ultimately, the job of protecting Daria would be left to either the US ambassador—a political appointee who didn't even speak Azeri and had been on the job for only four months—or the CIA's junior in-country officers. It occurred to Mark, however, that after what had happened at the Trudeau House, the CIA might not even have any officers besides Daria left in Azerbaijan.

In the wake of the Soviet Union's implosion, Azerbaijan had been deemed crucial because it had gobs of oil and bordered Iran and Russia; but after the invasions of Afghanistan and Iraq, the US focus had shifted to the war zones and the whole Azeri station had been downsized.

"Try going through Orkhan," said Mark. "He's the only guy we're tight with who can spring her."

"I said I'd handle it."

Mark thought again of all the people dead at the Trudeau House and concluded that Kaufman, safely ensconced in a nice house in suburban Virginia, wasn't up to handling squat.

"What was the Baku station working on that could have led to this kind of blowback?" Mark asked.

"Nothing."

"So this was just a coincidence?"

"Don't give me that crap."

Mark was about to end the conversation when Kaufman added, "So after we got the news about Campbell, I spoke with the Azeri ambassador. She told me Campbell specifically requested that Daria be his translator at the convention."

"Did they know each other?"

"You tell me."

"Not that I know of."

"Then why would he ask for her by name?"

"I've got no idea."

"You worked with Daria for two years," said Kaufman. "You know her better than I do. Any chance the Azeris are onto something?"

"Meaning?"

"Meaning Daria survived on the same day a former deputy secretary of defense, along with nearly all my officers in Baku, were killed. Do you think it's within the realm of possibility that she was somehow involved with what happened?"

"Listen to me, Ted. You need to lock down the entire Baku station and get your remaining ops officers under protection. Including Daria. She's your best asset over here, believe me. Then find out who hit us, and hit back hard. Blow them out of the fucking water. End of story. Daria's clean."

"It was a close call whether to even post her abroad."

The doubts about Daria's loyalty, Mark knew, stemmed from the fact that she was the product of a mixed marriage. Her mother was Iranian—hence her Iranian first name—and her father was American with English roots, hence the Buckingham.

The one time Mark had come across something vaguely suspicious regarding Daria—charges on a personal credit card that suggested she was traveling to a region outside of her declared area of operations—it turned out she'd been visiting an orphanage. On her own time. For the purpose of donating $500. When Mark had investigated the payment, he'd learned it had come from her modest personal bank account and had gone directly toward food and medicine for the kids. And when he'd investigated the orphanage, he'd learned that it was just a straight-up charity, with no ties to terrorists or corrupt money-launderers.

Mark knew, however, that fear often trumped logic at the CIA. As a result, most Agency officers were white guys like himself, men who had to struggle to blend in with the locals in Azerbaijan and Iran. And it was on Iran that Daria, with her honey-toned skin and fluent command of Farsi, had been recruited to spy, using Azerbaijan as a base. Her posting had been a welcome exception, an exception Mark had hoped would mark the beginning of a new way of thinking at the CIA.

That hadn't turned out to be the case. When Mark had quit the CIA, Daria was the only operations officer in Baku who wasn't vanilla white. And Kaufman had never liked, or trusted, her.

8

Washington, DC

Colonel Henry Amato eyed his boss—National Security Advisor James Ellis—from the opposite side of an oval table. Ellis was a tall man, with a prominent chin, deep-set eyes, and a patrician air that had been perfected at Harvard and elite think tanks. On television, when he was wearing makeup and standing side by side with the president, he looked distinguished. But at ten to midnight, in a basement conference room beneath the West Wing of the White House, under fluorescent lights that exposed Ellis's yellowing teeth and deep wrinkles, Amato thought cadaverous a better description.

And then there was the chewing.

Amato watched with disdain as Ellis methodically ground his jaw in small circles. It was a habit his boss lapsed into when other people were speaking, as if to suggest he was so engaged that he was literally chewing over what was being said. Which certainly wasn't the case now.

At the moment, Ellis was pretending to listen to the director of national intelligence. Reading from a file marked *Top Secret*, the DNI was sharing preliminary satellite evidence and intelligence reports that suggested a limited troop mobilization was underway in Iran.

Upon finishing, the DNI dropped the file on the table and shook his head. "Now maybe I'm grasping at straws, but I wouldn't be shocked to learn that Campbell's assassination has something to do with this activity in Iran. God knows what the Iranians are really up to, but the timing is too suspicious to ignore."

Ellis said, "What's your take, Henry?"

Instead of answering, Amato—who was Ellis's top Iran advisor—remained perfectly still, as though standing at attention before a superior officer. The fluorescent lighting above was unnervingly bright and flickering a bit, contributing to his feeling of nausea.

"Henry?"

He hadn't seen any of this coming. It was as if someone had cold-cocked him with a two-by-four.

He was a deacon at Saint Mary's. A volunteer at Walter Reed. His wife had died two years ago but he'd remained faithful to her since her death, just as he had for the twenty-three years they'd been married. What sins he committed, he regularly confessed to God. As of a few days ago, he'd thought that all he needed to do was to soldier on through a few more years in government and then tolerate a quiet retirement.

And now this.

Daria had survived, but they would hunt her down. They had the men and the resources. Good God, he wasn't prepared to shut down the whole operation, but he had to do something.

"Henry?" repeated Ellis, and this time his tone was sharper.

"Sorry, sir. I worked with Jack Campbell years ago and I confess the news of his death hit me pretty hard." Amato turned to face the DNI. "I don't see a link between the troop movements in Iran and

Campbell's assassination," he lied. "More likely what happened to Campbell is about settling old scores."

"Old scores?" said the DNI.

"Well, of course Campbell had a long history with Iran."

"I wasn't aware."

"Before the revolution in '79, he helped coordinate training for SAVAK, the Shah's secret police. After the revolution, when Ayatollah Khomeini ordered a review of all the old SAVAK records to see who'd been hunting down his followers, I'm sure Campbell's name came up. Add to that the fact that Campbell took a hard line with Iran when he became the deputy sec. def., and it's not hard to figure out why the mullahs might have targeted him. They've got long memories—they probably waited decades for the opportunity to present itself."

The DNI asked a few more questions, then said, "Well, you could be right. Maybe Campbell's assassination doesn't have anything to do with the troop mobilization we're seeing. But Campbell was a big player in his time, and if the Iranians think they can take him out and get away with it, they've got another thing coming."

9

Mark let himself out of the Trudeau House the same way he'd come in, walked the ten blocks back to his apartment, and sat down at his desk in his spare bedroom, intending to work on his book. But after five minutes of staring at his computer screen and seeing nothing but the mutilated bodies of his former colleagues flash across his memory, he realized he was kidding himself. He was in shock. He wasn't going to get any work done today. Nor could he just ignore all that had transpired since the night before.

Mark had helped train Daria. And as her station chief, he'd always looked out for her, just as he had the rest of his operations officers. Now that Logan was dead, she had no one in Azerbaijan to turn to for help.

But the thought of potentially sticking his neck out to help her any more than he already had was setting off alarm bells in his head. Don't go being some kind of delusional do-gooder, he told himself. Fifty-fifty he'd just make the situation worse by meddling. He'd seen it happen time and time again. Wait for the Agency to restaff. Let them handle this mess.

But by then it might be too late.

"Shit," he muttered and picked up his phone and dialed. After waiting on hold for a long time, his contact came on the line. Mark spoke to him briefly and then hung up.

Minutes later he was on the street, starting up his Russian-made Niva, a boxy four-wheel-drive car that he'd purchased after going on a professor's salary.

He headed north toward the center of the Absheron Peninsula, a scarred and grossly polluted spit of land fifty miles long that jutted out into the Caspian Sea. The roads were crowded with an unruly mix of sleek Western cars—BMWs, Mercedes, Land Cruisers—and old Russian jalopies that belched noxious fumes. He passed decrepit Soviet factories, some languishing, some completely abandoned, many of which sat right next to gleaming new high-rises. Gas pipelines, huge billboards with photos of the current president, and piles of garbage lined the sides of the road.

Near the Balaxani oil fields—a purgatorial wasteland of oil sludge and rusting nodding-donkey oil pumps—he pulled over and bought pistachios from a guy who was selling them out of the back of his battered truck.

Just beyond the oil fields the landscape opened up; interspersed among the hellish images of industrial waste were a few green fields. When Mark came to a collection of vacant buildings on the left-hand side of the road, he pulled into an adjacent gravel lot and parked in front of a tall cypress tree, next to a stray dog. A minute later a black Mercedes pulled up next to him. A driver got out of the car and opened the rear door.

"It is really you, Sava?" The dark-haired man who emerged spoke in heavily accented English. He wore a charcoal-gray suit, a conservative red tie, and long and pointed black leather shoes that reminded Mark of witches. His face showed the beginning of a very early five o'clock shadow and he had a large Turkic nose. "I see this car," he said, frowning and pointing at Mark's Niva, "and I think maybe a gypsy, or even a Kurd, has come!"

Mark smiled. "I've been downsizing."

"Downsizing, what is downsizing?"

"Downsizing is what you do when you start to teach," said Mark, switching to Azeri.

They shook hands.

"Ah yes. I remember. Western University. I have to admit I wasn't sure you were being completely—how do I put it—*open* with me when you told me of your intentions. But my people tell me you actually do teach classes. They learn much from you."

"I've wondered about some of my students."

"My men have been attentive, I hope."

"Very. Thank you for coming, Orkhan."

Orkhan Gambar was the Azeri minister of national security. Given that the United States and Azerbaijan were on good terms, Mark's affiliation with the CIA had been known to Orkhan and they'd frequently exchanged information. But since the CIA's presence in Azerbaijan wasn't officially acknowledged, their meetings had been held in secret. Often they had met here.

"Come." Orkhan lightly guided Mark by the elbow as his driver produced an M-16 rifle and began to stand guard. "We talk by the fire."

Mark followed Orkhan down a series of worn stone steps, into the bottom of a little depression. A white plastic table and three white plastic chairs had been set up a few feet away from a hillside that had been burning ever since an underground reservoir of natural gas had caught fire decades ago. A few enterprising Azeris had tried to set up a tea shop near the flames, but the tourists had proved few and the shop had gone out of business.

Orkhan settled into a chair and pulled it up close to the fire. On previous occasions he'd told Mark that getting extremely hot for a half hour or so made one feel cooler for the rest of the day. All Azeris know this, he'd said.

Mark sat down next to him now and pulled out the bag of pistachios, certain that Orkhan wouldn't be fasting during Ramadan.

"You remembered. This is why we get along so well."

That and the fact that the US government had sent an ocean of what was supposed to have been counterterrorism money Orkhan's way, thought Mark.

Not for the first time he considered that Azerbaijan was a country with a lot of things going for it. Though its people were predominantly Shiite Muslims, they were tolerant of Christians and Jews. Women could wear whatever they wanted without risking being stoned to death. In the south there were vast forests and lush groves of citrus trees. To the north, the snowcapped mountains and picturesque little villages almost could have been Switzerland were it not for the general lack of indoor plumbing. And the coastal center was rich with oil. But the country was also hopelessly corrupt. Mark had little doubt that plenty of America's money had gone directly into Orkhan's pocket. That was why they got along so well. But the pistachios didn't hurt either.

"How is your family, Orkhan?"

They exchanged pleasantries for a while. Then Orkhan asked about Nika. Although Nika had made the mistake of marrying a Russian when she was twenty-four—a marriage that had lasted only six months because all Russians are thieves and drunks—he indicated that she came from a decent family and that her job as a professor of English literature at Western University appeared to be secure.

"But you must tell her not to smoke around her child," Orkhan said. "This is very bad for children, I hear. I see she does this at her home."

"I wasn't aware."

Orkhan sat back and smiled, a hard smile that showed his teeth. Mark caught a glimpse of a gold crown in the back and recalled that the Ministry of National Security was the Azeri equivalent of the old KGB. They even occupied the same building that the KGB had operated out of, and had wound up employing many of the same people—people like Orkhan.

"Surely you know she and her child share a bedroom at her parents' house? It is in this bedroom that she smokes. You must get her to stop."

Mark shrugged, as though a little bored by the small talk. "You make a good point."

10

Mark had aged well, Orkhan observed with grudging admiration. Ten years ago, back when Mark had first been posted to Azerbaijan, he almost certainly would have expressed some pointless and typically American moral outrage at the news that his girlfriend's bedroom had been violated.

But not this older version of Mark. This Mark had perfected a look of cruel apathy, a dead-eyed look that reminded Orkhan of Uzbek sex-traffickers and Russian mafia assassins.

Of course, Orkhan suspected that behind his facade Mark was just as stupidly idealistic and dangerously sentimental as he and the rest of his American colleagues had always been. But he respected his counterpart's evolving ability to hide those weaknesses.

Mark said, "A prominent American was killed yesterday."

Orkhan studied Mark for a moment, then took a long drag on his cigarette and threw a handful of empty pistachio shells onto the burning hill where they crackled as they erupted into flames.

"Do the Americans blame us?"

"I doubt it."

"They'll fault our security, although the charges will be baseless."

"You already have someone in custody. She's a translator, does a lot of work with business clients through the hotels. Carries an Iranian passport."

"You are still in contact with your government, I see."

Orkhan had never believed for a second that Mark was really just teaching in Baku. For the past few years Mark had not only been the CIA's station chief, but for all practical purposes he'd been the US ambassador too because the actual US ambassador didn't speak Azeri. Orkhan hadn't thought the Americans would let an asset like Mark just walk away. The call he'd received last night, informing him that Mark was on his way to Gobustan, had proved him right.

Mark took a pistachio from the bag on the table, pried open the shell, and popped the nut in his mouth. "I thought you should know that your efforts would be better served if you looked elsewhere."

"And this information, it comes from Washington?"

"No. It comes from me."

"Why not from Washington?"

"You may hear from them soon."

"I thought you were retired."

"A friend requested my help."

"I see."

Orkhan sighed as he focused on the fire. The Americans were up to something, that much was obvious. The problem was that the Americans were schizophrenic. Their State Department was pushing for free elections, the Department of Defense for secret bases on the Iranian border, the CIA for better security on the BTC pipeline...Too many people were pushing too many agendas.

Orkhan felt a migraine coming on. He finished his cigarette, tossed it on the fire, and lit another.

"She is one of yours, I assume? This is why she is with this man Campbell?"

He stared at Mark, got the dead-eyed look back. Sometimes he missed the old Mark, he thought.

"I was led to believe that the American government and the Azeri government had an open relationship," said Orkhan with more than a little sarcasm. "You wouldn't have undeclared spies on my soil, would you? Spies using false identification, breaking Azeri laws?"

"I'm concerned her life may be in danger."

"And what gives you cause for such concern?"

"Intuition."

"Intuition? My intuition tells me my men did not watch you close enough when you were playing teacher."

"I really did quit."

"Then why do you talk to me instead of that fool Logan?"

"I stayed on in Baku because I was offered a good job here. And the reason Logan's not talking to you is because he's dead."

"Ahh…" Orkhan nodded his head as he stared into the fire, enjoying the feel of the heat through his light wool suit. The only sound was the sibilant hiss of the flames.

"I'm asking that you continue not to publicize her capture. It will make it harder for you to release her when she's cleared." Mark leaned close to Orkhan as he spoke. "And for now, guard her heavily. With men you trust."

"This is a concern for the minister of the interior. Why are you talking to me?"

"Because I don't know the minister of the interior. And you do." Mark paused, then added, "Please."

"Please?" Orkhan was genuinely surprised. His relationship with Mark had always been based on mutual self-interest. Azerbaijan needed the Americans to counterbalance the Russians, and the Americans needed his country to have access to Azeri oil, which had been accomplished in the form of a pipeline that led from the Caspian to the Mediterranean. *Quid pro quo.* Personal appeals were irrelevant at best. At worst they suggested vulnerability.

Orkhan wondered whether this girl at Gobustan meant more to Mark than he was letting on.

"If she is the slightest bit harmed while in your custody," said Mark flatly, "I can assure you my government will want to know why. Having Campbell dead on your soil looks bad enough already. Azerbaijan doesn't need to be known as an uncontrollable haven for terrorists. It would be bad for business and bad for you."

"Now that is the Mark I know. Back to issuing threats, are you?"

Orkhan was actually relieved. With a CIA station chief and former deputy US secretary of defense dead, the last thing he needed was for Mark—the only American in Azerbaijan he considered even remotely competent—to start acting irrationally just because of some girl.

"I'm just telling you there's the potential for more trouble."

Orkhan exhaled through his nose and clenched his jaw. "What am I dealing with, Mark?"

"I don't know."

"Who would want Campbell dead? And Logan? It certainly wasn't us."

"I know. That's why I'm here."

"The Chinese? The Iranians? The Russians?"

"All a possibility. The only thing I know for sure is that the woman you're holding as a suspect didn't do it."

11

Mark got back to his apartment a little before noon. He figured he still had time to get some work done if he could force himself to concentrate and get back to his real life. He'd done what he could for Daria.

But within less than a minute of sitting down at his computer, he walked over to a shelf in his living room. Tucked between two granite bookends was a miniature *long narde* board, a back-gammon-like game that was popular in Azerbaijan. He played it via weekly e-mail exchanges with a former agent, a colonel with Russian military intelligence who now lived as a pensioner in Tbilisi.

Mark picked up the dice, but instead of rolling them, he thought about Daria.

He remembered when, just two months after her arrival in Baku, she'd approached him about recruiting the counselor for investment affairs at the Iranian embassy. Kaufman had been skeptical, but Daria had pulled the operation off flawlessly. And the information she'd extracted had proved extremely damaging to Iranian business interests in Azerbaijan.

As station chief he hadn't been one to play favorites with any of his operations officers. Had he been forced to choose, though, it would have been Daria. She'd been a little green when she'd served under him, but she'd had guts.

He was finally about to roll the *long narde* dice when his landline rang. It was Kaufman.

"I'll call you right back," said Mark. He hung up, took out his cell phone, popped out the thumbnail-sized SIM card in the back, then replaced it with a new card. His phone now had a new number, one that the Azeris presumably didn't know about yet.

"Expect an FBI forensic crew," said Kaufman, when Mark had reestablished the connection. "They'll be in Baku as of tomorrow morning and they'll want to talk to you. Be at the embassy by nine. A legal attaché is flying in from Ankara and meeting with the ambassador tonight."

"You call in Logan's ops officers?"

"After what happened at the Trudeau House, we have only two left in the station. One is Daria, the second Peters. Daria I'm doing my best on."

"Meaning?"

"Meaning we're trying to open up a back channel to Aliyev through State."

"Then you should know I already talked to Orkhan about her." Mark gave Kaufman a brief synopsis of his conversation.

"You had no authority to talk to Orkhan. You could have fucked up what we're trying to do through State."

"Sorry, was just trying to help."

"Don't give me that crap, Sava. I mean it, there's a lot going on behind the scenes that you don't know about."

"Talk to me about Peters."

Kaufman was silent for a moment, as if debating whether to let the Orkhan matter drop. "I'm having trouble establishing contact."

Mark knew Leonard Peters—while studying international law at Stanford, he'd written a paper on the Iranian courts that had caught the attention of the Agency. So he was smart as hell, but the agents he'd recruited had been second-rate.

"How have you tried to establish contact?"

"Phone, embassy courier."

"You know where he's living?"

"I have him on Sarabski Street."

"He also used to keep an empty apartment on Aslanov," said Mark. "For meeting agents."

"See, that's why I called you, you know these things. Any chance you could swing by?"

Mark didn't answer immediately. Instead he stared out at his balcony, where he noticed that his potted tomato plants were wilting. He made a mental note to water them when he got off the phone. They'd been a house gift from Nika and keeping them alive had become a bit of a hobby.

Kaufman said, "I can have you put on the books as an independent contractor if you like."

There were two worlds out there, thought Mark. One was populated by normal people who believed that their lives were governed by natural laws that were knowable and consistent, if sometimes brutal. And then there was an underworld, populated by insane people who believed in no consistent set of laws, or even a consistent reality. When Mark had started with the CIA, he'd been up to his neck in that underworld. He'd even thought it was a more honest place—that the normal world was just a figment of people's collective imagination—and that by refusing to buy into the fantasy he was mustering the courage to see things the way they really were.

Now he didn't care whether the normal world was a fantasy, as long as he had a chance to enjoy it for a while. Which is why he'd quit the Agency.

Still, Peters could be next on the list. Someone should warn the guy.

"I'll see what I can do," said Mark. "But don't bother putting me on the books. I'm doing you a quick favor and getting Peters off my conscience. Nothing more."

"You have a conscience? This is news. By the way, I've arranged for a little extra security."

"No thanks." Mark figured that if anyone had wanted him dead because of his ties to the CIA it would have happened already, when his guard was down. And besides, when it came to personnel, he thought Kaufman's judgment sucked.

"Not for you," said Kaufman dismissively, as if the thought of protection for Mark had never ever crossed his mind. "For Peters. I want him under armed guard from the minute you find him."

12

Adidas, Polo, Tommy Hilfiger, Sony…hundreds of Western shops, intermixed with nightclubs and restaurants, lined Nizami Street in downtown Baku. High above, colorful advertising banners fluttered slowly in the waning breeze. The street was blocked off to cars and crowded with shoppers, which was why Mark had thought it would be a good place to meet John Decker, the man Kaufman had contracted to protect Peters.

He could see Decker's head now, a hundred feet away, bobbing up and down above the crush of people around him. It was an unusually large head, complemented by a chiseled face and topped with soldier-short dirty-blond hair. For brief moments, when the crowd parted, Mark caught glimpses of Decker's bright blue short-sleeved shirt, easily spotted in what was otherwise a sea of dour brown and black fabric. Equally conspicuous was the broad smile on Decker's face.

People in Azerbaijan smiled plenty—just not while they were walking around by themselves in public.

Mark couldn't help but smile briefly himself, thinking this was the CIA he remembered. Former Navy SEAL John Decker would be the perfect person to act as a bodyguard for Peters, assuming Peters never attempted to meet any of his agents, conduct any clandestine work, or do anything that involved blending in with native Azeris. Which was to say Peters wouldn't be able to do anything that a CIA operations officer investigating Campbell's death would be required to do.

Decker approached a line of cabs—mostly old Russian-made Ladas—on Vurgun Street where it intersected with Nizami. He began to look inside each one, eliciting bored looks from the cigarette-smoking drivers who were lounging around next to their vehicles.

Mark, who was sitting in his Niva behind the line of cabs, tapped on his horn, but Decker didn't notice. So he drove forward a few feet and rolled down his window.

"Need a ride?"

Decker waved him away without making eye contact.

Mark looked out his windshield for a moment, then said, "Buddy! Get in the damn car."

This time Decker turned.

"I'm your contact," said Mark quietly.

Decker's eyes widened and he gave a significant nod of his chin. He climbed in the Niva, although it was a tight squeeze for him and his head nearly touched the ceiling. He offered his hand to Mark and in a serious, I'm-all-business tone, said, "Pleasure to meet you, sir."

Mark ignored Decker's hand—he needed both of his own to muscle the manual steering. On top of that he was irritable and worried about Peters and Daria.

He estimated that Decker was in his midtwenties. One more guy out of thousands drawn to Baku by the oil money, looking to cash in on his Navy SEAL experience. Only Mark thought Decker was too late. A decade ago Baku had been like the Wild West during the gold rush. But the big security firms had long-since discovered Baku and taken over.

"You don't look like a SEAL. You're too big." Six four, Mark guessed. And broad-shouldered. Guys the size of Decker were usually too slow and awkward to handle the training.

Decker screwed up his face a bit. "Are you always this friendly?"

"Are you armed?"

Decker lifted his pant legs, revealing a snub-nosed Glock holstered on one ankle and a five-inch double-bladed combat knife on the other.

Mark shrugged. "OK, John Decker. You'll do. Let's go find your protection detail."

Peters's apartment—the allegedly empty one he kept on Aslanov Street—was locked, but Mark had brought a couple of small lock-picking tools with him.

"Old-school. That's pretty slick," said Decker as Mark went to work. After a few minutes of watching Mark unsuccessfully try to pick the lock, he said, "You know they make electronic picks now. I trained on one a few years ago. They're great."

"That so?" said Mark.

"Yeah, you just stick it in and it does the work for you."

"You got one now?"

"No, sir."

"Then what's your point?"

"Ah, no point I guess."

After another minute the door swung open.

Mark, for one, wasn't overly surprised at the state in which they found Leonard Peters. Even before discovering the body in the bathtub, he'd noted the scratch marks around the lock. Then there was the overturned ashtray in the living room and Peters's ridiculous pipe—Mark always suspected Peters had fancied himself a bit of a Sherlock Holmes—broken in two on the living room floor.

It was a small apartment, but Peters evidently had started living there, for it had been furnished with care—supple leather couches from Turkey, a fancy espresso maker, dark blue curtains…The bed had been made. Other than the few things in the living room and kitchen that appeared to have been disturbed as the result of a struggle, nothing was out of order.

Mark went back into the bathroom and examined the body. Decker stood behind him, Glock drawn. There were gunshot wounds on Peters's arms, but also precise shots to his head and chest, reminiscent of the clustering Mark had seen at the Trudeau House. The body rested in a seated position with one arm hanging over the side of the tub, like a modern-day *Death of Marat*.

Mark noted the purple livor mortis on the hand outside the tub. He squeezed it gently between his forefinger and thumb. Peters's skin remained purple. The arm and fingers were stiff. He was no expert and he knew that estimating the time of death, especially in a stiflingly hot apartment, was a crapshoot in the best of circumstances. But he guessed Peters had been dead for around as long as the people at the Trudeau House.

"You better call your contact at the embassy." Mark glanced at Decker.

"Yes, sir."

But Decker didn't move. His lips were pressed tightly together and he was breathing through his nose as he stared at Peters. Sweat glistened on his forehead. The air was hot, easily in the upper nineties. Behind Decker, sunlight streamed into the apartment through large sliding glass doors that led to a balcony. Mark had noticed a window-unit air conditioner in the living room, but it wasn't on.

"Come on," said Mark. "We've seen enough."

Decker still didn't move, so Mark turned around and grabbed his elbow. "Come on, buddy, let's get some air."

They retreated to the balcony, where Decker crouched down and cradled his big head in his big hands for a moment. "It's just the heat," he said.

"Compared to last week this is nothing."

Decker took a deep breath. "I'll call the embassy."

"I think that's a good idea."

Just then Mark noticed an irritating flash of light, like an errant ray of sunshine, fixing on his eye. The next second he was rocketing sideways, tackled by Decker.

He blacked out momentarily. When he came to, Decker was on top of him.

The wind had been knocked out of his lungs, rendering him unable to speak. He tried to lift his hands up to Decker's throat, intending to choke him, but Decker pushed them down.

"Keep below the wall." Decker gestured with his chin to the waist-high brick parapet on the edge of the balcony.

Mark kept quiet until the excruciating pain gripping his chest subsided a bit. "Get the fuck off me."

"Someone just took a shot at you, sir."

"I said get off me!" The remains of Mark's crushed reading glasses slipped out of his shirt pocket. He could smell lamb meat—probably from a *döner* kebab—on Decker's breath.

"Check out the door," said Decker.

Mark looked up and observed a tiny bullet hole right around where his head had been.

"I saw the red sight dot on your face." Decker rolled off him but stayed below the balcony wall. "The bullet hit the far wall at about the same height it penetrated the glass. Judging from the angle, whoever took a shot at you has to be almost right across from us."

That would be the Kura Araksvodstroi apartment complex, thought Mark, with a constricting feeling of dread and anger. A run-down 1950s-era Soviet behemoth, it was a veritable rabbit warren of dilapidated apartments. A shooter could hide for weeks in that building and never be found.

He looked at the sliding glass door again, just to confirm that he wasn't going insane. The bullet hole was still there. He suddenly felt old. He wondered what underworld he'd let himself get sucked into, and how he could get the hell out.

They rolled into the apartment, keeping close to the ground. But when Decker went to open the door to the common hall, Mark blocked him silently with his hand.

He reminded himself that the carnage at the Trudeau House almost certainly hadn't been inflicted by one person. Which meant the guy who'd just taken a shot at him was probably part of a team.

A few seconds later the door handle moved almost imperceptibly, as someone gently tried to twist it open. But Mark had locked the door behind him before entering the apartment, and now the lock engaged. He put a finger to his lips and gestured to the rear bedroom.

When he and Decker were behind the bedroom door, Mark whispered, "Your gun."

"Screw that. I'm the protection."

"That closet," said Mark, pointing. "The wall inside it abuts the next apartment. Cut a hole and crawl through it. I'll watch the door. Your gun. Now."

Decker handed it over. Seconds later, there was a screeching sound as he used his knife to saw through the drywall.

From the crack he'd left in the open bedroom door, Mark had a clear view of Peters's front door. He kept Decker's pistol trained on it.

"I'm good, boss. Going through," whispered Decker from the closet.

Then the front door popped open. A guy with a crowbar was pushed aside by two clean-shaven men who charged into the apartment with silenced assault rifles.

Mark scurried cockroach-like into the closet. Decker was already through the hole in the wall, on his belly in the bedroom of the adjacent apartment. They crawled on their knees through the kitchen and out into the common hall. At the end of the hall was a stairwell, which they descended four steps at a time.

"What are we talking for exits?" called Decker, in a loud whisper.

Mark pictured the building in his head. "A main one in the front, a small one in back, and a main one on the west side. East side, nothing."

When they got to the second floor of the building, they tried doors to apartments on the east side until they found one that was open.

Decker ran past a woman holding a crying baby. As she screamed at him to get out, he raced to the open balcony and vaulted over the edge without even pausing. Mark followed in Decker's footsteps, but when he got to the balcony himself, he hesitated. The drop was about fifteen feet.

"Lower yourself over the side." Decker was standing unhurt on the pavement. A few pedestrians had stopped to gawk. "Relax as you fall, keep your knees bent, and roll on the ground if you need to."

"Yeah, that'll work," said Mark, but he jumped anyway. Instead of rolling he hit with a sack-of-potatoes thud and wound up twisting his ankle. Decker pulled him up and they started to run.

13

Before the latest oil boom, Fountains Square had been where the prostitutes hung out, but now it was just an extension of the Nizami Street shopping bonanza. Well-tended flower gardens lay planted around the central fountains.

Mark stopped short in the center of the square. Bent over and panting, he rested his hands on his knees. A veiled woman in a black skin-tight T-shirt, skin-tight jeans, and high heels bumped into him. Mark eyed her—she was chatting on a cell phone, which made him suspicious, but decided he was just being paranoid.

His ankle was killing him and sweat dripped off his forehead. He noticed Decker, who had stopped beside him, wasn't even breathing hard.

"I think we're clear," said Decker.

Mark wondered—had the shooter been waiting for them specifically, or had he just been watching the apartment to see who showed up? Because if the whole thing had been a chance encounter, then Mark figured he could risk going back to his apartment, back to his life. But if he'd been specifically marked, if they knew he was the former chief of station/Azerbaijan and had been helping Daria…

"You want to tell me what that was all about?" said Decker.

"I don't know."

Decker had been out on the balcony too, completely exposed, standing directly to his right. Had the shooter simply flipped a coin when deciding who to go after first? Or had he, Mark, been the primary target?

Mark considered the laser sight, the lookout point in the Kura Araksvaodstroi apartment block, and everything he'd seen at the Trudeau House. It all pointed to a disturbingly high level of professionalism and planning. But any professional worth his salt would have tried to take out Decker first. Then he would have gone after the weak guy.

But the shooter hadn't done that. Which meant he'd been specifically targeted.

Mark took a minute to catch his breath. As station chief he'd spent all his time behind a desk. The last time he'd been in the field was six years ago. "Listen, I need to take off but I want to thank you for what you did back—"

"Where are you going?"

"I'm perfectly cognizant of the fact that you saved—"

"If you need me, I'm available. I can help. You're CIA, aren't you?"

"Who said that?"

"One of the embassy marines. He was just guessing."

"I don't work for the government anymore," said Mark. "The best thing you can do for yourself is to get back to the embassy, tell them what happened, and then hop on the first plane out of town. It's possible you're a target now too."

"I can take care of myself."

"Evidently."

"And I need the work."

Mark remembered the speed with which Decker had reacted on Peters's balcony. After taking a moment to think, he said, "You're way too young to have retired from the SEALs. Why'd you leave?"

"There were opportunities here."

Mark studied Decker, observing his discomfort.

Decker added, "I was stationed here for a while. I made some contacts."

"Like who?"

"One of the secretaries at the embassy." Decker gave a name Mark didn't recognize. "She works in the ambassador's office."

"You know her professionally?"

"Ah, I would say more personally."

"And that's how you got this job? Because you were screwing a secretary in the ambassador's office?"

Decker shrugged. "I think they tried to get somebody from Xe first. I was the only person available on short notice."

"How long were you a SEAL?"

"Three years."

"What team?"

"Five."

"What'd you do in Azerbaijan?"

"Training."

"Who, Azeris?"

"Actually, I'm not allowed—"

"To guard the BTC?" said Mark. The BTC was the thousand-mile-long oil and gas pipeline that ran all the way from Baku to Tbilisi to the Turkish port of Ceyhan on the Mediterranean Sea. Mark remembered that, a couple years ago, a SEAL crew in Azerbaijan had been sent over to train a special Azeri naval unit to guard it. "Don't answer if that's what you were doing."

Decker looked as though he'd just taken a bite of something rancid, but he didn't answer.

"Look around, John. Are any of these people dressed like you?"

Decker didn't respond.

"You can't do anything about the fact that you're twice the size of everyone here, but you can do something about your clothes. Go shopping. Buy black pants, black shoes, and a brown shirt. Dye your hair brown. Fit in."

"Yes, sir."

"And if you want, meet me back here in three hours. By then I'll know if I have work for you."

"I'll be here."

"No guarantees," said Mark.

"I understand."

14

Mark walked to the McDonald's on the perimeter of the square. A grubby yellow payphone stood not far from the entrance and he used it to call Nika.

"Dinner won't be ready until five thirty," she said. "But come at four anyway."

"Listen, I'm not going to be able to make it."

The line went silent, then Nika said, "I already bought everything."

"Where are you?"

"Inside my apartment, in the kitchen."

"Don't go near the windows. Where's Sabir?"

"At the kitchen table, doing his homework. I'm looking at him right now. You're scaring me."

Mark rested his head on the interior wall of the phone booth. The cool metal on his forehead felt good. "I just think it would be better if we played it safe."

"Played it safe? I'm making dinner, Mark. What's not safe?"

"A little while ago someone took a shot at me. I'm afraid they might try again."

"Took a shot at you? You mean with a gun?" Nika's voice was incredulous.

"Ah, yeah."

"You're telling me someone tried to kill you?"

"That's exactly what I'm saying."

"Because of something to do with your drunk foreign service friend?"

"It's actually more complicated than that. I can't get into it now, you're just going to have to trust me on this."

"Are you hurt?"

"No."

"Did you call the police?"

"This isn't a matter for the police."

"Of course it is."

"I can deal with it. I know people, from when I used to work at the embassy."

"This is crazy, Mark."

"The reason I'm calling is that I'm worried that whoever's after me will try to use you to get to me. You're going to need to leave for a while, until I sort this out. You have a sister in the north, in the mountains."

"What am I supposed to do about work? I'm teaching summer classes. Sabir is in summer school. We can't just pick up and leave."

"I'm sorry."

"You're sorry?" said Nika, raising her voice.

"You need to pack your bags. Now. Then veil yourself and go down to the parking garage. Put Sabir in the trunk of your car—"

"No, Mark."

"Don't fight me on this, Nika! Put him in the trunk of your damn car so that if anyone's watching your apartment, waiting for a woman and her son to leave, they only see a single woman. And make sure your face is completely veiled. If they try to get to me through you, both you and Sabir could be in danger."

"Who's 'they'? Who would want to kill you? And what does Sabir have to do with this? He's just a boy."

Nika was whispering frantically, reminding Mark that her son was probably within a few feet of her, listening. What a mess. And what a delusional mistake it had been to have let his mess of a life get intertwined with the lives of these two decent, normal people.

"He doesn't have anything to do with this. Nor do you. But this is a seriously ugly situation and I don't want to take any chances. Drive directly to your sister's place—"

"Who are you?"

"Don't tell anyone you're leaving. Don't tell your sister you're coming. You can let Sabir out of the trunk when you're twenty kilometers clear of Baku."

"I could lose my job," said Nika, plaintively.

"I'm sorry." Mark scanned the crowds in Fountains Square, wondering if anyone out there had a fix on him. He was sorry, genuinely so, but he had to go. "I'll contact you through your parents when it's OK to return. In the meantime, get out. I mean it, Nika. Get out now."

15

Mark watched from a distance as Nika's car exited from the parking garage underneath her apartment building. She was wearing a black veil and there was no sign of Sabir. He looked to see if anyone took off after her as she pulled onto Vagif Avenue in the direction of the Baku Zoo. She appeared to be clear.

From a bench in front of the Nizami Cinema he called Ted Kaufman and told him about what had happened at Peters's apartment.

Then he gave Kaufman two options.

First, Kaufman could hire him back temporarily as an independent contractor. In return, the CIA would receive a report on any progress he made in figuring out what was driving the violence in Baku. Second, he would investigate anyway and keep his findings to himself.

"I've got no problem hiring you as an independent," said Kaufman. "We'll have a new Agency team in Baku by tomorrow. You can work with them."

"I'm not working with any new team," Mark said. "And I'll need money." He mentioned a figure he knew Kaufman wouldn't like.

"We're not funding your retirement," said Kaufman coldly. "Show a little patriotism for Christ's sake."

"That's the going rate for independents."

"Going rate, my ass."

"And then I have to figure expenses on top of that, expenses that I anticipate will include lots of bribes—"

"I don't want to hear about it."

"—and subcontractor payments. That figure's a weekly rate by the way, payable in advance."

"What subcontractors?"

"That's my business."

"Not if you're on my payroll."

"Take it or leave it."

"What is it with you?" said Kaufman. "I mean really, you think now's a good time to go asshole on me?"

"This new team of yours that's flying in, anybody on it speak Azeri?"

Kaufman didn't answer.

"Anybody who's ever set foot in Azerbaijan?" After that last question was met with more silence, Mark said, "I'm not good with Daria and me playing the sitting-duck routine while you send over a couple jackasses who have no intention of doing anything other than holing up in the embassy and writing reports based on what the Azeri government feeds them or what they read in the English-language newspapers. We can either agree to use each other, or you can ignore me and take your chances. Your choice."

The line was silent for a while. Eventually Kaufman said, "Hold on."

Fifteen minutes later, Mark had his answer: the Agency had agreed to his terms. So after stopping off at the British-owned LPM International Bank and withdrawing $50,000 from a numbered CIA account—the five hundred-dollar-bill bank bundles fit easily into a small canvas shoulder bag—he called Orkhan again.

16

Martyr's Alley, a long open-air memorial to all the Azeri protestors killed by the Soviets in 1990, was perched on a ridge high above the old walled city of Baku. A limestone tower, under which burned an eternal flame, anchored one end of the memorial.

Orkhan walked purposefully toward the flame and placed a red carnation inside an eight-pointed Azeri star at its base. After a moment of feigned reverence—he thought the protestors who'd died had been stupid not to just wait for the Soviet Union to collapse—he strolled to a point a few feet away from Mark.

"This is not an ideal place to meet," he said tightly.

Martyr's Alley was just a short walk away from the Ministry of National Security. The whole area was infested with Russian and Iranian spies. Orkhan wondered whether any were watching now.

He glanced down at the yellow cranes that lined the enormous shipping docks far below them.

"Thank you for seeing me again," said Mark.

Mark, Orkhan observed, was still wearing the same filthy shirt he'd had on earlier that day. And he hadn't bothered to shave.

"What do you want?"

"Since we spoke this morning, I've encountered complications."

The Americans were a bloodthirsty people, Orkhan thought, as Mark described what had happened at Leonard Peters's apartment. More so even than the Russians. Ask any one of them and they'd deny it. They'd claim to regret the necessity of whatever violence they were in the process of inflicting and point to some righteous cause that had forced their hand.

But always there was blood.

"Baku is a safe city," he said. "You brought this with you."

"I brought nothing with me."

"Then your government did."

"We're the ones getting killed, not doing the killing."

"Why are you telling me this?" said Orkhan.

"The woman you have in custody. I fear—"

"I have arranged for extra protection, as I said I would. I spoke with the minister of internal affairs."

"Still, I worry that her guards may not share your commitment."

"I have personally spoken with the commander of the prison. If she is harmed his head will roll."

"I also need to question her about Campbell's assassination."

"I thought she knew nothing about that."

"At this point I don't know what she knows."

"Did she kill him?"

"No."

"But you think she's holding back information."

"I want her out, Orkhan."

"Impossible. The Interior Ministry controls Gobustan."

"When I find out who killed Campbell, you'll be the first person in Azerbaijan to know."

Orkhan didn't respond. It was true that he and Mark had proved useful to each other over the years, in ways that had benefited them both. But Orkhan sensed something was different this time around, that the stakes were much higher.

"She's going to be a problem for you," said Mark. "Eventually the US embassy will have to get involved."

"So she is an American."

"If the Iranians find out that she was carrying a fake Iranian passport, they'll investigate. When they discover she has ties to the Agency, they'll assume that you knew she was spying for us in Azerbaijan, helping us collect intelligence on Iran."

"We knew nothing of the sort." Orkhan felt that migraine threatening again in the back of his head as he recalled that Mark could be an absolute bastard when he wanted to be. Iran didn't worry him the way Russia or the US did. But Azerbaijan was a tiny nation of nine million people—Iran, seventy million. And the Iranians were paranoid; they had to be treated delicately. And Mark knew it.

"The Iranians already know you let us use Azerbaijan as an intelligence base because we help keep the Russians at bay. This will just feed their suspicions."

Orkhan's jaw tensed. "It would be unfortunate for both of our countries if there were to be supply disruptions on the BTC."

"Unfortunate for both of our countries is right," said Mark.

After a decent silence, Orkhan added, "I don't want to hear any more threats about Iran."

"Point taken. But that still leaves the girl."

Orkhan sighed.

17

This was the point in the conversation when Mark had envisioned offering Orkhan a bribe—to the tune of $25,000 or so. But now he wasn't sure how to go about it. In the past, bribing Orkhan had just involved transferring funds earmarked for combating terrorism from the Americans to the Azeris, at which point Orkhan would take whatever he saw fit off the top.

But Mark couldn't offer official funds now, and he wasn't sure how Orkhan would react to a big, crass bag of cash. Orkhan had rules concerning what was honorable and what wasn't, and sometimes those rules were hard for Mark to figure out.

"If there are any incentives I can provide on my end to help facilitate this, let me know." The strap of the cash-filled shoulder bag crossed Mark's chest like a bandolier. To drive his point home, he tapped the strap and added, "I am not without means."

This brought a hard smile to Orkhan's face. He said, "I like you, Sava. But you are an American through and through. You think a few dollars solves all problems."

Mark nearly choked on that one. His best guess was that Orkhan had skimmed around a half million dollars off the top of military assistance from the Americans. A few dollars indeed.

"Just something to consider." Mark stared back at Orkhan.

"Unfortunately, my friend, I'm afraid this time I am powerless to meet your request."

"If it would—"

"It is not to be negotiated."

Mark thought for a moment. If Orkhan couldn't be bribed, he'd bribe the guards at Gobustan.

"Well then, I won't take up any more of your time." He started to walk away, then added, "I appreciate your meeting with me."

"You may," called Orkhan, "be interested to know that as part of the increased protection I mentioned, I will be moving the girl from Gobustan Prison to a detention center here in Baku. We must keep her safe not only from potential attackers, but also from the other inmates. And sickness. Tuberculosis is an unfortunate problem at Gobustan."

"I see."

"I will order her moved later today."

Mark studied Orkhan. "I suppose she will be guarded."

"Of course. But how many guards I can get on such short notice, I don't know. Maybe one, two?"

"I should think one would be plenty."

"Perhaps you are right." Orkhan checked his watch. "I will see who is available for a five o'clock departure."

Mark knew not to thank Orkhan. It was better just to walk away. But he'd only taken a step when Orkhan spoke again.

"I have told you of my son?"

"Sure. Heydar." Mark had met him once. He remembered a mean-spirited teen who'd talked a big game about following in his father's footsteps but was probably too stupid to do so. "How is he?"

"When he finishes his studies in Baku, he hopes to go to America. He'll be applying to the University of Texas next year.

Wants to get a degree in geosystems engineering and hydrogeology." Orkhan enunciated each word clearly, as if he'd taken great care to memorize the exact phrasing. "Petroleum engineer," he added. "It will help him when he returns to Azerbaijan."

"That so?"

"Of course, his grades could be better." Orkhan shook his head. "He's a bright boy—"

"That was my impression."

"But he should apply himself more." Orkhan stuck his hands in his pockets. "I understand to go to an American university, one needs to fill out long applications, get letters of recommendations, take tests—what do you call them, the SAT? A very, very difficult test I hear."

"I'll help him." Jesus, thought Mark.

"He could use it. The teachers here, they mean well, but they don't know the American system. You could be good for Heydar."

Or not, thought Mark. But he also thought it would be a smart move for Orkhan to send his son abroad. Many of the best jobs in the oil industry went to Westerners, with their Western educations. The average Azeri was often shut out.

Not that Orkhan's son qualified as an average Azeri. But to Mark it said something that even the minister of national security felt his son needed to leave the country for a while to get ahead in life.

"Have him call me. When I finish with this, I'll see what I can do."

18

John Decker sat on a bench in Fountains Square, wearing black leather boots, a tight-fitting brown button-down shirt, and black jeans that were way too small.

"They don't have big-and-tall shops in Baku," Decker said preemptively as Mark approached.

"Thousand dollars a day. First week in advance."

"Damn. That works."

For himself, Mark had figured $2,000 a day. "Starting now."

"Am I still taking orders from the embassy?"

"No. You're working for me."

"Ah, I guess that's OK," said Decker. And then, "Who are you?"

"I've been hired by our government as an independent contractor to investigate the murder of Jack Campbell and some other things that have been going on in Baku."

"Like what happened to that guy Peters?"

"Yeah, like that."

"I'm your guy."

"I'm not done yet. I have no intention of sharing anything but the most basic information with you. We're not partners. You're a hired gun. If you're not comfortable with that, and you're not comfortable taking orders, now's the time to tell me."

"I can follow orders."

"Good."

19

Washington, DC

Colonel Henry Amato didn't like the CIA.

He didn't like all the lies and the sneaking around. By his reckoning, nine times out of ten it was better to just have the balls to say what you believed up front, back up those words with a military that could pack a serious punch, and let the chips fall where they may. To be sure, he hadn't always followed those principles himself, but at least he hadn't made a career out of being a sneak—the way CIA Division Chief Ted Kaufman had.

"Thank you for coming," said Amato as he walked out from behind his desk and extended his hand. They were in his office at the Old Executive Office Building, across from the White House. It was seven in the morning, on a Saturday. Amato had been awake all night. "I've been asked to extend the president's appreciation for all you're doing during this difficult period."

Kaufman was a short guy, with a thin neck, spindly arms, and a little belly that popped out over his belt. Amato had met him a few times before, at obligatory Washington social functions. Kaufman had always struck him as a tired bureaucrat who'd climbed up about as high as he was ever going to get on the CIA ladder.

After answering a few questions about the attack on the CIA's Baku station, Kaufman said, "You can assure the president we'll have a replacement team in place by the end of today. I brought the personnel files you requested."

"I understand you're also coordinating with the FBI's forensic unit?"

"We are. A team will be landing in Baku shortly." Kaufman took a folder out of his briefcase. "These are the Agency assets en route."

Amato grabbed the file a little too eagerly and began to page through it. A former Baku-based operations officer was being transferred from his desk job in Istanbul; a young operations officer—an alleged Central Eurasia counterterrorism expert—was on his way from Uzbekistan; and a deputy chief of station from Moscow was being flown in. The investigation would be based out of the US embassy in Baku, said Kaufman.

Amato nodded as he flipped through the pages, decidedly unimpressed.

Then he came upon Daria's photo. He leaned forward a bit, trying to mask his reaction. "What's her status?"

"She's the woman I told you about, the one who was with Campbell when he was shot. The Azeris arrested her and brought her to a prison on the outskirts of Baku—"

"Arrested her?"

"That's what I've been told by our ambassador in Baku."

"They don't think she had anything to do with what happened to Campbell, do they?"

"We're not sure yet what they think."

"What prison?"

"Gobustan. It's outside of—"

"I know where it is."

"We believe she's still alive—which would make her our only operations officer in Azerbaijan to have survived the purge."

"What are we doing about her?"

"Well, you have to understand that she was operating under nonofficial cover—"

"She's also an American citizen. The president—"

"Not according to her Iranian passport. But we do have a former operative who's looking into who killed Campbell who might be able to help her too. Go to the next file."

Amato turned the page and found himself looking at a picture of an unremarkable man—a good quality in a spy, he conceded— with graying brown hair and dark brown eyes.

"Mark Sava," said Kaufman. "He was my chief of station/ Azerbaijan until six months ago. I persuaded him to come back on a contract basis."

Amato skimmed the first page of Mark's file. *Education: Rutgers State College of NJ... Thespian Society... Fulbright scholarship, Soviet Georgia... Place of Birth: Elizabeth, NJ... Mother deceased (suicide), Father...*

Sava's father, Amato read, was a devout Eastern Orthodox Christian who owned a gas station in Elizabeth, NJ. Amato glanced at the photo again and this time noted that Sava wasn't quite as unremarkable as he'd first thought. It was his eyes—they were wide set, in a way that made him look a little reptilian.

The second page of the file included a list of countries in which Sava had operated. "He's certainly been around the block a few times," said Amato.

"In addition to investigating this Campbell business, I authorized Sava to do what he could to help Daria Buckingham. As a result, he's put some feelers out to his contacts in the Azeri government."

"What contacts?"

"If the president wants us to share that information with the National Security Council he'll have to put in an official request."

"Is Sava going to be doing anything to actually secure her release?"

"That wasn't my impression and I don't see what good it would do even if he could. We haven't claimed her as our own, but realistically her cover's as good as blown. So even if we were to get her out tomorrow, she wouldn't be able to operate in-country. In the meantime, Gobustan might not be the worst place in the world for her to hole up in. At least she'll be safe there."

"I wouldn't be so sure of that."

"You know something I don't, Colonel?"

"Let's say I just don't share your optimism about her safety given your recent track record."

"No one's denying that we got hit pretty bad—"

"*Pretty* bad—"

"But now we're gearing up to play offense and—"

"Find a way to get her out."

"Talk to me in a couple days."

"All I can say is that if anything happens to Buckingham, there'll be hell to pay. I hope you understand that. I hope the DCI understands that. We—and by we I mean the president," lied Amato, "don't abandon our own."

Since Amato's boss was James Ellis, the president's personally appointed national security advisor, and since the president did indeed direct national security largely through Ellis, and Ellis in turn directed much of the president's policy through Amato, it could genuinely be said that on matters related to Iran, Amato usually did speak for the president.

But Kaufman wasn't easily bullied.

"No one's abandoning her, Colonel. She's alive and safe and we've let the Azeris know we'd like her to stay that way. If the president feels we should be doing otherwise, have him contact the DCI. Meanwhile, I've got other priorities."

20

In a vast desert south of Baku, Mark lay hidden amid an elevated cluster of mud volcanoes—bizarre little cratered hills that popped out of the desert like acne and burped up gray mud and methane gas. He held a pair of Zeiss binoculars to his eyes, focusing on an isolated collection of low-slung buildings visible in the far distance. Decker lay a few feet to his right.

The summer sun remained a brilliant, blinding white. No shade existed for miles around and the heat rising up from the baked earth was brutal. Beyond the mud flow in front of him, Mark could see patches of white salt crystals, the desert equivalent of a dusting of snow. The rest of the expansive landscape was dotted with dry scrub brush, wild lavender, and black puddles where oil had oozed naturally out of the ground. Gobustan Prison looked like a lifeless island surrounded by a sea of desert.

The road leading up to it was lined with steel pylons, remnants of the jail's former incarnation as a stone factory. Just beyond the prison lurked the bottom half of a mountain—its top half had been blasted apart and carted off to Baku in the form of limestone blocks. Mark wiped the sweat off his forehead and thought about all the poor schmucks who must have slaved away at that factory for their Soviet overlords. A couple decades of hell and then dead by forty. His life hadn't always gone as planned but at least he hadn't been born into that.

He refocused on a point just past the pylons where there was a gated break in the high chain-link fence surrounding the prison compound.

At ten past five, an olive-green van with military markings on it passed through the gate. It was similar to the one Mark had been stuffed into the night before.

"That's us," he said.

They hopped in Mark's Niva and took off across the desert, bouncing over rocks and smacking down scrub brush until they intersected the road ahead of the van at a secluded railroad crossing. Mark pulled over in a cloud of dust and parked the Niva in the middle of the road where it narrowed just before the train tracks. He popped open the hood as though he were having engine trouble. When the van came into view, he told Decker to get out.

"Flag him down. He should know what to do."

It was all supposed to be a big charade, so that Orkhan could cover his ass. A fake ambush.

Decker got out and raised his arms, but the van just sped up.

"Uh, he ain't stopping, boss."

"Fire a warning shot above him."

Decker did, but the van just blew by them at top speed.

"Well, shit," said Mark.

"Game on."

Mark wondered whether they had the right van. He held up his binoculars and looked down the road toward the prison. It was empty.

"Get in. We'll take him out on the road."

But the van reached the highway to Baku before they could catch up and as they drove through Gobustan, Mark kept his distance. Other cars were on the highway, weaving in and out of their lanes. On the edge of town they passed a collection of modest houses and then the landscape opened up again—just desert and power lines to the left and the Caspian Sea and a couple offshore oil platforms to the right.

"I'll get you close enough to take out the tires," Mark said. "Be ready."

But then the van made a sharp turn off the highway and started bouncing along a dirt road, headed east toward the sea. Mark turned off as well and floored it. The Niva's engine screamed and the rear shocks sounded like gunfire. Decker's gear bag fell from the backseat to the floor.

At the water's edge, the dirt road turned into a decrepit wood platform held up by rotting stilts. The platform skimmed the surface of the water, snaking as far as the eye could see out into the Caspian. Mark had seen roads like it before—they were decaying relics of the Soviet empire and inevitably led to aging offshore oil derricks.

He followed the van onto it, slowly gaining ground.

"I don't like this," said Decker.

"Me neither."

As the Niva bounced over the rickety wood planks, Mark squinted, leaned forward in his seat, and gripped the steering wheel even tighter. They were about ten feet above the sea. In some places, there were holes in the road where the wood had fallen away.

"Ah, you want me to drive, boss?" asked Decker.

"I got it."

"You sure? Because I'm pretty good behind the wheel."

"I said I got it. Where the hell are you going?" Mark said, thinking aloud. What was out here? He guessed that the road would dead-end at the last oil derrick, but that could be miles away. The blue sea that surrounded them was disturbingly vast.

Decker picked up the binoculars and did a 360-degree scan. There was no one behind them and no one other than the people in the van in front. They passed a series of rusting derricks, each one rising forty feet out of the water. Little iridescent oil slicks were visible under most.

When they'd gone about five kilometers, and the coast was nothing more than a distant brown blur in the heat, Decker said, "Fuckin' A, there's a boat out there. Two o'clock."

Mark couldn't see anything. Just waves, a few whitecaps, and an indefinite horizon blurred by low clouds. "Where are they headed?"

"Toward us."

"What kind of boat?"

Decker fiddled with the binoculars. "Looks like a Zodiac. Hauling ass."

Mark's plan had been to drive to the end of the stilt road, block the way back, and then confront whoever was in the van. "Can you take out the tires from here?"

"Maybe, but it could send them swimming."

Mark glanced down at the water. It looked shallow, but twenty feet was plenty to drown in. "Check the boat again."

"Same course," said Decker. And then, "I can see three men."

Mark considered—had someone gotten to Daria's guards? Someone who inspired more fear, or was shelling out more money, than Orkhan? "Take out the tires."

Decker retrieved his Glock from his ankle holster, rolled down the window, leaned his head out, and then shot twice without even appearing to aim. Both rear tires on the van burst. The van veered to the left, but then the driver overcompensated and sent the vehicle careening over the right edge.

21

For an instant Daria felt weightless, and then suddenly the bottom of the van slammed up into her with an explosive smack.

She bolted up in the darkness and fumbled for the rear door handle, hoping the force of what had to have been a crash had somehow popped open the lock. It hadn't.

Then came the water—first lapping at her ankles and seconds later rising to her shins. As it reached her knees, she swiveled and waded toward the front of the van, finding in the dark the locked metal door that led to the driver's compartment.

She was about to cry out for help when someone ripped it open.

Blinding sunlight spilled in. A face slowly came into view. Through the windshield of the van all she could see was open sea. She wondered whether she was losing her mind.

They'd been driving. On a dirt road, she'd thought, bumping over what had felt like potholes.

A huge hand encircled her arm and yanked her into the open water. The van was sinking, its driver swimming away at top speed. A strange wood road loomed above her.

"Can you swim?"

The man who'd pulled her out had an enormous rectangular head and blue eyes. He smiled at her in a goofy way that put her at ease.

"I think. Who are—"

"John Decker! Mark sent me!"

"He's here?"

"Up on the road."

Daria saw him now. He was staring down at her, looking worried.

"Get your ass up here!" Mark yelled. "We're going to have company!"

Daria crawl-stroked to the road and began to shimmy up one of the thick wood stilts just as Mark appeared from above and extended a hand down. With a wiry strength that surprised her, he hauled her up onto the road.

Decker joined them a second later.

"I can't outrun them in reverse," said Mark.

Daria saw the boat—a distant black Zodiac filled with armed men. And that was when she understood how disastrously she'd miscalculated. Dragging Mark into this had been wrong, so wrong. She'd been deluding herself—thinking that it had been some kind of bad-luck coincidence that she'd been with Campbell when he'd been shot.

It hadn't been a coincidence. It had been blowback for what she'd done. She'd been a target then, just like she was now.

"Turn the car!" said Decker. He groaned as he leaned his barrel chest into the front fender. When Mark joined him, the Niva moved a bit.

"Push!" said Decker through clenched teeth.

Daria threw her weight into it too and together the three pivoted the car so that it was facing the shore. They all jumped in. Mark threw the car into gear, slammed his foot down on the gas pedal, and didn't look back.

22

A half hour later, Mark pulled onto a narrow dirt road that intersected the highway to Baku and cut between two shallow salt lakes.
He stopped at a pumping station near the south lake and parked
between the empty building and an enormous wastewater pipe that
had once drained toxins from a nearby Soviet factory into the lake.

"We need a little privacy," he said to Decker. Then he remembered how the guy had vaulted over the side of the stilt road, and
added, "Please."

He hadn't told Decker anything about Daria's relationship to
the CIA, or why she'd been imprisoned at Gobustan.

"Where do you want me?"

"Take cover somewhere, watch the road. And let us know if
anyone's coming."

Once they were alone, Mark told Daria about the carnage at
the Trudeau House, and about what had happened at Peters's apartment. He finished by saying, "Aside from the support staff at the
embassy, the two of us are the only CIA personnel in Azerbaijan.
For now at least."

Daria put her hand to her mouth as she listened. She was in
the passenger seat, still soaking wet. With her black silk blouse
plastered to her body, she looked thin and fragile. Eventually she
whispered, "I can't tell you how..." She put her hand to her mouth

again, as though trying to stuff the emotion back inside her. He could hear her breathing through her nose. "...how grateful I am."

The sun was beginning to go down; it hung low in the sky, a red ball suspended just above the bleak desert.

Her fingers lightly touched his shoulder.

Mark was reminded of when they'd met up a year ago, at a crowded bar. She'd touched his shoulder then too—just before slipping a thumb drive loaded with Iranian bank records into his hand. Their faces had been inches from each other when she'd whispered the encryption code, and they'd both lingered in that intimate space for a few beats longer than they should have.

Afterwards Mark had reminded himself that thinking with one's dick was a dangerous way to collect intelligence. He reminded himself of that again now.

"Listen," he said, "I need you to tell me what was going on between you and Campbell."

She pulled her hand away.

"Nothing. I'd never met him before."

"Well, he knew you."

She looked confused. "No, he didn't."

"Campbell requested that you translate for him at the convention."

"*Me?*"

"Yeah, Kaufman told me he called up the ambassador and asked for you by name. Now why would he do that?"

"I have no idea. Campbell wasn't even here on government business, he worked for himself as a consultant. It was a joke that I was even assigned to help him, like he couldn't just hire his own translator. I figured the ambassador owed him a favor or something."

"Well, there has to be a reason that a former deputy sec. def. wanted you as his translator."

Daria shot him a look.

"By the way," said Mark, "I still have my security clearance. And Kaufman authorized you to talk to me." Which wasn't quite true.

"I'm not lying to you."

"I didn't say that you were."

"You were thinking it."

Mark reflected on the contradiction inherent to Agency field-work: that so much of an operations officer's life involved deception and lies—indeed, being a good liar was a central job requirement—but that when it came to intra-Agency communication, those same officers were suddenly expected to be scrupulously honest. Of course, that didn't always happen. When he'd been an operations officer, he'd sometimes had difficulty respecting that sharp line between acceptable conduct in the field and acceptable conduct in the office.

Which is to say that he'd frequently lied his ass off to Langley. There were some things they didn't need, and in truth probably didn't want, to know. He'd always thought that Daria was more of the straight-shooter type, but now he wasn't so sure.

"What were you working on before this happened?" he asked.

Daria stayed quiet for a while, then, with some reluctance, said, "Not long after you left, I discovered through one of my agents that China and Iran have come to an agreement regarding an oil pipeline." She looked out the windshield instead of at Mark as she spoke.

"From where to where?"

"From Iran, up through Turkmenistan, then east through Kazakhstan and into China."

"They've been talking about something like that for a while. And Kazakhstan and China are already connected."

"Not at the level they're planning now. This isn't just any oil pipeline. It's huge—four million barrels a day."

"Jesus," said Mark. He knew something about pipelines. A key focus of his job as station chief had been the safeguarding of the BTC—it was the West's crucial energy link to the Caspian region. But the BTC could only handle around one million barrels a day.

"Yeah. That's what I thought." Daria ran her hand through her hair and glanced briefly at Mark with a worried look on her face.

"How are they going to fill the thing? Iran hardly even pumps that much oil."

"Once it's built, they'll get other countries to tie into it. With Kazakhstan's Kashagan field flowing into it, they could fill the thing. Turkmenistan will probably sign up too. Of course, China's a long way away and it would be cheaper for the oil to go through the BTC or to get shipped out of the Persian Gulf."

"But the Chinese are willing to pay a huge premium for the security of knowing that they'll be able to get a steady supply of oil," said Mark.

"If that pipeline gets built, most of the oil that Iran exports will go to China for the next thirty years. The US and Europe can say good-bye to pressuring Iran through oil embargoes."

"How definite is this?"

"Construction has already started in China and Iran. They won't make any official announcement until they have to, but it's well past the planning stages."

"Did Washington order you to take any countermeasures? Something that could have resulted in blowback?"

"No. But I was worried to hell the agent who told me all this would get caught. That's why I was armed at the convention, by the way, even though Logan hadn't authorized it. I was worried, Mark. For good reason it turns out."

"What about the rest of the station? Were they taking countermeasures?"

"I would have known about anything big. If you ask me, we should have been taking countermeasures, but you know Kaufman. He's not going to stick his neck out. Maybe the Near East Division was doing something, but if they were, Central Eurasia was out of the loop."

Daria went back to staring out the front windshield, looking worried. And angry.

As Mark studied her face, the feeling of dread that he'd felt in Peters's apartment washed over him again. He wished that Daria would just walk away from all this. Go back to the States, get a real job, marry someone decent, have a few kids, and enjoy life. She was young enough that she could still do it.

It's not worth it, he wanted to tell her. People had been killing each other over control of Central Asia and its resources for nearly two hundred years. First it was the British versus the Russians, then it was the Americans versus the Soviets, and now it was a free-for-all, with Russia, China, and the West all clawing at each other's throats over oil. It was the latest incarnation of the Great Game—and it would be played the same way it always had been played, with or without her.

She wouldn't get out, of course, any more than he would have packed up and gone home himself if someone had told him to twenty years ago. She still believed that there was some larger purpose, that she was making a difference, that it wasn't just people killing each other over money.

Mark said, "So Iran and China have a huge pipeline deal going on, we're not doing anything about it, and that's all you know?"

"That's all I know."

"Fuck it. I'm gonna get to the bottom of this, Daria."

23

They bought clothes and essentials in Baku and paid cash for two rooms at the Absheron Hotel. A sixteen-story monolith, it had been the place to stay during the Soviet era but was now a worn-out has-been. It suited their purposes perfectly, though, because the different floors were managed by different hotel operators who barely noticed who was coming and going.

Inside Daria's room on the eleventh floor was an ancient refrigerator that sounded like a diesel truck when it kicked on and a stained carpet that looked as though it had been installed around the Brezhnev era. The bathroom, another Soviet relic, featured rusted pipes, a wobbly toilet, and cracked tiles.

But there were clean sheets, hot water, and a view. The Absheron overlooked the Caspian Sea and the hulking Dom Soviet, the old communist government building which was now a largely deserted curiosity, still waiting its turn, along with the Absheron itself, to be gentrified with new oil money. In front of the Dom Soviet lay a vast asphalt parade ground where the Red Army used to goose-step behind missile launchers.

Mark followed Daria to her room. He walked to the balcony and drew the blinds closed as she stuck a new SIM card into his cell phone and proceeded to make a series of calls. She spoke in

Azeri, Farsi, and even a little Chinese, reflecting the multiethnic composition of her foreign agents, of which she had many.

Using coded language, she was able to set up meetings with the few agents she dared to call directly; the plan was to see if they had any leads on the source of the violence. Then she announced she was going to cut and dye her hair.

"What time's your first meeting?"

"Ten tonight."

"Decker and I will follow you, play backup."

"Thanks, but my agents expect me to meet them alone."

"We'll be discreet."

"I said my agents expect me to meet them alone."

With that she went into the bathroom and shut the door.

After a minute, Mark knocked. Daria cracked the door and he opened it the rest of the way. She was standing in front of the mirror with a pair of scissors in her hand, cutting four inches off her hair and letting the clippings fall into the sink below. The faucet was shut off but a drip was making a sound like a metronome, slowly boring a hole in the base of the sink.

Mark had read Daria's 108-page personnel file twice. And she'd reported directly to him for over a year. So he figured he knew her pretty well. An idealistic overachiever who was plenty smart enough to drive herself nuts was how he'd pegged her. She was also a bit of a loner, probably due to the fact that she was half-Iranian by blood and that as a kid she'd been mocked for her ancestry—until she hit puberty that is. After that no one cared where her mother had come from. Instead it was her beauty that set her apart.

On the flip side, he didn't think Daria really knew him. For starters, she'd had no access to his personnel file. And as her boss, he'd presented himself as a by-the-books, asexual, analyst-type guy who came to work on time, rarely drank, was scrupulously honest with his operatives, and wholeheartedly believed in whatever mission he was sending her out on. They'd only met in person a couple of times a month, for maybe an hour at a time, so it had been relatively easy to maintain those fictions.

Now he wondered whether his professional persona was preventing her from telling him everything she knew. Or whether there was something else going on.

"Did anything happen at the prison that you want to talk about?"

"No."

"*No* nothing happened, or *no* you don't want to talk about it?"

"They pushed me around at first, but after you came last night there was no more of that."

She clipped off another lock of hair and it fell into the sink.

"Did you know any of the other ops officers well?"

He didn't think she had. In Baku, security concerns had limited the ability of CIA personnel to interact, especially for those operating under nonofficial cover.

"Well enough."

"Is that what's bothering you?"

"Isn't all this bothering you? I mean, the entire station got wiped out. Are you human?"

He considered her reactions to his questions: she was making eye contact; she wasn't touching her throat or face; her expressions seemed genuine. But Daria knew the obvious signs of lying as well as he did. The fact that she wasn't exhibiting any didn't tell him much.

"I'm just trying to figure this out, Daria." Was he just letting Kaufman's doubts about her get to him? Making something out of nothing?

Or had he been a complete idiot to have trusted her in the first place?

Because there had to have been a reason why Jack Campbell, just a few hours before getting shot in the head, had requested that she be his translator.

They stood there silently, with Mark looking at Daria and Daria looking at herself in the mirror, until Mark said something he hadn't planned on saying.

"Listen, Daria, I know the way the system works. It's easy to get in over your head." He remembered when they'd first met, how she'd come charging in, twenty-nine years old and all fired up to fight the good fight after being deskbound as a CIA analyst for three years. He'd found her enthusiasm, while naive, to be refreshing. But now he wondered whether that enthusiasm had led her to do something she shouldn't have. "I've been there myself, I'm not perfect."

The drip from the sink ticked off a few seconds.

Eventually Mark said, "I care about you, Daria. I'm trying to help."

He was actually telling the truth, but his voice sounded patronizing and false even to himself.

"You are helping, Mark." She spoke with forced politeness. "Thanks again for coming for me."

"Anything you tell me will stay in this room," he added.

For a moment her face seemed to soften, as though she were actually considering confiding in him. But then she went back to her hair, and to whatever dark thoughts were eating away at her.

24

Duke University, Fourteen Years Ago

"Miss? Oh, Miss? Just a moment?"

Daria eyed the little man walking toward her with suspicion. At first glance there was nothing alarming about him—he was clean-shaven and wore rumpled khaki pants and an ill-fitting brown blazer. Maybe a professor, she thought, looking at the little crow's-feet wrinkles around his eyes. But the unnerving intensity of his smile made her wary.

"Miss, I apologize for the intrusion. If I could just have a minute of your time."

He spoke in an overly formal tone.

"I'm actually kind of busy."

"It concerns a matter of utmost importance to you."

She was on her way to visit a friend at Alspaugh Hall. The slender leaves of the nearby willow oaks were a vibrant spring green. The afternoon sun shone brightly in the cloudless sky. A few classmates lay reading nearby on the lawn. She sensed no immediate danger.

So she stopped. "OK…Why are you staring at me like that?"

"You remind me of someone I haven't seen in a long time."

"I didn't get your name."

"*My name is Reza Tehrani.*"

An Iranian name, she noted. Which explained the olive skin similar to her own.

Tehrani unzipped a leather-backed folder and removed a square, faded color photo. "*This is the woman you remind me of, dear. That's me standing next to her, over thirty years ago.*"

Daria saw that Tehrani's hand was trembling. She clutched her biology textbook a little tighter to her chest.

"*Please, take it.*"

Hesitant but curious, Daria took the photo. The petite woman in the pale green sundress did remind her a little bit of herself.

"*Who is she?*"

"*That, my dear…*" *Tehrani paused for a moment.* "*That is your mother.*"

"*Ah, I think you have the wrong person. That's not my mother.*"

"*I know this comes as a shock—*"

"*I said that's not my mother.*"

"*If I knew of another way—*"

"*I really am busy.*"

"*You have her eyes, her hair, her nose, her skin.*" *Tehrani's eyes were tearing up.* "*She died when you were young. You never knew—*"

"*You're wrong. I have a mother. She lives in Geneva with my father.*"

"*You refer to the good woman who raised you. And raised you well from what I can see. But the woman who gave birth to you is the woman you see in this photo.*"

"*Are you crazy?*"

"*Look at her. She looks like you, dear. You must know it.*"

"*I'm going to have to ask you to leave.*"

She tried to hand the photo back to him but he wouldn't take it.

"*The people who raised you—*"

"*I'm outta here—*"

"*Adopted you when you were a baby. You are old enough now to know the truth. I have waited so long.*"

"*I said leave!*"

Daria began to walk away.

"*I am your uncle, my child! Your mother's younger brother! I mean you no harm.*"

She broke out into a jog.

"*My phone number, I wrote it on the back of the photo!*"

"*Get the hell away from me or I'll call the cops!*"

"Do these people remind you of anyone?"

Daria stood in her friend's dorm room. Through a window she could see the lawn outside of Alspaugh Hall, but the man who'd accosted her was no longer there. She laid the old photo he'd given her on her friend's desk.

"Julie thinks her brother can get us stuff for margaritas tonight. Can we use your blender?"

"Yeah, fine."

"Yuck, you're all sweaty. Did you run here?"

Daria realized she had been running. All the way up to the third floor. "Take a look at the woman in this photo. Who does she look like?"

"Gimme a second, I'm almost done." Daria's friend typed a few more words into her computer, then glanced at the photo. "I'll pick up some frozen strawberries too. Is that you?"

25

Mark paid a visit to Decker in a room across the hall.

He was lounging on a narrow twin bed that sagged under his weight. One hand was channel-surfing with the TV remote and the other was wedged in his pants above his crotch.

"News have anything about Campbell?" asked Mark.

"Negative. Hey, I forgot to buy toothpaste. Can I bum some of yours?"

Instead of answering, Mark pushed a few buttons on his cell phone, trying to retrieve the list of calls Daria had just placed to her agents. He saw that she had taken the precaution of deleting them. "Change of plan."

"Yeah?"

"Daria's going to be meeting someone tonight."

Decker kept watching the television. He was a bit of a strange bird, thought Mark. A guy who gave the impression that he'd like nothing better than to hang out with his buddies in a frat basement every night, playing beer pong until three in the morning. But instead he was hanging out in Baku. By himself.

"I'd like you to help me keep an eye on her."

Decker turned his head. "I'm game."

"Yeah, I figured you would be." Mark pocketed his phone and sat down on the twin bed adjacent to Decker's. He took the remote from Decker's hand and shut off the TV.

"Actually, I was watching that," said Decker.

"Why are you here, John?"

Decker looked up at him from the bed. "Uh, because you're paying me, sir."

"I mean here in Baku, working on your own. You were only a SEAL for three years."

"So?"

"So were you discharged honorably?"

"It was a general," said Decker.

"That explains a lot."

"What's that supposed to mean?"

"It means you're working on your own because no big security firm would hire someone with just general discharge papers. Because they know that the navy doesn't spend over a million bucks training a SEAL just to kick him out early unless they have some serious problems with him."

Decker made a lousy attempt to conceal his discomfort.

Mark said, "I want to know what those problems were."

"I tell you what," said Decker. "You start filling me in on all you know about what's going on with this Daria chick and people taking potshots at us and I'll get into my deal. Unless you're willing to do that, back off and let me do my job."

Mark took out his wallet, pulled out $3,000, and placed the money on the end table between the two beds. "There's a bonus payment in there as an extra thanks for your service," he said. "Really, I mean it. For what it's worth I'll tell the embassy that I wouldn't be here if it weren't for you."

"Oh, come on."

Mark was walking out of the room when Decker said, "I'm here because if I go back to the States with a general, it's like I might as well have never been in the military. I can't put that shit on my resume. Not to mention I got family."

"Where are you from?"

"New Hampshire. My father was a marine sergeant, my brother is a marine corporal. We don't do general discharges."

"They know you left the SEALs?"

"Fuck no."

"You planning on telling them?"

"After I get my general upgraded to an honorable."

"That's what this is all about? That's why you're hiding out in Baku?"

"General discharges are upgraded all the time, and in three months I'll be eligible to apply for an upgrade myself. If I help out the US government over here, it'll only help my case."

"I'm out of the loop, John. Nothing you do while working for me is going to help you in the slightest. Even what you did in Peters's apartment. I wish I could say otherwise."

"Did I ask for your help?"

"No, I guess you didn't." Mark picked up the remote control again and tapped it on his knee for a few seconds. "Want to tell me what you did to deserve a general?"

"It was a rules of engagement issue. You don't have anything to worry about."

"Meaning?"

"Meaning I refused a bullshit order."

"To do what?"

"Take out this Afghani dude."

"Why'd you refuse?"

"Because the guy wasn't a threat."

"Was he armed?"

"Everyone's armed over there."

"Was it your first time in combat?"

"I'm telling you it was a bullshit order. My CO was just jumpy and wouldn't admit it. They offered me a demotion to regular navy, I told them to go screw themselves."

Mark tapped the remote on his knee a few more times. Then he shrugged, turned the television back on, and gave the remote back to Decker. "The thing is, Daria can't know you're going to be helping me."

"I'm not working for her. Just tell me where you want me."

"You up for a long night?"

Decker cracked a wry smile and clicked the TV to a Russian food channel. A fat chef in a white hat was carving up a chicken with a meat cleaver. "At this point, sir, I'm game for almost anything."

26

Daria watched with something bordering on alarm as Mark strolled back into her room, tossed a bag with his stuff in it on one of the two twin beds, and slumped down into a dirt-brown easy chair with squeaky springs.

"Figure I'll crash here for tonight if you don't mind," he said. "I was thinking we could help protect each other."

Daria wondered whether that was just Mark's way of saying he didn't trust her. Or whether he was trying to come on to her. Or whether he thought she was incompetent and needed protection. She tried to read his face but found she couldn't. She should have tried to run while he was next door talking to Decker.

"I thought you were staying next door. With Decker."

"I sent him away."

Daria closed her eyes for a moment, relieved. One less person to run from.

"Why'd you change your mind about him?"

"I don't need him anymore. I was just keeping him around for protection when you met your agents, but you made it clear you don't want us around, so I let him go."

"Where's he going?"

"If he's smart, he'll hole up in the embassy and fly home. Anyway, I figured it'd be safer if we were in the same room."

"Fine."

The sooner she could get to Astara the better, thought Daria. She should be driving there now.

"Nice getup."

She was wearing designer jeans, gold hoop earrings, a tight T-shirt that accentuated what little chest she had, and a modest amount of glossy red lipstick. She couldn't tell whether Mark was being sarcastic or not. It bothered her that he'd become so inscrutable, at least to her.

"It's how my agents know me. Minus the new hair."

What she was wearing, she knew, also had the benefit of lulling older men into thinking she was some naive twenty-five-year-old who was probably loose with her affections, easily impressed by classified information, and too dim-witted to be deceitful. Tonight, though, the only person she was trying to fool was Mark.

"I know," he said.

"I hate wearing makeup."

Mark was still staring at her, and it was putting her on edge. She started looking for something in the shoulder bag she'd bought earlier that evening.

Mark stood up. "I was gonna order us some dinner. There's a restaurant on the sixteenth floor. They'll bring it down."

"First we're changing rooms. If someone picks Decker up and he talks, this place'll be compromised."

"Good point. By the way, even though Decker won't be tailing you tonight, I will be."

"I told you, my agents expect—"

"It's not open for discussion. You won't see me, but I'll be there."

She gave him a look that said back off, but he either didn't get it or didn't care. She wondered whether he was intentionally making it hard for her to run or just being stubbornly protective.

"I don't want your help, Mark."

She looked at her watch, thinking she *had* to get to Astara.

"Yeah, I'm getting that."

27

Washington, DC

"The Azeris just let her go?" asked Colonel Amato, upon hearing that Daria was no longer imprisoned at Gobustan.

"Her release was arranged by Mark Sava, the contract operative I told you about," said Kaufman.

"I thought you said we were looking at a couple days, minimum?"

"Evidently he saw an opportunity." Kaufman spoke with little enthusiasm.

"Excellent." Amato nodded his head as he held his phone to his ear. "Excellent work. I assume that upon her release, Ms. Buckingham was taken to the embassy, for a debrief?"

"In fact she was not."

After a silence, Amato said, "So when's she coming in?"

"Whenever Sava decides he doesn't need her anymore for his investigation."

"He's using her? After what she's been through?"

"Our assets in Azerbaijan are limited. He's doing what he has to. And since Ms. Buckingham was carrying an Iranian passport when she was picked up by the Azeris, it could get sticky if she's seen approaching our embassy. We haven't officially acknowledged her as one of our own and the embassy is almost certain to be under surveillance."

"Is she at least under protection? After what happened in Baku, under your watch I might add, I'd think protecting your remaining assets would be paramount."

"Well, yes. If you count Sava as protection. He's still with her, and he's an experienced operative. One of our best."

Amato recalled the section of Mark's file that had detailed his history as an operations officer. "I didn't see any military experience in his file, nothing to suggest he's qualified for a real protection detail."

"Are you kidding? In the nineties he served as an advisor to our Special Activities Division. Abkhazia, Tajikistan, Nagorno-Karabakh…that's three civil wars right there that he was in the thick of. The file might not have spelled out all the details, but I can assure you, the guy knows what he's doing."

Amato sighed. "Where are he and Buckingham now?"

"Baku, I think."

"You think?"

"He didn't say and I knew better than to ask. He was on a cell phone. It was a thirty-second conversation."

"Call him—immediately. If he's half as good as you seem to think he is, he should be able to find a way to safely bring both Daria Buckingham and himself to the embassy for a debriefing. If he still needs her to help with the investigation she can do it from the embassy."

Kaufman sighed. "I have the last cell number Sava used. But this guy changes his phone number practically every time he makes a call." He explained about SIM cards. "He's obnoxiously obsessive about it. I doubt I'll even be able to reach him until he calls me."

Speaking slowly, as if addressing a hapless private, Amato said, "Both Buckingham and Sava need to be questioned about what happened in Baku. And quickly, so the president can properly instruct State on how we can get ahead of this mess. Campbell's assassination has got the Azeris worried that an intelligence war is about to break out in their country between us and the Iranians. If we don't play this right, it's possible the Azeris will restrict all our in-country assets, including the military's. So I don't care how you do it, you bring Sava and Buckingham in ASAP."

"If that's the way the president truly feels, I'd advise you to have him communicate the same to the DCI. Because right now you're the only person who's pressing me on this. And I don't take orders from you, Colonel. We'll hear from Sava when we hear from him."

28

Mark forced himself to stay awake, secretly keeping watch over Daria as he stared up at the swirls in the dark textured ceiling and turned everything over in his head. The Iranians, the Chinese, the pipeline, Campbell, Daria...nothing was in focus.

She'd returned at midnight from an unproductive meeting with a middle-aged Chinese diplomat and now lay in the twin bed next to his own, curled up into a fetal position. He suspected she was still awake because her breathing was irregular and every so often the sheets rustled in a way that suggested consciousness. They were both fully clothed, ready to bolt at a moment's notice if need be.

At one in the morning he got up to go to the bathroom. As he was taking a piss, he dialed Decker's number.

"I'm up!" said Decker.

Mark hung up without speaking and went back to bed. And this time, knowing that he'd transferred the rest of the night watch to Decker, he fell into a deep sleep—until four thirty in the morning, that is, when his cell phone started ringing.

He fumbled for it in his front pocket. When he finally flipped it open, Decker said, "Get your ass moving, boss!"

Mark jumped out of bed and turned on the light. Daria was gone. "Where is she?"

"On foot, already walking north on Pushkin."

"Why didn't you call earlier?" He grabbed his bag, opened it to see if Daria had stolen any of his cash—she hadn't—and limped toward the door, still stiff from having jumped off the balcony. Taped to the door at eye level was a note:

Please drive straight to the embassy and stay there. I'm sorry I put you in danger. DO NOT try to find me.

Daria

"I did," said Decker. "You didn't answer."

"Don't lose a visual."

Through the lobby windows, Mark saw the gray Lada sedan that Decker had rented parked in the circular driveway in front of the Absheron. The keys would be in the ignition. When he was about twenty feet from the lobby doors, he stopped. "How we looking?"

"Still good."

But Mark stayed where he was.

A moment later Decker said, "Hold up! She's turning, heading right back to you." And then, "Shit, she's staring right at the entrance to the Absheron. I think she's onto you, boss."

"No, she's just being careful, doubling back to trip up any tail that might be on her."

He sat down on a couch that faced away from the windows and waited.

A couple of minutes later Decker said, "OK, she's moving again."

Mark walked through the lobby doors and got into the Lada. Inside was a faded navy-blue beret, a dirty brown blazer a size too big for him, a baseball cap, and a black windbreaker.

He started the engine. "Fall back. I got her."

Mark drove past Daria, turned right a couple of blocks later, and then parked the car. That early in the morning, the streets of Baku were empty and dark. He followed her on foot. Taking parallel streets, he was able to monitor her from a distance at the intersections, using walls and bus shelters as blinds. He changed his appearance frequently, rotating the brown blazer, blue beret, baseball cap, and windbreaker in different combinations.

She took surveillance-detection action on a couple occasions, slowing down and then speeding up, stopping and pretending to search for something in her shoulder bag as soon as she'd turned a corner. At one point she took a circuitous route through the massive railway station, circling back on her tracks a couple times.

But while Daria was a natural when it came to recruiting and manipulating foreign agents, Mark noted she was still a bit of a rookie in the countersurveillance department. To him, her movements were often obvious and easy to anticipate—good enough to flush out a tail of even above average skill, perhaps, but not someone with his kind of experience.

She walked the streets for over two hours. As she did, the city slowly came to life. Men pulled back metal grates covering their storefront windows and soon the smell of baking bread began to mix with the stink of diesel fumes.

Finally she ducked into an alley, pulled a headscarf and a black chador robe from her bag, and came out dressed as a conservative Muslim woman. She walked straight down Azadlyq Avenue until she came to the Central Bank of Azerbaijan, an angular modern building clad in brilliant copper-colored reflective glass. In front of the bank lay an open square with a long central wading pool awash in the delicate sunlight of dawn.

Using his binoculars, Mark observed Daria from a distance as she sat down on a bench by the pool. Then he called Decker and asked him to retrieve the Lada.

When Decker showed up, Mark got into the driver's seat and parked the car a couple of hundred yards behind Daria. The morning commuters were beginning to come out, providing some cover.

"She'll wait until seven when that bank, the Credit Azerbaycan, will let her in for off-hours access." Mark pointed to a small brick building on the perimeter of the square, barely visible because it was tucked behind the much larger Central Bank.

"How would you know?"

When Mark didn't answer, Decker said, "She a CIA agent?"

Mark hesitated, then said, "Operations officer." Noting the blank look on Decker's face, he said, "Operations officers get hired by the CIA in Washington and are then sent abroad to spy. Agents are the foreigners they recruit to spy for them. The other thing you should know is that she's been operating in Baku under nonofficial cover. Which means she has no diplomatic immunity, no special protection, nothing. The embassy can't even officially acknowledge her. Needless to say, you are not to repeat—"

"I can keep my mouth shut."

"I know she kept a safe deposit box with her original US passport here at the Azerbaycan. The CIA has a relationship with the bank that allows her and other ops officers access outside of normal hours."

"You know a lot about her."

"I used to be her boss."

"Why'd she run?"

"I couldn't tell you."

29

Daria swiped her thumb across the fingerprint scanner and waited for a beep but none sounded.

The bank teller, a woman in her twenties who wore thick makeup caked over her acne-scarred face, frowned then pushed the reset button.

"Again."

Daria did. Still no beep. "Is there a problem with the machine?"

"Sometimes it's slow."

"I'm actually in kind of a rush."

And she was god-awful hot in her heavy chador. She wiped a bead of sweat from the top of her forehead, reminded herself to breathe normally, and glanced at her watch—five minutes after seven. Mark would almost certainly be awake by now.

She hoped he'd have the good sense to take refuge at the embassy.

"Should I try it again?"

The machine beeped. "There it goes. Now enter your password."

Daria did so and was led to a room in the back of the bank. A minute later the teller placed her safe deposit box on a table in the center of the room.

"Ring me when you're done."

Daria locked the door from the inside and quickly opened the box. After confirming that a long strand of her hair still lay undisturbed across the top, she pushed her real US passport aside, revealing $2,000, an Iranian passport, an Iranian driver's license, a second US passport, and a US driver's license.

She hastily pocketed the altered documentation and the money and was about to put her real US passport back in the safe deposit box when she stopped herself.

At this point she should just throw the real one out, she thought. She couldn't use it again, she'd burned her bridges. And although it had been obtained legally, in reality it was just as fake as the others—just as fake as the first eighteen years of her life had been...

The drive from Duke University to the little town of Wolf Trap in Fairfax County, Virginia, usually took Daria over four hours, but tonight she pushed her mom's old BMW hard and did it in nearly three.

As she turned onto the wooded suburban road where she'd grown up, she wondered whether she was losing her mind. There was the stream she'd tried to dam up with rocks and branches when she was ten, there was tree she'd fallen from and broken her arm...

She recalled the pushy little man who, just hours ago, had claimed to be her uncle, and shuddered at the thought that he might intrude on this world.

The large brick Georgian house sat at the end of a cul-de-sac. No light shone from inside. With her parents abroad, the family house was only used these days as a place to gather for holidays.

And a place to keep records.

She opened the door, flipped on the lights in the long front foyer, and disabled the burglar alarm by typing in "Penguin"—the name of the rescue-shelter cat she'd picked out on her fifth birthday.

Everything was deceptively, comfortably normal—the Persian carpets, the pale yellow walls, the photos of her and her family on the walls. This was her home.

Still, she felt like an intruder as she climbed the steps to the second floor, taking care not to make too much noise.

Her parents' bedroom was cavernous, thirty feet long and nearly as wide. On her mother's side stood a tall antique armoire, made from gorgeous burled walnut.

She opened one of the lower drawers and found an expired membership card for the Corcoran Gallery of Art, her mother's voter registration card, an expired driver's license, and there, in the back, the card that Daria had remembered seeing years ago, when she'd retrieved her mother's passport from the very same drawer. She hadn't examined it closely back then, but she did now: It read American Red Cross Volunteer Blood Donor ID Card, and then it gave her mother's name, and her blood type: AB.

Daria hung her head as she crumpled the card in her hand.

Three months ago, she had given blood at Duke as part of a freshman class blood drive and learned she was type O. And from the advanced placement biology course she'd taken as a senior in high school, she knew that an AB parent couldn't have a type O child.

Unless, of course, that child had been adopted.

After staring dumbfounded at the card for several minutes, Daria lifted her head and noticed her old field hockey stick propped up in a corner of the room. She'd used it in the regional tournament her team had won last year. Her mom had wanted to frame it.

Without pausing to think, she stood up, retrieved the stick, settled on a good grip, then faced the wall where a framed studio photo of her and her alleged parents hung at eye level. Intellectually, she realized that they'd probably been the good guys. Certainly they'd cared for her as though she'd been their own for eighteen years.

But they'd also lied to her, and she was furious.

She swung the field hockey stick into the photo frame, shattering the glass and impaling the photo.

"Fuck you," she said, leaving the stick stuck where it was in the wall. "Fuck you all."

⊠

By eight o'clock Daria was well south of Baku, hurtling down the M3 highway at over a hundred and fifty kilometers an hour in a rented Fiat subcompact.

She stripped off her headscarf and chador and drove with the windows open, so that the wind rushed though her hair. But every time she blew by a town where there was cell phone reception, she rolled up the windows and placed a call to her uncle in France, the same uncle who had told her who she really was. No one ever answered.

She told herself she should eat something, that she needed the energy, but she had a sick feeling in her stomach that just wouldn't quit. Food was the last thing she wanted.

The coastal desert region gave way to marshland, then wheat fields, and after several hours, to lush green forests with occasional views of the steep, wooded Talysh Mountains to the west.

In the town of Astara, which sat right on the border with Iran, she parked across from the coral-colored district chess school, on a road that ran through the center of the town. After walking a few blocks, she turned down a partially paved street choked with overgrown grass and crisscrossed from above with low-hanging wires. Weed-strewn piles of bricks lay in front of a few half-built houses. Poorly stocked shops and dilapidated two-story apartment houses lined the rest of the street.

When Daria finally reached her destination, she put her hands to her mouth, seemingly paralyzed by what she saw.

Don't cry, she told herself. You half expected this, didn't you? Hold it together.

Hold it together? After all that had happened, what was the point?

30

Mark watched with confusion as Daria dropped to her knees.

Above her loomed a bombed-out building with gaping black holes where windows had once stood. It looked sinister and ugly. A few charred palm trees stood to either side of it. Police barriers had been set up in front of the building, to prevent gawkers from entering, but no one was manning them. The stink of ash and smoke was strong, as though embers from a fire were still smoldering.

Mark edged closer and saw that Daria was weeping.

A moment later a tall, gangly man with jet-black hair ran up to her. They embraced and began walking.

Mark followed but they soon ducked into one of several cafés situated between the Caspian Sea and a long line of diesel trucks waiting to cross the border into Iran.

He looped around to the rear of the café and hid behind the ruins of an old Ferris wheel that lay rusting on the gray, driftwood-littered beach. From there he had a clear view of the café's outdoor terrace where a few plastic tables had been set up. Daria and her companion argued for a moment before choosing a table in the corner, as far away as they could get from three men who sat on the terrace playing dominos and smoking.

Daria's friend was animated and gesticulating with his hands. He looked young, Mark thought. A bearded waiter brought them tea in clear glasses.

Mark called Decker and told him to meet him behind the Ferris wheel.

"And don't hang up," he added. "After I stop talking just keep the line open, put your phone in your pocket, and keep quiet."

Mark looped back around to the front and approached the café from the street side, so that he remained hidden to Daria and her companion. Inside were a few tables and a deli-style display case sparsely stocked with lamb stew, some wedges of fresh feta cheese in water, and a few packs of imitation Marlboro cigarettes.

The middle-aged man who'd been waiting on Daria's table asked Mark if he also wanted to sit outside. Mark said he wasn't there to eat. He took out his cell phone and two one-hundred-dollar bills from his wallet. He was there, *Insh'Allah*, to learn the truth about his unfaithful, scheming, lying whore of a wife.

31

"What was the leadership's reaction to the bombing?" asked Daria.

"I don't know."

"You didn't call them?"

"I couldn't."

Daria was about to ask why not, but instead she studied Tural. His eyes were bloodshot, his nose a little runny. And he kept tapping his foot under the table. She'd only met him twice before but recalled that, by the time he was ten, he'd lost his mother in a car accident and his father to the Iranian regime. The older brother who'd raised him had just died in the bombing.

He was a scared nineteen-year-old kid going through absolute hell and she'd hardly noticed because she was so upset herself. One of the women who'd been killed in the bombing had been a friend.

She put her hand over his own, trying to comfort him. "I'm sorry. I know this hasn't been easy for you."

"I'm OK."

He said it in a way that made Daria certain he wasn't. So she kept her hand on his and grieved silently with him until their waiter arrived with a large basket lined with a checkered cloth and full of flatbread. "We didn't order bread," she said. "Only tea."

"But you see we have cooked too much."

From his long beard and his ring stamped with the name *Ali*, she figured he was a religious nut who'd taken a fancy to her because she was wearing a full chador.

He flashed her a creepy smile. "There is no charge. Please."

The waiter stood there with the bread basket.

"OK, OK, leave it," said Tural, sounding agitated.

The waiter placed the bread in the center of the table.

Daria felt exposed here. She needed a refuge, a place to regroup and plan and think. But Tural was afraid his apartment was being watched. She cast a suspicious eye over the men playing dominos. There was no place she felt safe.

"So why couldn't you contact the leadership?"

"My *masoul* didn't trust me with the contact information."

"Was Yaver able to contact them?"

"Maybe. I don't know."

"You said he was hurt. How badly?"

"Some burns, that's all. The two of us are the only ones left. So he's the head of the cell now."

"Where is Yaver?"

"The mountain house."

"I've never been. Take me there, Tural."

Tural hesitated. "How do you know you didn't bring this on us?"

"I don't."

"What if the CIA knows you're working with us?"

"Even if they did, they'd never have done something like this. Never. I know them."

At that point Daria noticed a fly buzzing over the flatbread. Because she was frustrated and distraught, she flicked her hand at it with more anger than she might have normally. But the fly returned to settle on the bread.

"Disgusting." She picked up the basket and moved it down the table.

She was about to turn her attention back to Tural when she stopped herself, sensing that something wasn't right. So she picked up the basket again, this time assessing its weight.

"What are you doing?" asked Tural.

Daria removed the rest of the bread, and then the checkered napkin, revealing a cell phone. It was open and on. And she recognized it.

"Mark! Where are you!"

32

"Stay hidden," Mark told Decker.

He stood up. After a few moments, Daria began marching toward him across the gray sand beach. They converged in a barren area between the café and the ruined Ferris wheel.

"Working with the MEK behind the CIA's back? Nice, Daria. Really nice."

The MEK, short for Mojahedin-e Khalq, was an armed Iranian resistance group that had been trying for decades to get rid of the Islamic regime in Iran.

"You don't know you're talking about."

"Your buddy Tural used the word *masoul*. A *masoul* is an MEK supervisor. You were the one who briefed me on it. Remember that?"

"Then you should know I was looking to recruit agents from them," she shot back. "To get information for the CIA. Which is to say, to do my job."

They were staring each other down but keeping their distance.

"How did you find me?" she said.

"I followed you, how else?"

"You were sleeping when I left."

"Evidently not."

"I would have seen you."

"You didn't. You know why?"

Daria declined to speculate.

"Because I'm damn good at tailing people." Mark hoped the binoculars on his chest would distract her from considering the possibility that he'd had help from Decker, who'd rented a second car in Baku. The fact was, she should have spotted at least one of them. It had been poor countersurveillance work on her part that had allowed them to go undetected for so long.

She looked at him as though he were the one who'd betrayed her.

Mark said, "Was that an MEK safe house that was hit?"

"Yeah. With people in it."

"It's not a coincidence that this MEK cell was taken out around the same time as the Baku station."

"No shit. But I don't know how they're related. Yet."

"Why did you come down here now?"

"For the same reason I talked to my agents in Baku last night—to try to find out why Campbell was assassinated." A tone of exasperation crept into Daria's voice. "If the Iranians killed him, the MEK might know something about it through their sources in Iran."

"And that's why you want to talk to this guy Yaver?"

"Yeah. He was second in command of the cell that got hit and now he's the leader. And you know what? If you're hanging around, he's not going to talk to me. And if the guy waiting for me now suspects I'm in league with you—"

"That would be Tural?"

"—he won't even take me to Yaver."

"Get ready, I'm going to push you."

Mark suddenly sprang into Daria and shoved her hard, so that she fell backward on the sand.

DAN MAYLAND

She looked up at him, shaken. "What the fuck is the matter with you!"

"If you're armed, get out your gun now and point it at me."

Daria didn't need much prompting on that account. She lifted up her chador, pulled out a small pistol from between her jeans and her waist, and pointed it at Mark's chest.

"Tural is coming up behind you," said Mark. "Tell him to back off."

"Up yours."

"I pushed you so he won't think we're working together, Daria."

"We're not."

But Daria stood and gestured for Tural to back off, which he did. She kept the gun pointed at Mark. Her arm was shaking a bit.

"I saw you crying outside that MEK building. You cared a lot about those people who died. They weren't just agents you were running."

"Don't go there."

"You know, Daria, after I found out Logan was dead, I called Kaufman. I told him what had happened and that you were in trouble and that he damn well needed to help get you out of Gobustan before you wound up dead too. You know what he said?" Daria just stared at him. "He said he didn't trust you. He even thought maybe you had something to do with Campbell's death."

"That's bullshit."

"The reason he didn't trust you is because you're half-Iranian. I told him to go stuff it—that you were one of my best officers and that I believed in you. And when it was clear that Kaufman wasn't going to bend over backward to get you out of Gobustan, I did it myself by cutting a deal with Orkhan."

"I didn't ask you to do all that."

– 126 –

"Kaufman would have let you die there. I wasn't going to let that happen."

From the pained look on her face, Mark could see the guilt trip he was serving up was having the desired effect.

"What do you want from me, Mark?" She sounded weary.

"The truth."

"And then you'll leave?"

Mark pretended to consider her proposition. She really didn't know him that well, he concluded. "OK. You have my word on that."

"You're not going to like it."

"I'm not expecting I will."

"I'm not who you think I am. You should have listened to Kaufman."

"Get on with it, Daria."

"I need to talk to Tural first. He's freaking. Wait here."

"I gotta take a leak, but I'll be right back. Hey, how would you feel about giving me my phone back?"

"You've got to be—"

"Please."

She threw up her hands as she walked away.

33

Mark swung by the Ferris wheel.

"How'd it go?" asked Decker, who'd remained hidden behind it. "You guys patch things up?"

"Ah, I'd say we still have a few outstanding issues to work through." Mark crouched behind the metal axle tower and lifted his binoculars to his eyes. As he watched Daria argue with Tural, he explained about how Daria had been two-timing the CIA and secretly sending information to the MEK.

"Who the hell is the MEK?"

"Iranian opposition group, trying to overthrow the regime in Iran."

"So, they're the good guys?"

"Kind of. Not really. You remember the Shah?"

"The who?"

"The Shah of Iran, guy who used to rule Iran."

"Oh, yeah. Him."

Not convinced that Decker really knew who the Shah was, Mark said, "He got overthrown by Ayatollah Khomeini in '79?"

"You know, I was born in the eighties."

"Anyway, the MEK started out trying to kick the Shah and the US out of Iran. They killed a few Americans and supported the Iranian revolution at first, but then they broke with Khomeini and thousands were executed. Now they claim to support democracy, but they have jack for support among regular Iranians and the organization is run like a militant personality cult. You ask me, the mullahs in Iran and the MEK deserve each other. They're both fucking nuts. Daria's gonna be back soon, I gotta blow."

"She know I'm here?"

"I suggested I was just good at following her. Don't know if she bought it or not. Get back to your car, wait for me to call."

34

Daria handed Mark his cell phone.

"Hey, thanks."

"Walk with me."

"Where are we going?"

"What do you know about my mother?"

Mark ran a few steps through the sand to catch up to her. "She had to leave Iran right after the revolution, because she was married to an American diplomat. Lives in DC and Geneva now."

"Wrong."

"What does this have to do with Campbell's assassination?"

"I was adopted as a child."

"That wasn't in your file." Mark glanced behind him and saw Tural was following them. "Where are we going, Daria?"

"The mother you read about in my file isn't my birth mother, she was the woman who adopted me."

"The Agency checks these things—it would have come up."

They reached the street. Daria didn't even break stride as she crossed the line of trucks waiting to enter Iran. She was headed west, toward the center of town.

"Well, it didn't."

"Why not?"

Daria told him about her uncle's revelation. "I was a normal kid back then, Mark. I had a boyfriend, I thought I was going to be a doctor..." As they reached an intersection and waited for a break in the traffic, her eyes closed for a brief moment, as though she were hoping to transport herself back to that time of innocence. "I wasn't like I am now..."

"You're telling me that's why Campbell and Peters and everyone at the Trudeau House were killed?"

"I don't need your sarcasm."

"I don't have time for bullshit."

She glowered at him.

"Say what you have to say, Daria. Just get it out."

"Fine. My real mom was murdered. End of story. Don't worry, I won't waste any more of your damn time."

"Who did it?"

"The mullahs. In 1979, during the revolution."

"Why?"

"Because she and her family backed sane people during the revolution and—"

"The National Front?"

"Yeah."

"I was with my mom when it happened, in our home."

"Why didn't you tell the CIA this?"

"After it happened, a neighbor took me to the US embassy and dumped me on the first American she saw heading for the entrance. She told him he needed to find this piece of shit Derek Simpson and make him take responsibility."

"Whoa, back up. Who's Derek Simpson?"

"The guy who got my mom pregnant. My real father."

"He worked at the embassy?"

"Yeah. He'd dated my mom for like half a year, everybody knew him, but he ditched her right after she told him she was pregnant. I was a mistake."

"Nice guy."

"He could have helped her. He could have helped me. Instead he ran. Anyway, the guy I got dumped on was a diplomat named John Buckingham—"

"Who told you all this? Your uncle?"

"He and his Iranian wife never even officially adopted me, they just brought me to America after the hostage crisis hit, claimed me as their own, and filed for a birth certificate. Yeah, my uncle told me most of it."

Mark just shook his head. He didn't know what any of this had to do with the current mess, but it was clear she was up to her neck in old grievances and abominations. It didn't bode well for her, he knew. Or for him. She stopped walking and turned to face him. They stood in the middle of a garbage-strewn alley.

"Did you ever confront your adoptive parents?"

"Oh yeah. They admitted everything. They even said they'd tried hard to find Derek Simpson, both in Iran and back in the States. But it was like the guy had never existed. The embassy wouldn't even acknowledge that he'd worked there."

"Was he CIA?" said Mark.

"Probably."

Daria looked down at her feet for a moment, then pulled her chador tightly to her chest.

"How'd you take the news?" asked Mark.

"How do you think?"

"I don't know."

"I made peace with my parents but I was still furious—at the mullahs for killing my mother and at my father for what he did to my mom. I wanted to do something to make things right."

Out of the corner of his eye Mark saw Tural approaching.

"Why have we stopped walking?"

"After the revolution my uncle joined the MEK—that's how he found out what really happened to my mother, because he had access to MEK spies in the Revolutionary Guard. Anyway, I told him I wanted to join too. He said I was too young, but I kept bugging him and eventually he suggested that as an American citizen I might be more useful in another capacity."

"Working for the CIA."

"The MEK wanted someone on the inside, someone who could let them know what America was really up to. So I studied Farsi and international law. I practiced taking polygraph tests. It worked. I applied to the CIA and was accepted." She paused before saying, "That's it. Now you know. Kaufman was right—you shouldn't have trusted me. I'm sorry I used you. I'm sorry for everything."

Mark considered how oblivious he'd been, how easy he'd been to fool. "Did you ever sell out any of your CIA agents?"

"No, never. I just had multiple loyalties, that's all."

"Multiple loyalties," Mark repeated, remembering the slaughter at the Trudeau House. Treason was another word for it.

"You know as well as I do that I gave the Agency a lot of good information." Daria jabbed a finger at him. "Information I would never have been able to get if it hadn't been for my relationship with the MEK. And the MEK and the CIA both want to take down the mullahs. They should be working together anyway. It's stupid that they're not."

Mark said, "You have ties to the CIA and MEK, and both were hit. The attacks have some connection to you, Daria."

"But I don't know what the connection is. Nor do I know why Campbell was killed. Or why someone tried to kill you."

"But you still know a lot more than you're telling me, don't you?"

This time Daria didn't even try to lie.

By now Tural had reached them. Mark stepped back a foot, prepared to defend himself, but Tural breezed by him on his way to a beat-up Russian version of a Vespa motor scooter. It was parked in front of a run-down hotel that catered to Iranian men looking for cheap sex just over the border—*Love Rooms* read a sign in Farsi. Tural hopped on the scooter and Daria took a seat behind him.

"I can't just let you just go," said Mark.

Daria turned so that she was facing him. Her face was contorted into an expression that fell somewhere between despair and rage. Her chador slipped open, and she gripped the handle of the pistol, holding it so tightly that Mark worried she was going to inadvertently shoot herself. She didn't point it at him, but said, "You don't have a fucking choice."

35

Mark stuck a new SIM card in his phone and called Decker.

"They just took off. Watch the road leading back out of town. She's probably headed for the mountains and that's the only way to get there."

He jogged back to his Lada, which was still parked by the café. As he started driving out of town, Decker called back.

"They just passed me. They're now in a black Land Cruiser, an old beater with a roof rack."

"They see you?"

"No way. I haven't even pulled out yet."

"Follow them, but stay far back. I'll be coming up behind you."

A few minutes later, Decker called again to say that the Land Cruiser had turned left onto a dirt road.

"I see it and I see you. Fall off, I'll lead from here."

The road was a muddy and rutted disaster. Mark's Lada labored through enormous potholes and up sharp inclines as it tackled the foothills of the Talysh Mountains, where thick hardwood forests grew between citrus groves and fields planted with tobacco and tea leaves.

Little private roads frequently branched off, leading to farmhouses with sedge-grass roofs. And unlike the relatively straight coastal highway, where sight lines of a half mile or more were common, this road twisted and turned, rendering Mark's binoculars useless. Which meant that, once he caught up to the Land Cruiser, he had no choice but to stay close behind, sometimes within a couple hundred yards.

36

"I think someone's following us," said Tural, sounding a little panicky.

He'd been staring intently out the back window for the last minute.

"The gray Lada." Daria glanced at the rearview mirror. She'd insisted on driving, given how agitated Tural was.

"You've seen it?"

She had—several times on the more open stretches of road. "It's a common car."

"What if it's that CIA guy?"

Daria checked her rearview mirror again but couldn't see anyone behind them now. "It couldn't be."

"He followed you all the way from Baku."

"We left him on foot in Astara."

"He could have run back to his car."

"Fast enough for him to see where we went? To follow us?"

Tural went back to peering anxiously out the back window. "If it's not him, then—"

"Then it's just a farmer—"

"Or whoever hit us in Astara."

It was a possibility, Daria knew, although she hadn't wanted to alarm Tural by voicing her fears. She wondered whether someone had been watching the burned-out safe house in Astara.

"Go faster!"

The Land Cruiser was already bouncing all over the road. But Daria sped up a bit more anyway.

"Are you armed?" she asked Tural.

"No."

They skidded around several turns before rounding a tight curve and nearly driving into a pile of rocks that had slid down a steep bank, blocking the road.

She threw the Land Cruiser into reverse and backed up, preparing to gun it through a narrow detour had been cut into the lower bank.

Just then, the gray Lada rounded a corner and stopped suddenly, fifty feet or so behind her, close enough that she was able to see, and recognize, the driver.

No, it couldn't be.

But it was. Somehow he'd found her. Again. And she'd let it happen.

"Asshole!" she yelled, slamming her hands down on the steering wheel, infuriated at herself, and him. "Asshole!"

She flipped Mark the bird, threw the car into drive, and slammed her foot down on the accelerator.

No more screwing around, she told herself. This time she was going to stop him for good.

37

After ten minutes, the road dead-ended without warning. Mark had lost sight of the Land Cruiser for the last mile, and there was no sign of it now. In front of him rose a steep rocky out-cropping, marking the end of the foothills and the beginning of the real mountains. He got out of the car and climbed it, and from the top had a decent view of the land below—a vast green expanse that ended sharply in the distance at the blue sea's edge.

Maybe a half mile or so away he saw a farmhouse, in front of which the black Land Cruiser was parked.

Mark called Decker then jogged back down the road, looking for the turnoff he knew he must have missed. It came up soon on the left, hidden by large oak-tree branches that had been dragged in front of the entrance. He pulled them away, revealing a path. The long grass that covered it had been recently matted down by car wheels in two long parallel strips.

Mark walked for a quarter mile along the edge of an overgrown citrus grove where unpicked lemons and oranges were rotting on the trees. Eventually a modest one-story house appeared in the distance. It was surrounded by a clay privacy wall common to Muslim homes. The Land Cruiser was parked in front of the wall.

Behind him, Daria said, "That's far enough."

Mark turned around slowly. Daria was gripping a pistol with both hands, and she was pointing it at him.

38

Washington, DC

Colonel Henry Amato and his boss, National Security Advisor James Ellis, were alone in Ellis's West Wing corner office when a call from the deputy director of the FBI was patched through on speakerphone.

"Campbell was shot twice, once in the chest, once in the head," said the deputy director, reading from a preliminary forensic report. "Spent shell casings recovered at the scene were from a 7.62 mm rifle cartridge. Same goes for the casings we recovered at the Trudeau House."

"All fired from the same gun?" asked Amato.

"Two guns were used at the Trudeau House. Whether one of them was the same gun used to kill Campbell, we don't know yet. The bullets that killed Campbell are still in him and we won't be able to do a ballistics analysis until after the autopsy later today. The one thing I can tell you about the bullets we recovered from the Trudeau House is that they indicate there were significant flaws in the barrels of the guns from which they were fired. Which leads us to believe they were probably knockoffs, likely of an M-14 or Heckler & Koch G3."

"Both models the Iranians have been known to copy," said Amato. "Has your forensic team in Baku gotten in contact with Mark Sava yet?"

"That's the guy who discovered the bodies at the Trudeau House?"

"The same."

"We're still waiting for the Agency to reel him in."

"Did they say when that's going to happen? I mean, you have told them you need to talk to Sava, no? And this Buckingham woman who's with him?"

"I share your frustration, sir."

Daria and Sava wouldn't survive for long alone out there, thought Amato. Not with the resources Aryanpur had in Azerbaijan.

Amato felt the tightness in his chest again. And the need to do something.

39

Daria moved to the center of the path. Tural stood to her left, his eyes darting nervously from Daria to Mark.

On Daria's right stood a dark-haired man with a large rabbit-like overbite and bright white teeth. He wore brown dress slacks, a short-sleeved button-down shirt, and plastic sandals that revealed dirty toes. And he was gripping a scuffed-up AK-47 with a relaxed confidence that Mark found disturbing. The man's trigger finger rested just outside the trigger well, and the rifle barrel pointed slightly downward. His feet were about shoulder-width apart and staggered. To the untrained eye, he might have looked like a guy just casually holding a gun, but Mark recognized a classic firing stance when he saw one.

It was Mark's first inkling that he'd miscalculated yet again. The MEK consisted largely of ragtag soldier wannabes. This guy, despite the civilian getup, seemed more like the real thing.

Mark said, "I take it you're Yaver?"

"You tell him my name?" Yaver asked Daria, with evident derision.

"I didn't tell him. Like I said—"

"Hands so I can see," said Yaver to Mark. "Walk."

"Do what he says," said Daria.

So Mark walked until he reached a clearing about ten feet in front of the farmhouse's privacy wall, in a rutted section of the driveway.

"Turn around," said Yaver.

Daria said, "I told you not to follow me. You were warned."

Ignoring her, Mark looked to Yaver. "I'm Mark Sava. I'm the former chief of—"

"Yes, yes, I know who you are."

"The MEK's people were killed in Astara, probably by a team from Iran. The CIA was hit too, in Baku. Our interests overlap—I came here to propose that we work together."

"Why do you say the Iranians do this in Baku and Astara?"

"Who else would?"

"You have no evidence?"

"I'm gathering it."

Yaver handed Daria a set of steel handcuffs. "Bind him."

Daria said, "You're going to be staying here for a while, Mark. Locked up."

"I wouldn't be so sure."

"You'll be given food and water and you'll be treated well. But you will not be following me any longer. I've had it."

"You are stupid, Daria *joon*?" said Yaver, as she approached Mark. "You bring your weapon near this man?"

Daria handed her pistol to Tural, then started handcuffing Mark's hands together in front of him.

"Behind his back," said Yaver.

"He needs to be able to eat," said Daria, and she continued to bind his hands in front.

"*Marg. Sag madareto begaad*," said Yaver. *May a dog fuck your mother.*

He spoke the words with more disdain than real anger.

"Back off. I know what I'm doing." Daria clicked the cuffs tight.

And then, for a brief moment, everything was silent. So silent that Mark could hear the wind in the orchard and Daria's breathing. A small flock of starlings settled in a nearby field.

"I'm not your enemy," Mark said to Yaver, although as soon as he said the words, he was hit with a powerful feeling that no, *he actually was this guy's enemy.* "I came here because I thought we could work together."

Yaver gave him a who-gives-a-shit look, then suddenly stepped to the left and popped Tural hard on the side of his head with the butt of his AK-47. The hit was sharp and professional, and Tural collapsed.

"What the hell?" said Daria, turning.

"I change the plan." Yaver stooped down to retrieve Daria's pistol, which had fallen near Tural's feet. With one hand he removed the magazine from the gun and threw it fifty feet away, into the field of lemon trees. "On knees, both of you. Hands to heads."

"I gotta give it to you, Daria. You sure can pick 'em," said Mark as he knelt. "This guy's a real winner."

Tural started to moan so Yaver kicked him and told him to kneel next to Mark, which he did.

Daria just stood there. "Yaver, I told you we didn't bring him here intentionally."

"Hands to your head, Daria *joon*. Now."

Mark studied Yaver. His gun hand was steady and his eyes were boring into Daria. This clearly wasn't the first time he'd ordered people around like this.

Daria put her hands on her head and dropped to her knees. "He was following us, Yaver. I tried to lose him in Baku and I thought for sure I'd lost him in Astara…I did my best, I didn't mean to bring him here."

Yaver searched each one of them from behind, keeping his AK-47 aimed at the back of the head of the person he was searching. When he came to Mark, he removed a bundle of hundred-dollar bills from each of his front pockets—$20,000 total.

"Thank you for the tip. Very generous."

Then Yaver produced a cell phone and dialed a number, keeping one eye on his phone and the other on his prisoners. In Farsi, he read off the date, time, and GPS coordinates, said that he had Mark Sava and Daria Buckingham in his custody and was requesting instructions. Mark thought he sounded like a highly trained soldier communicating with a superior officer.

"You bastard," said Daria to Yaver. "You're not MEK, you're a plant."

Yaver stared blankly at his three captives as he held the phone to his ear, waiting.

By now it was oppressively hot. Mark could feel trickles of sweat running down his neck.

"Was that your work in Astara?" asked Daria. "And in Baku?"

"I understand," said Yaver, speaking into his phone, which he then snapped shut. His face hardened as he slipped the device into his back pocket.

Mark had seen executions before. He knew the look professionals got before they pulled the trigger, the way their eyes deadened, as though they were looking at a paper target.

He saw that look now and wondered where the hell Decker was.

"How much are the Iranians paying you?" Mark asked, stalling. Before Yaver could answer, he added, "You should know that I have evidence that Iran was directly involved in Campbell's assassination. And if you kill me, that evidence will be transferred to the CIA within a day."

"You lie, *tokhme sag*—" *Seed of a dog.*

"I'm willing to make a deal. That money you took, it's only the beginning. I'll give you thirty thousand more, in cash, to let us walk."

Mark still had nearly that much hidden in the Lada back on the road.

Yaver paused. "This money, where is it?"

"First we need to come to an understanding."

"There is no understanding. There is no deal. There is only—"

Tural suddenly jumped up, fully panicking, and began to run, prompting Yaver to fire two expertly placed shots into his head.

The instant Yaver turned, Mark ran at him, lunging for his neck with his bound hands. They both fell, rolling in the dirt as Daria sprinted away.

Mark tried to ram his head into Yaver's face, but he wasn't strong enough to keep his grip on Yaver's neck and he wound up falling back in the dirt. He gripped the barrel of the AK-47 and pushed it away from his body just as Yaver fired off a few rounds. The barrel was hot and it seared Mark's hands.

"Drop your weapon!" yelled Decker from about fifty feet away.

Mark struggled to keep the barrel of the AK-47 away from his body as Yaver yanked on it. He dropped to his knees and jammed the barrel into the dirt.

The crack of a pistol rang out. Decker hit Yaver's leg.

Then Daria came back. In her hands was the pistol that Yaver had thrown away. She jammed the magazine she'd recovered into the grip frame, aimed quickly, and fired two shots. One hit Yaver in the gut, the other in his chest.

Yaver fell to his knees and Mark wrenched the AK-47 out of his hands.

40

As Yaver lay there moaning, curled up into a fetal position on the ground, Daria watched Mark pull back the action on the AK-47, confirm there was still a bullet in the chamber, then switch the rifle to semiautomatic with a flick of his finger.

He pointed the AK-47 at Yaver's head. Daria noted his hands were steady, his mouth set in a sneer. A couple of veins on his forehead had popped out.

"Patch him up!" he yelled to Decker.

Decker knelt down and started ripping Yaver's shirt into strips to use as a field dressing.

Daria stood a few feet away holding her pistol.

"Put it down," Mark ordered.

Daria looked at her gun hand. She'd never shot anyone before. It was an awful feeling.

"Now!"

She eyed the AK-47 in Mark's hands and, for the first time, was afraid of him.

"Take it."

She handed over the pistol and he flipped the safety on without even glancing at it.

Yaver's eyes were open, but they were glassy and unfocused. His mouth was moving, but in such a way that he looked like a starving baby bird asking for food.

"Fuckitall, he ain't gonna live," said Decker.

Mark wedged Daria's gun into his waist belt, then yanked his $20,000 and Yaver's cell phone out of the dying man's back pockets. When he pushed the button for recently dialed calls, no numbers appeared.

Decker finished packing the chest wound, raised Yaver to a sitting position, wrapped it, then started working on the gut wound.

"Who is he, Daria?" asked Mark.

She heard the question but was too dazed to respond. Mark gripped her arm.

"You're hurting me."

"Who is he? And spare me the bullshit version."

"I knew him as Yaver Mustafa. Until now I thought he was loyal to the MEK. I came here to ask him whether he knew anything about what happened in Baku and Astara. I wasn't lying to you."

"How long had he been a member of the Astara cell?"

"Maybe a year."

"And before that?"

"I was told was he used to work in Tehran exporting carpets, and that his brother was executed by the regime for organizing protest marches. He had money and he helped bankroll a lot of resistance operations. Which was probably why we weren't more suspicious of him than we should have been."

Decker finished with his second improvised dressing and gave it a hard yank so that it was tight around Yaver's waist. There was more moaning.

Mark bent down. "Yaver! Can you hear me!" He slapped Yaver's cheek. "Wake up here, buddy. I need to ask you a few questions. After that we're going to drive into town, get you some medical help. You help us out here, we'll help you out."

Yaver didn't respond.

"Who did you report to, Yaver? You Qods Force, buddy?" said Mark, referring to the elite special forces unit of Iran's Revolutionary Guard.

Yaver didn't answer. Bubbles of spit formed at the corner of his mouth as he struggled to breathe. Mark lightly slapped his cheek again. "Stay with me."

For a moment Yaver's eyes focused on Mark, but then he went slack.

Mark let his head drop into the dirt. "Dickhead. Stick him in the back of the Land Cruiser," he told Decker. "Find some way to secure him, in case he gets a second wind." He pulled out Yaver's cell phone. "And see if you can get anything off of this. When you're done, shut it down so the signal can't be triangulated. Be quick about it."

Watching Mark operate, Daria realized she hadn't been the only one hiding things about her past. Because it was rapidly becoming clear that he hadn't just risen through the ranks of the CIA as some analyst. No, he was way too comfortable, way too sure of himself around violence for that.

41

Mark ran to the farmhouse. He figured he only had another minute or two before whoever Yaver had called started wondering why it was taking so long to get an execution confirmation.

Daria followed him to the bright blue front door. Mark briefly considered having Decker drag her back to the Land Cruiser and tie her down to one of the seats.

"Anyone inside?" he asked.

"I don't know."

The front door opened onto a kitchen, where a battered samovar sat on a bare-wood kitchen table and unwashed pots filled the sink. Mark rifled through the cabinet drawers and ripped food off the open shelves but found nothing of interest. He moved on to the small living room, where a worn couch sat behind a coffee table cluttered with oil lamps, aging newspapers from Baku, and a worn volume of poetry by Hafez—a fourteenth-century poet still wildly popular in Iran. The walls were covered with dark hand-knotted carpets.

Behind another wall-hung carpet in the back bedroom, Mark found a metal door with a sophisticated-looking lock on it. He tried the handle and it wouldn't turn so he fired a shot into the lock and threw his shoulder into the door. It stayed shut. He fired two more shots and kicked it open.

A rickety wooden staircase led down to a small cellar with clay walls. Mark turned on a single fluorescent overhead light, revealing a series of bright stainless-steel tables lining the perimeter of the room.

On one of the tables lay a set of night-vision goggles, an infrared strobe light, and a digital camera with an enormous telephoto lens. On another, a collection of listening devices and a miniature GPS tracker. On still another, a pistol belt, boxes of ammunition, two 9mm Glocks, a mini-arsenal of old AK-47s, a Heckler & Koch MP5 machine pistol, a few limpet mines, and what looked like a halfway decent knockoff of a CAR-15 automatic rifle. From the ceiling hung a black wetsuit, fins, a scuba-related contraption, and waterproof chemlites.

"Holy shit," said Mark to Daria, who had followed him down the steps.

"This isn't MEK stuff," she said slowly. "I mean, we had a few weapons, but nothing—nothing like this."

"Did the Astara MEK know this basement even existed?"

"I know I didn't. I thought this was just an auxiliary site. It was used as a safe house for Iranian defectors. Yaver arranged it all."

Mark pulled out a couple of canvas duffel bags from under the stainless-steel tables. He stuffed everything in them except a few beat-up AK-47s and hauled it all back to the Land Cruiser.

Yaver was in the rear seat, lying on his back between the two doors. His feet and hands had been bound together with duct tape and tied to the armrests. But his eyes were closed and he wasn't moving. Decker was taking his pulse.

"Is he dead?" said Mark.

Decker shook his head. "Not yet. But give it a few minutes and he will be."

"He's not faking?"

Decker pointed to the sizable pool of blood collecting on the seat of the Land Cruiser and dripping onto the floor. "I can't completely stop it, I can't get enough pressure on his gut."

"Shit," said Mark. He suddenly felt lightheaded. God, what a mess, he thought. What a world.

"We lost our chance to interrogate him," said Decker, sounding slightly accusing. He gave Daria a look.

"I did what I had to," she said.

"There was a reason I just tagged him in the leg."

"Then you were playing with fire."

"Leave it be," said Mark.

He placed his hand an inch away from Yaver's mouth. He could hardly feel the man's breath.

"Listen, buddy! Last chance here. Tell us who you report to and we get medical help. Hold back on us, and you're screwed."

Daria translated what Mark had said into Farsi, but Yaver was beyond hearing.

Decker, who was looking through the duffel bags, said, "I gotta say, some of this is crap but a lot of it reminds me of what I used to carry." He pulled out something that looked like a piece of scuba equipment. "This is a Draeger rebreather. You can dive without releasing bubbles. Standard SEAL gear."

"Would Qods Force use it?" asked Mark.

"They might." Decker picked up the Heckler & Koch MP5 machine pistol. "I wouldn't be surprised if some of this gear was lifted from our guys who've gone down in Iraq and Afghanistan."

"Pack it back up, we gotta get out of here."

Mark climbed into the driver's seat, Daria slid into the passenger seat, and Decker got in back. After picking up the rest of

Mark's cash from the trunk of the Lada, they started hauling ass toward the coast, bouncing all over the rough road and skidding through a few curves.

But they'd only gone a couple of miles when they heard the distant thumping sound of a helicopter's rotor blades.

"You've gotta be kidding me," said Mark.

"It can't actually be coming for us, do you think?" said Decker.

Mark swerved off onto a narrow trail that paralleled a tea field and dead-ended at a dense grove of oak trees.

He backed the Land Cruiser into the trees, raised his binoculars to his eyes, and scanned the sky. He saw nothing. Suddenly there was silence.

"They touched down," said Decker, who'd opened the back door of the Land Cruiser and had been listening intently.

"At the farmhouse?"

"Could be. Yeah."

"They're looking for us," said Mark.

He continued to search the sky as a breeze rustled the leaves behind him. Daria stood on the other side of the car, silently scanning the tea field and the surrounding sky.

He considered the logistics of getting a helicopter to a rural part of Azerbaijan within what—ten minutes? Whoever they were dealing with had access to some serious resources.

In the backseat, Yaver was dead. Mark dragged him out of the car and let him flop to the ground. Then he picked up some downed branches from the forest floor and piled them on the roof of the car.

"We'll lay low here for a while," he said. "In the meantime maybe Daria will finally deign to tell us more about what the hell is really going on."

42

"No more lies," said Daria. "No more secrets."

"No more secrets," Mark agreed.

"No, look at me. I mean it this time. I tell you what I know and in return you don't bullshit me, like saying you sent Decker away. Or telling me you were a CIA analyst."

"I was an analyst. For six months."

"Over a twenty-year career."

"You never asked for how long."

"I mean it, Mark. We come clean with each other for real now or no deal."

"Fair enough," he said, although in truth he was thinking that any opportunity to reestablish mutual trust was long gone.

Daria glanced around her, as though someone might be eavesdropping even in the middle of the woods. "So this is the deal—as part of that pipeline agreement I told you about, the Chinese gave the Iranians help with their nuclear program."

"What kind of help?" Mark said slowly.

"Enriched uranium."

"High grade or low grade?"

"Most of it low. Around four percent uranium two thirty-five."

Good enough for a reactor but not for a bomb, thought Mark. Besides, the Iranians were already making plenty of 4 percent 235 on their own. "And the rest?"

"Some at sixty percent uranium two thirty-five, some as high as eighty. Not the ninety-plus percent considered weapons-grade, but—"

"Eighty percent is concentrated enough to be used in a weapon. Not a very efficient weapon, but a weapon that might work. I can't believe the Chinese would have been so fucking reckless."

But he actually did believe it. The Chinese hadn't balked at arming the genocidal government of Sudan in return for access to oil, or dealing with the deranged generals of Myanmar in exchange for an oil pipeline; arming Iran would be right up their alley.

"The low-enriched uranium was given with the understanding that the Iranians would use it to produce electricity. The rationale was that, with the Chinese buying so much of Iran's oil, the Iranians would need the extra energy capacity."

"And the highly enriched uranium?"

"Supposedly for use in a research reactor and in two nuclear-powered subs the Iranians want to build to patrol the Persian Gulf."

"What safeguards were there, so that it's not used for a bomb?"

"Real ones? None. The Chinese want the Iranians to have the bomb, so that the US and Israel will think twice before attacking their gas station. The BS about the research reactor and subs is just so that, if this ever comes to light, they can deny that they meant to give Iran the bomb. Anyway, what it comes down to is that China got its oil and the Iranians got enough highly enriched uranium to make three small fission bombs in the ten kiloton range."

"That's big enough," said Mark. Ten kilotons was only about two-thirds of the explosive power of the bomb dropped on

Hiroshima—nothing compared with the destructive force of modern nuclear weapons, but more than enough to destroy the better part of a city. "What about delivery systems?"

"They're going for something small that can be smuggled over borders or onto a cargo ship, or better yet a cargo plane. A poor man's version of an ICBM since their long-range missile technology sucks."

"They've already built these bombs?"

"No. At least I don't think so. And when they try to, they'll be short some enriched uranium." Daria's mouth tightened into something approximating a smile. "I helped a physicist in Tehran smuggle two blocks of it out of Iran."

"My God, Daria." You are in way, way over your head, was all Mark could think. It occurred to him that he was now, too. "And where did this uranium wind up?"

"It was supposed to have been transferred to the International Atomic Energy Agency. The MEK wanted to use it to prove that the Iranians were lying about not developing nuclear weapons."

"This transfer to the IAEA, was it actually made?"

"I have no idea. All I did was bring the physicist and the uranium from Tehran to Esfahan. The MEK contact I met in Esfahan was supposed to have smuggled it outside of Iran."

"But the IAEA never broke the news," said Mark.

"No. And now it's been six weeks."

"Which suggests the uranium didn't get from Esfahan to where it was supposed to go. You stole a bunch of uranium from the Iranians and now it's disappeared."

"Yeah, you know, I figured that much out."

"So have you tried to call the MEK leadership?"

"I've tried my uncle ten times today. He's not answering or returning my—"

43

Mark put his hand up, silencing Daria as the sound of the helicopter started up again.

After a minute of listening to it wax and wane in the distance, Decker said, "They're searching for us."

The sound of the helicopter faded, to the point where it was almost inaudible, but then gradually it grew louder. And louder. Until suddenly it was within a few hundred feet of them, sending gusts of wind whipping down through the trees.

Mark could see portions of its black silhouette through the leaves but couldn't make out any identifying marks. He wished he'd piled up more branches on top of the car. Then it was gone, off to circling in a new area.

Until a cell phone started ringing.

"Shut that thing off," snapped Mark, thinking it was either Daria's or Decker's.

"Not me, boss," said Decker.

"It's not mine," said Daria. Then she stared at Decker. "It's Yaver's. You forgot to turn it off."

"No. No, tell me you didn't," said Mark.

"Fuck me."

"I told you. The signal can be triangulated."

Decker pulled out Yaver's cell phone from his front pocket and shut it off.

"Fuck me," said Decker again.

"Maybe they weren't tracking it," said Daria.

"Guys, I'm sorry."

"Maybe they didn't have time to get a lock," said Mark.

Moments later the helicopter came screaming back toward them.

Decker jumped out of the car and grabbed the equipment bag. "You guys blow."

"No one gets to play the martyr," said Mark. "We ditch the car and run together."

Decker unzipped the equipment bag and pulled out the Heckler & Koch MP5 machine pistol. "I'm not planning on a suicide mission! I'll just keep them busy for a few minutes and then bolt. There's plenty of tree cover—I'll be fine. You guys take off."

Mark quickly calculated that his best chance of finding out who'd attacked the CIA in Baku was to first find out who had stolen Daria's uranium, because it was a near certainty that whoever had done it would be at or near the center of this mess. And that meant retracing the uranium trail, starting in Esfahan, Iran. He estimated the times and distances involved in getting to Esfahan.

To Decker, he said, "If you make it out of here, go to France."

Decker was dragging Yaver back to the Land Cruiser. Mark saw the helicopter through the trees.

"I'll make it."

"Find out what happened to Daria's uncle. I'll call you sometime after you get there. Daria and I will be in Iran."

Mark handed a $10,000 bank bundle to Decker, who quickly stuffed it in his pocket.

"You'll find my uncle at the MEK compound in Auvers," said Daria. "On Saint Simon Road a mile out of town. His name is Reza Tehrani. There's a photo of him on the MEK's website. He's an advisor to the leader of the MEK, a woman named Maryam Minabi. She should be on the website too. Are you going to remember all this?"

"Auvers, Saint Simon Road, Reza…"

"Tehrani. Tehrani. Like the city."

"Tehrani. Got it."

"Advisor to Minabi, who's the head of the MEK."

"I'll remember."

"Just go to the website if you forget."

Decker took Yaver's cell phone, switched it back on, and threw it into the front seat of the Land Cruiser. With Mark's help, he heaved Yaver's dead body into the driver's seat.

The helicopter was just a couple hundred feet away now, hovering over the empty tea field just past the forest, circling and searching. Decker turned on the Land Cruiser and jammed a spare AK-47 between the gas pedal and the front seat.

"Good luck," said Mark, just before Decker threw the Land Cruiser from park into drive and aimed it through a break in the trees.

Mark grabbed two pistols and full clips from the equipment bag and started to run. Daria kept close on his heels. After he'd gone a hundred yards or so, he turned and, through the trees, caught a glimpse of the Land Cruiser careening out into the middle of the tea field. Shots were fired from the helicopter, followed by shots from Decker, still hidden in the woods.

Daria looked up at the sun. "If we keep going south we should hit a road I know in a few minutes. From there I can take us to a trail through the mountains and get us over the border without running into guards."

"How long are we talking?"

"Border crossing's not more than a mile away. That's why we had the safe house up here."

"I'll follow you," said Mark, and then they both turned and ran.

- 162 -

PART III

Port of Jebel Ali, United Arab Emirates

The two-story steel warehouse was one of thousands of freight stations clustered on the eastern edge of the port. It was remarkable only in that on the inside, instead of being crammed full with goods for import or export, it lay empty save for a thirty-foot-long powerboat and a group of soldiers.

Three of the soldiers wielded spray guns and were painting the boat, which had been propped up on jack stands and blocks.

A fourth, the leader of the group, stood in the background observing his men and occasionally glancing at a photo of an actual United Arab Emirates Coast Guard boat that he held in his hand. Tomorrow, when the gray paint had dried, two red stripes would be affixed to either side of the hull, and the marine radar dome and other antennas would be installed. The details would have to be perfect, he thought, because anything approaching the USS Reagan *that was perceived to be a threat would be blown out of the water.*

Under normal circumstances, not even the Emirates Coast Guard would be allowed to get too close. But if the coast guard was in direct pursuit of a hostile craft... well, the soldier couldn't see the Americans firing on the coast guard until it was too late.

44

Washington, DC

A man in his midtwenties, wearing khakis and a wrinkled Oxford shirt, sauntered up to the office of Vision Financial Consulting and Cash Advances on Georgia Avenue. In one hand he held a set of keys, in the other a giant Dunkin' Donuts coffee cup. He took a sip and nodded to Henry Amato, who was standing on the sidewalk in front of the locked entrance to the building.

Morning rush-hour traffic was noisy and a car alarm was going off nearby.

"You were supposed to open at eight," said Amato.

"It is eight."

"It's five after."

The guy shrugged. He was tall, with floppy brown hair and an untrimmed soul patch under his lip. Amato noted the enormous metal-ringed hole in the guy's earlobe and scowled. Why people chose to deface their bodies like savages was beyond him.

"Sorry. We're open now." He unlocked the door. "Come on in."

It was a small store. The gray carpet was black with street grime in front of the main counter, over which hung a sign that read *Paychecks Cashed Here*. An old air conditioner stuck out from the wall. In the back lurked an office separated from the main area by glass partition walls and a flimsy wood door.

"Here to cash a paycheck?"

"I'm a retired colonel in the US Armed Forces," said Amato, standing tall. "And I need a cash advance on my pension."

"Colonel, huh? Don't see many of those down here."

It disgusted Amato that this kid who, if he had even gone to college, had probably spent the time drinking himself silly and smoking marijuana, and who had certainly never seen military service—probably even looked down on those who served—it disgusted him that this kid would, for even this brief moment in time, hold the key to something Amato desperately wanted. It was a prime example of the degeneration of values across the nation, Amato thought. A degeneration he'd tried but had so clearly failed to prevent. This punk, he thought, was what America had become.

"I'm in a bit of a rush."

"You bring a copy of your most recent pension statement?"

"I did."

"You working now?"

"For the government. I brought pay stubs."

"How's your credit?"

"It's fine," said Amato sharply.

He was ushered into the back office, told to take a seat in front of the desk, and handed an application. Amato filled it out in five minutes.

The guy leafed through it. When he got to the last page, he whistled. "That's quite a figure."

"Can you do it?"

Since Daria and Sava clearly didn't plan to take refuge at the embassy, Amato figured his only hope was to pay private contractors to intercept Aryanpur's men. But private contractors were extraordinarily expensive.

When it came to money, Amato had never been a saver. With social security and his government pension due to kick in soon, he'd always figured he didn't need to worry about socking money away.

And anyway, too much money was an affront to God.

"I'll need to confirm your pension of course, and run a credit report and all that. But if everything checks out, you should be OK."

"What kind of timing are we talking about?"

"Two weeks or so."

"Your website says immediate cash advances."

"Yeah, on paychecks. The pension buyouts are another animal."

"If I can't get it today, it won't do me any good! How long does it take to run a credit check and confirm my pension? You should be able to do that in ten minutes."

"You can pay for us to expedite it, but honestly sir, I wouldn't recommend it. You'll take a huge hit in fees, see. You'd do better to wait."

"Expedite the application, son. I'll pay what I need to."

"I don't know if we can even do this figure this quick. I'll have to call my boss."

"I'll wait."

45

Mark recalled that there had once been a border fence separating Iran from Azerbaijan, a mini-Berlin Wall that had stood for decades during the Soviet era. But there were more Azeris in northern Iran than there were in Azerbaijan itself, so as the Soviet Union was collapsing, Azeris on both sides of the fence had just ripped the thing down.

Ever since, illegally crossing into Iran from Azerbaijan had involved little more than racing along a well-trodden path from one side of the border to the other. Which is exactly how he and Daria did it.

Not far from where they crossed stood a cluster of well-kept farmhouses. Inside a mud-walled garage attached to one of them, Mark hotwired an old Paykan—a cheap Iranian car—and left $2,000 in its place on the dirt floor.

They raced south toward the city of Esfahan, passing perfectly symmetrical green rice paddies, tea fields planted on steep mountain terraces, roadside kebab restaurants that smelled of grilled lamb, and roadside stores that displayed open barrels of dried fruit amidst unruly stacks of blue oil drums.

Soon they hit the cool air of the craggy Alborz Mountains, followed hours later by the intense heat of the westernmost tip of the vast Kavir Desert. They chose roads that kept them far from the crush of people and stink of cars in the cities. On the wide open stretches, where Mark could be sure there were no cops for miles around him, he kept the gas pedal pinned to the floor.

As he stared out across a dry desert salt marsh, Mark was reminded of the desert south of Baku, which in turn led him to start thinking about Nika and her son. He remembered the last dinner they'd all eaten together. It had been at an unpretentious little Georgian restaurant south of Baku, not far from the beach where they'd spent the day. After dinner, Nika had put her son to sleep at her parents' house. And then she and Mark had gone back to his place to drink wine and have sex on the balcony. That must have been just about the time everyone in the Trudeau House was being slaughtered, he realized, struck by the absurdity of his own obliviousness. He hoped Nika was safe.

He turned to Daria. "Tell me more about this physicist who helped you steal the uranium."

She was sitting in the passenger seat, still wearing a black chador robe that covered her hair and upper body.

"His girlfriend was an Iranian-Kurd reporter who was murdered by the regime."

"What's his name?"

"He's a source."

"Who's already bolted."

"His disappearance was made to look like he was abducted by the Mossad or the CIA. I'm not going to put his extended family in danger. If you were ever captured—"

"Who are we meeting in Esfahan?"

"An MEK courier. Whose name you also don't need to know. I should go to meet him alone."

"Give me a break."

"I protected my sources even when I was with the CIA. You know that. I'm not treating you any different now than when you were my boss."

"We'll go together—I'll back you up like I did when you met your agents in Baku. You want some advice?"

"No."

"Tell me everything you know about this mess and then walk away, or better yet, run before you do any more damage."

"I already did tell you everything I know. We made a deal, remember?"

"Create a new identity and start a new life somewhere. The world's a big place, you're resourceful."

"Try taking your own advice, dude."

"You've had your revenge on the CIA. You've settled the score. Leave it at that."

A long time ago, her CIA father had betrayed her Iranian mother and to return the favor, she'd betrayed the CIA. So the Agency had suffered a little bit of blowback. And in truth, Mark thought the CIA deserved a certain amount of blowback when it came to Iran—overthrowing Iran's democratically elected government in the fifties, for example, hadn't exactly been a stroke of genius. Supporting the Shah and his secret police probably hadn't been such a hot idea either. But the operations officers who'd died at the Trudeau House hadn't been involved in any of that. They'd died for other people's old mistakes, other people's old grievances.

Daria said, "By the time I was working for you, it wasn't about settling scores anymore. I'd moved on from that."

"Enlighten me, Daria. What did you move on to?"

"Do you always have to be so sarcastic?"

"Only when it's called for."

"Toppling the mullahs could help a lot of people in Iran. A lot of good people."

"You don't think maybe people get the government they deserve?" When Daria didn't respond, Mark said, "I do. Let the Iranians deal with Iran."

"I'm half-Iranian. I'm dealing with it."

"You're American."

"Whatever."

Mark sensed that she wanted him to sympathize with her. To say he understood what she was going through, that she wasn't a traitorous backstabber after all because her ultimate cause was just.

Screw that, he thought. Too many people had died, likely as a result of her actions, for him to have any sympathy left.

So they sat without speaking for a while, as the Paykan rattled violently and the oven-like wind coming off the Kavir Desert buffeted the little car. Finally, Mark said, "Did you ever actually learn anything about other operations officers, or anything about the Agency's policies, that I wouldn't have told you under ordinary circumstances?"

"No. I tried. You were too careful with your files. And if I had, I wouldn't have compromised any individual agents or operations officers. I wasn't out to hurt people. I'm not a monster."

After a long time, Mark said, "I didn't say you were."

46

At over half a kilometer in length, Imam Square in downtown Esfahan was a vast space. The Grand Imam Mosque, with its enormous four-hundred-year-old dome and millions of hand-painted blue tiles, anchored the southern end. To the west stood an ancient palace; to the east, the Sheik Lotfollah Mosque, a delicate masterpiece built for a king's harem. In between, hundreds of little shops were nested into an arcade that ringed most of the square.

When Daria and Mark arrived, it was near dusk. Several middle-aged men were rolling up red carpets in front of the Grand Imam Mosque—loading them into the back of a pickup truck while old women scurried around mouselike beneath their black chador robes, helping to clean up after the massive Friday prayer gathering. Farther away, clusters of young men and women in jeans sat talking by a fountain.

Daria passed by the fountain dressed in a colorful but ragged chador, her face fully covered by a red mask that looked as though it had been salvaged from a Mardi Gras parade. Mark observed that she drew a few amused stares and raised eyebrows along the way. Although some maybe mistook her for a gypsy, he figured that most recognized her as an Arab *bandari,* a woman from the southern coast of Iran—the daughter, no doubt, of smugglers and thieves.

She turned down a crowded alley that snaked off from a corner of the square near the Grand Imam Mosque. It smelled of rosewater and sweat, and was lined with shops that sold enameled brassware and hand-knotted carpets. Mark followed behind her from a distance, assessing the stares she attracted for signs that she'd been recognized. He saw none.

After turning down several more alleys, Daria slipped into a shop whose front window was obscured by ceiling-high stacks of folded tablecloths. A minute later, Mark ducked inside the cramped shop too. Near the rear of the store, a stooped old woman with crooked, wrinkled hands was securing a bundle of tablecloths with twine. Her back was to Daria.

"Fatima, I know you can hear me," Mark heard Daria say. "I come in peace. I mean you no harm. *Salaam Aleykum.*" *Peace be upon you.* Daria pulled her red *niqab* mask away from her face. "We met six weeks ago. Do you recall?"

The woman wore a black chador pulled tight around her head. She lowered her gaze and kept tying her bundles, but now she handled the twine in a rough way that suggested she was sick to hell of dealing with people like Daria.

It wasn't lost on Mark that Friday was a weekend day in Iran. And that it was nearly eight in the evening. And that this old woman had likely been fasting all day for Ramadan. Yet she was still working.

In the front of the store, another woman sat at a table, using a wooden paisley stamp and various brushes to apply paint patterns to a tablecloth in the making. Like the older woman, she too wore a black chador with a veil. But her paint-stained fingers were slender and smooth, pink and purple Nike sneakers poked out from beneath her robe, and the black fabric beneath her neck was secured with a metal binder clip, a trend Mark knew to be common among young Iranian women.

When young Iranian women even wore the clumsy chador, that is. In a cosmopolitan city like Esfahan, Mark figured that a woman wearing pink and purple Nikes would only grudgingly wear even a light headscarf—the bare minimum allowed by law. She certainly wouldn't wear a veil. Unless...

The young woman noticed him. "We don't take deliveries on Fridays," she said. "Especially not at this time."

Unless she were grieving.

On his back, Mark carried a battered wood-frame porter's pack laden with an enormous stack of dun-colored cotton fabric. The fabric fell down around his head as if it were a veil, obscuring most of his downward-cast face. He lowered the pack to the floor now, slowly closed the store's front door with his foot, and began to scan the room for a weapon. The best he could come up with was the pointed end of a long paintbrush that lay on the table where the young woman was working.

"We don't take deliveries on Friday," the young woman repeated. "And give that back. I'm using it."

"I apologize for the intrusion," said Daria to the old woman, "but your husband and I worked on a design together and now I need to speak with him."

In Farsi, the old woman whispered, "That will not be possible."

"How many days is it?" called out Mark to the old woman. He spoke in broken Farsi.

She glared at him with undisguised hatred.

"You are in mourning."

When Daria shot him a look, Mark gestured to the young woman. She'd just smacked her wooden stamp down hard on the fabric. Daria appeared to study the scene for a moment. The stamp smacked against the fabric again. For forty days after a death, the family members of the deceased wore black. The old woman likely wore a black chador every day anyway, so evidently Daria—whose focus had been the old woman—hadn't noticed that anything was amiss. She did now.

"Oh…I see."

"They found your contact and killed him," said Mark to Daria. Remembering how Peters's apartment had been watched, he said, "This place is compromised. We should leave."

"Yes, yes, go," said the old woman. But this time her voice cracked with emotion.

"What happened?" pressed Daria.

"Go!"

"Fatima, Fatima…" Daria said and tried to put her arms around her. "You are not alone."

Mark heard footsteps just outside the shop. He positioned himself behind the door.

Daria said, "I need to know where he took the package I brought him, Fatima. They're after me too. I need your help."

The door cracked open. Mark saw a heavily muscled forearm on the handle. Without waiting for the door to fully open, he swung the pointed end of the paintbrush up to where he guessed an eye would be. He connected—although he had no idea whether it was with a potential killer or an unlucky customer.

He slammed the door shut as the man he'd stabbed cried out in pain.

"We're outta here!" Mark said.

"Fatima," said Daria. "Please. I need to know where your husband took the package."

Mark started running. When he got to the locked door in the back of the store, he threw his shoulder into it and popped it open with one quick push. Daria took off after him.

They ran through a series of dark, mazelike back alleys, until they came to a street crowded with people eating and celebrating the end of the day's Ramadan fast. Within seconds, a green Peugeot screeched to a stop in front of them. A strikingly attractive woman of maybe twenty sat behind the wheel, gasping for breath. She wore a flimsy blue headscarf that barely covered any of her hair, but what Mark really noticed were her slender paint-stained fingers. He glanced down at her feet and saw purple Nikes.

"How'd you find us?" he asked.

"All the alleys lead to one exit. Get in."

Mark and Daria did so. The young woman took off without a word, cut in front of an orange bus, then sped down Ferdowsi Street. By now it was dark. The unbroken lines of tall plane trees on either side of the street made Mark feel as though he were racing through a tunnel.

"The MEK is useless!" the woman said. "Fossils! You couldn't have sent someone to protect him, to warn him? To watch the store? You use him for twenty years and then leave him to the wolves?"

"I'm so sorry about your father," said Daria. "If I had known—"

"Why would he become involved with you people? Why?"

"I don't have anything to do with the MEK," said Mark.

They came to an intersection and the car jerked to a stop. In front of them, a pedestrian bridge that looked centuries old spanned a river. Brightly colored flags, illuminated from below by spotlights, fluttered near its entrance.

"Cross that bridge," said the young woman. "If someone has been following us, it will force them to cross too, on foot, and you will be able to see them. After that, you should be safe enough if you get off the streets."

The bridge had two levels, each with multiple tiled alcoves. Yellow light from inside the alcoves spilled onto the river below. In the center of the bridge, a man was singing a plaintive song, his voice echoing across the water. Couples were out on the river in yellow duck-shaped paddleboats.

"When I last saw your father," said Daria, "it was to give him a package. Do you know where—"

"Ashraf. He took your package to Ashraf, and then came back to Esfahan the next day. They didn't kill him until a week ago."

"Did he tell you what was in the package?"

"No. And I don't want to know."

"Thank you." Daria gripped the young woman's hand. "Please, be careful. I wouldn't go back to your shop tonight, maybe not for a long time. If you want a place for you and your mother to stay, I can arrange it. You both may be in danger."

"Find a way to get to Kermanshah," said the young woman. "It's six hundred kilometers west of here. Go to an Internet café called the Emperor and ask for Rahim. If it's closed, ring the bell until he answers; he lives upstairs."

"Who's Rahim?" asked Daria.

"A friend of my father's. He may be able to help you cross the border into Iraq. From there you'll have to find your own way to Ashraf. Now go."

"Are you sure we can't help?"

"I said go."

47

Washington, DC

Colonel Henry Amato sat to the right of James Ellis at a long oval conference table in the newly renovated White House situation room. Mounted on the sound-dampening fabric walls were six flat-screen plasma video monitors. To the sides of two of the monitors were smaller screens that displayed the date, the time, and the words *NSC/57 Top Secret*.

"This meeting is called to order," said the president.

The vice president, the director of national intelligence, the secretary of defense, the secretary of state, the secretary of the treasury, the chairman of the Joint Chiefs of Staff, the president's own chief of staff, his national security advisor, and all the attendant advisors gave the president their attention. In the back of the room, the two watch officers responsible for running the technical show sat up a little straighter behind their computer screens.

"We're here to discuss how to respond to reports that indicate Iran has mobilized more of their armed forces over the past twenty-four hours. James's team…" The president gestured to his national security advisor. "…is going to bring you up to date on the latest."

Ellis frowned and looked over his bifocals. "I'll cede the floor to my assistant, Colonel Henry Amato."

For the second time in as many days, Amato didn't respond when prompted by his boss.

"Henry?"

"Sir?"

"Your presentation?"

Amato had just heard from the contractor he'd hired in Iran. The man had called from a hospital—apparently someone had stabbed him in the eye as he'd tried to intercept Daria and Sava.

Amato's hope was that in the confusion, Daria hadn't been able to figure out where the uranium had been taken after it left Esfahan. That would be the best outcome, one that might lead to her going into hiding.

"Of course."

He stood up and walked to the front of the room. When he spoke, it was with something less than his usual confident precision: New intelligence reports suggest regular army troops and millions of Revolutionary Guard Basij paramilitaries have been ordered to gather weapons and food supplies...two of Iran's Kilo-class submarines have been detected by the US Navy near the Strait of Hormuz...At this time, however, Iran's military posture appears to be a defensive one. No troops are massing on the borders. The situation is something to watch closely, for sure, but still no cause for immediate alarm.

48

Iraq, Near the Iranian Border

Mark sat on an old truck tire in front of a boarded-up roadside store. In back of him lay a pile of empty oil drums and a bright tangle of abandoned concertina wire. He checked his watch.

"They'll be here," said Daria.

After what had happened in Esfahan, Mark figured the only hope he and Daria had was to move so fast that the enemy—whoever it was—couldn't keep up. So they'd driven through the night to Kermanshah, and then instead of sleeping had pushed on to the border with Iraq—which they'd crossed in the dark where their contact Rahim had told them to. After that, it'd been hurry up and wait.

Mark checked his watch again.

They'd been lounging around by the side of the road since dawn had broken about twenty minutes ago. He was beginning to feel like a piece of bloody chum thrown out to attract sharks.

Even this early in the morning it was frighteningly hot out, just shy of a hundred degrees. Across the road, behind more swirls of abandoned concertina wire, a couple of boys were playing in what looked like an old guardhouse. The roof had caved in and there were no longer any windows.

Mark wondered how long it would take the boys to announce to the neighborhood insurgents that a couple of American tourists were waiting to be sacrificed. One of the boys was staring at him, so Mark waved and the kid waved back.

Then his phone rang.

"Hey, boss," said Decker. "Guess where I am?"

Before Mark could answer, Decker said, "Paris, man!" and launched into a play-by-play of his daring escape, and bus trip to Baku, and—

"Well, I'm glad you made it," said Mark. "That's awesome, buddy. We're on track too. Keep us posted."

"All right. I've never been to France before, kind of wild, I can see the—"

"Really kind of tied up right now, Deck."

"OK, OK. Well, we'll talk soon."

After Mark clicked his phone off, Daria said, "You still trust that guy?"

"You don't?"

"I don't know. He left Yaver's cell phone on after you told him to shut it off."

Mark considered himself a pretty good judge of people. And all his instincts, plus the two minutes he'd spent back in Baku Googling Decker's name, were telling him that Decker was on the level. Then again, his instincts had also told him Daria was on the level.

"People make mistakes," he said.

Five minutes later Decker called again.

"Hey, boss, remind me again, what's the name of Daria's uncle?"

"Tehrani." Mark spelled it out.

"And where was the MEK headquarters?"

"Auvers. On Saint—"

"Saint Simon Road, got it."

A reasonably new-looking white Toyota pickup truck pulled up and skidded to a stop. The MEK contact Daria had lined up, Mark assumed.

"You good now?" Mark asked Decker. "Because I have to go."

"I'm gonna shoot up to Auvers today."

"Fantastic. Be careful."

"Should I call you when I get there?"

A middle-aged woman with tobacco-stained teeth rolled down the window of the pickup truck and spoke to Daria in Farsi.

"Why don't I call you."

"OK, that works. When do—"

"Deck, I have to go."

This time, after shutting off his phone, Mark switched out the SIM card.

They drove absurdly fast, first along a dirt road and then down a two-lane highway. The engine whined at a high pitch and the wind roared through the open windows, so no one talked. Mark sat in the passenger seat and Daria sat wedged between him and the driver. The land was arid and flat and there was little to see except other cars and an occasional convoy of military vehicles.

On the outskirts of Baqubah they stopped at a service station and parked behind a row of rusting gas pumps. The woman with the tobacco-stained teeth got out of the pickup and opened the back of a nearby white refrigerator truck. She removed some cartons of processed chicken parts from it, and beckoned to Mark and Daria. When they climbed up into the back, they discovered a trapdoor that lay flush to the floor. The woman pulled it open, exposing a long shallow smuggler's compartment, and gestured for Mark and Daria to climb in.

They lay down as instructed, squeezed up next to each other. The trapdoor was lowered. When the chicken parts were stacked back on top of it, the inside of the trapdoor just touched Mark's nose. The air was cold but he found it preferable to the heat outside. The darkness was absolute.

Daria gripped his hand. "We're close now," she whispered. "This is just to get us past the gates."

They drove for maybe ten minutes before the truck came to a stop, at which point Mark heard the muffled sound of Iraqi soldiers talking outside. Which told him they'd arrived at Camp Ashraf, a plot of land Saddam Hussein had given to the MEK decades ago. More recently it had been limping along as a diplomat's nightmare, with four thousand or so rabidly antiregime Iranians huddled inside and no country willing to take them off Iraq's hands other than Iran—to kill them. The Iraqis had wanted to shut the place down for years but had defaulted to treating it as a refugee camp/ prison until someone figured out what to do with all the MEK soldiers.

The Iraqi soldiers standing outside the truck posed a series of routine questions—what was the truck carrying, where was it coming from—and then asked for documentation. Mark heard the back door open and observed a sliver of light as it widened around the perimeter of the trapdoor. Then all was darkness and the truck started moving again.

Two minutes later, it came to a stop. This time the engine was turned off and Mark heard people pulling out the chicken cartons. When the trapdoor was finally pulled open, he saw that he was in a warehouse, surrounded by an unimpressive cadre of unarmed soldiers. They were clad in olive-green uniforms and gathered in a big clump behind the truck, frowning and looking nervous. Half were women.

A squat, ugly woman stepped forward. She wore a headscarf and prescription glasses that magnified her eyes so that they looked unnaturally big.

"Sister Daria," she said, opening her arms. "It has been too long."

Her expression conveyed genuine warmth but was tinged with worry. And maybe fear, thought Mark.

"Welcome to Ashraf," she continued. "I rejoice that you reached out to us in your hour of need." When she turned to Mark, her expression turned hard. "And who is your friend?"

49

Mark wondered whether this was another of Daria's double-cross deals.

Within minutes of getting to Ashraf, she and the squat, bespectacled woman—who turned out to be the camp commander—left to meet privately while he was taken to the other side of the camp, possibly as a prisoner, to have tea and cookies with a couple of grim-faced MEK soldiers.

They sat in the shade on a concrete patio, just outside an all-male residential unit.

The soldiers were jumpy, glancing at Mark then scanning the perimeter of the camp, as though they expected to be attacked at any minute. In the distance, across an expanse of flat, burnt desert, stood an Iraqi guard tower.

"Did my friend say when she was coming back for me?" asked Mark.

"No."

Just past the patio lay a vegetable garden. After sitting in silence for a few minutes, one of the soldiers explained with aggressive pride how they grew much of their own food, and that the MEK had built this camp up from nothing over the years and that the Iraqis would never succeed in shutting it down. Did Mr. Sava know there was a swimming pool?

Mark had gotten a fleeting glimpse of the "swimming pool" on the way over. All the water had been drained out, and weeds were growing out of cracks in the concrete apron that surrounded it. And the vegetable garden in front of him consisted of little more than a feeble collection of green beans and rows of what looked like wilting lettuce.

Even the soldiers looked wilted. They were too slender and their uniforms hung too loosely on their frames.

No, there was nothing in this refugee camp to be proud of, thought Mark. It was a pathetic, dusty, miserable shithole-under-siege in the middle of the desert. And the people who lived here were deluding themselves if they really thought they could topple the regime in Iran. It was a testament to the folly of hanging on to a dream for too long.

He found the occasional mixed-gender squads of MEK soldiers marching by on a nearby road, going double time—as if it mattered—to be dispiriting, as he did the framed photo of Maryam Minabi, which hung from a post on one corner of the patio. She had green eyes, and her broad smile was framed by a green headscarf. Mark recalled that she'd taken over the leadership of the MEK after her husband had disappeared in the wake of the Iraq War. Now she hung out in France at the MEK headquarters, giving speeches that hardly anyone listened to.

He gestured to the photo. "She ever leave France to come visit you guys here on the front lines?"

His question was met by silence and a glare from the soldier closest to him.

"It must be difficult, not being able to leave the base," Mark offered a little while later, after he got tired of sipping his tea in silence.

"One must be willing to pay the price for freedom," said the soldier, sounding a bit like a robot.

"Hmm," said Mark agreeably.

"I will show you something." The soldier left and returned with a three-ring binder. Evidence, he said, of atrocities the mullahs had committed against the MEK and the people of Iran. The soldier flipped through photos of gruesome executions and clear evidence of horrific torture: mangled bodies, burnt limbs...

It was all true, Mark knew, all of these awful tragedies. And every one no doubt was a mini-holocaust for the families involved. But he'd heard so many similar stories coming out of Iran—and Iraq, and Armenia, you name it—that he'd become numb to the misery.

He wished Daria would show up.

50

A half hour later she did, moving quickly.

"Follow me."

Daria started walking off at such a fast clip that Mark had to jog a few steps to catch up.

"Where are we going?"

"So the original camp commander, the guy who might have really known whether the uranium ever made it to Ashraf, was shot by a sniper three days ago. People are blaming the mullahs and the Iraqis. Everyone is in a panic."

"Anybody got any evidence?"

"No. They just always blame the mullahs and Iraqis when something goes wrong."

"This time maybe they're right." Mark wondered whether the sniper was still around, and whether his and Daria's arrival had been detected.

"Anyway I explained to the new commander why we're here and got her to check Ashraf's records. Turns out that the day after I brought the uranium to Esfahan, one of the unit leaders here was smuggled out of Ashraf."

"To pick up the uranium."

"Maybe. All we know is that he came back the next day, was smuggled out again a week later, and then disappeared. In between he apparently spent a lot of time at the repair shop. It's our one lead."

She gestured to the large steel-sided warehouse in front of them. "We're here, now."

Mark and Daria stepped into a large bay, where a few disabled armored vehicles and stripped-down Brazilian Cascavel tanks were stored, the sad remnants of what had once been a sizable battalion. One of the armored vehicles was up on a hydraulic lift. Around the perimeter of the bay were tool shelves, a large drill press, a milling machine, welding equipment, and a large waist-high electroplating bath.

Two machinists, looking slightly disheveled and apprehensive, stood in front of the tanks. Next to them the new camp commander slouched on a tall three-legged stool. Unruly strands of hair stuck out from under her headscarf and her mouth was set in a deep, tired frown.

She ordered the machinists to share everything they knew about the unit leader who'd disappeared, and in particular to explain why he'd been visiting the weapons shop in the week prior to his disappearance.

One of the machinists stepped forward. In Indian-accented English, he recounted that this unit leader, acting under the authority of the old camp commander, had ordered him to help create two replicas of a heavy block of metal.

"What kind of metal?" asked Daria.

"Depleted uranium, my sister. He brought it with him."

"*Depleted* uranium?" said Mark.

"Yes, sir."

"Are you sure?"

The machinist shrugged. "He told me it was depleted uranium. And it was very, very heavy. I could barely lift it."

"It was just a block?"

"No, it had six holes in it, I think to accept bolts. Around this big." With his hands, the machinist indicated it had been about the size of a large tissue box.

Mark looked at Daria. "Did the package you brought to Esfahan have holes in it?"

"No."

"Sir, it also had the name Lockheed Aeronautics stamped onto it. This means it is from a military airplane, no? Made by the Americans?"

Depleted uranium was used in armor-piercing bullets and armor plating because it was dense, cheap, and only mildly radioactive, but Mark hadn't heard of a use for it in planes. "Was this *depleted* uranium kept in a lead case or anything?" He still wondered whether it was actually the highly enriched uranium.

"No, it was just wrapped in a towel."

"And the unit leader handled it himself?"

"He did."

"And you did what he asked you to? You made the replicas?"

"Yes, out of lead, as I was ordered to do. And since the block of depleted uranium was plated with cadmium, I plated the lead replicas with cadmium too." He pointed to the electroplating bath and added, "We used to use cadmium to refinish old weapons that take rust. And molds for lead, they are easy to make." Almost as an afterthought he said, "The only difference between the original block of depleted uranium and the lead replicas I made was that the replicas were hollow, with a cover that was easy to screw on and off."

"Can you draw us a sketch of what this block of depleted uranium and your replicas looked like? To scale?"

"Yes, of course."

51

The camp commander's office was a drab room, located in a desultory concrete monolith called the castle, near the center of Camp Ashraf. The carpets were worn and the poorly constructed Chippendale furniture looked ready for the dump. A dim incandescent bulb glowed overhead.

In the corner sat an old Compaq computer, which Daria used to Google "depleted uranium cadmium aircraft."

The computer was connected to the Internet through a phone line and it took several minutes to spit out the information. But when it finally did, thousands of search results came up. The first was a US Federal Aviation Administration memo.

Mark pulled a chair up next to Daria's. The memo explained how some planes still used depleted uranium as ballast, either in the tail or the wings, because depleted uranium was remarkably heavy relative to its size. When it was used, it was always plated with cadmium to prevent rust.

"That's it," said Mark. He turned to Daria. "You get it?"

"That means the uranium could be anywhere in the world by now," she said.

"Get what?" said the camp commander.

Mark stared at the screen for a moment longer. "This is what happened. Your missing unit leader did bring the stolen uranium from Iran back to this camp. The problem then was how to deliver the uranium to its final destination." Mark tapped on the computer screen. "And this tells us how it was smuggled out of Ashraf and probably out of Iraq—depleted uranium ballast from a Lockheed airplane was replaced with enriched uranium ballast that was encased in lead. Now, even encased in lead the enriched uranium might still have thrown off some radiation. Enough maybe to set off airport sensors if the plane was ever checked. But if the sensors went off, no one would think anything of it, because the original ballast was made of depleted uranium, which also would have thrown off a little radiation. That plane probably could have gone anywhere in the world and no one would have known what it was really carrying."

Daria did a series of new searches and discovered that, while most new planes used tungsten as ballast, thousands of Lockheed C-130 military planes still used depleted uranium. Even a few of Lockheed's civilian planes—older DC-10s and Jetstar business jets—still used it.

Mark tapped his knee with his hand as he thought. "Do a search of airports in Iraq."

At that point, the commander said, "Sister Daria. I tried contacting Paris again while you were retrieving Mr. Sava. There was still no answer."

"I have tried many times as well," said Daria.

"Something terrible has happened."

Daria turned from the computer to face the camp commander. "I fear it."

"It was brought on by the mullahs who are looking for this uranium we stole."

"I fear that too."

"Do you also fear that the wishes of our leaders were not honored? That this uranium was taken somewhere it should not have been?"

"I do."

The commander seemed torn, but only for a moment. "Then I must tell you that while you were retrieving Mr. Sava I spoke with a sister who claims she helped smuggle our missing unit leader out of the camp on the day he disappeared. She believes she was the last person in the camp to see him."

For a moment the room was silent.

"She told me he was traveling with two extremely heavy trunks, and that it took all her strength to help him lift just one. She brought him to Jalaula—it's a town north of here, not far away."

"And from there," said Mark. "Do you know where he went?"

"In Jalaula there is a road that branches off and leads to Kirkuk. He was dropped off after this intersection and the sister saw him get in a car with two other men and drive north. If you are right and he was headed for an airport, then they must have gone to Sulaimaniyah. It is the only airport in that direction."

Sulaimaniyah was north of their current position, Mark knew. In the Kurdish region of the country.

"The airport there is new," said the camp commander. "It was built after the invasion."

"What kind of planes can it handle?"

"Any of the planes you're looking for."

52

If there was one thing Mark had learned in his twenty years of working for the CIA, it was that most people would believe almost any lie you told them provided that you followed two rules.

The first was that the lie had to be within the realm of plausibility. The second was that the lie had to be framed in such a way that it didn't appear to be in the self-interest of the person who was telling it.

With those rules in mind, Mark handed the deputy director of security at Sulaimaniyah Airport a business card. It had his real name on it, along with a phony title—executive director of security, US Embassy, Baghdad, and a version of the Great Seal of the United States that he'd downloaded from the Internet.

"Your purpose?"

Mark pulled out his black diplomatic passport.

"A joint investigation is being conducted by the US embassy and the Iraqi Department of Border Enforcement." He gestured to Daria. "This is my assistant."

He explained that he needed records of all arrivals and departures from May and June of this year. "For both commercial and charter flights."

Mark wore a charcoal-gray pinstripe suit. A cell phone hung on his belt.

The security official, a middle-aged man with a Saddam Hussein mustache, frowned. He said he thought it could be arranged—eventually—if the request were made through the proper channels.

"They're not classified documents and Border Enforcement and the US Embassy want them now."

"For what purpose?"

Mark glanced around the terminal—it was empty except for himself and Daria, a handful of airport workers, and one family sitting in a waiting area off to the right next to a pile of luggage that consisted of cellophane-bound cardboard boxes. He wrote down a telephone number on the back of one of his business cards. "This is the direct line to the ambassador's office. His people can answer your questions."

The number was actually for a telephone at Camp Ashraf that would be answered by a twenty-two-year-old MEK soldier who'd once studied at the University of Illinois.

The security official stared uneasily at the number for a moment before saying reluctantly that he would consult with his director of security, who was in Mosul for the week.

"I can see you are uncomfortable giving Border Enforcement access to your records," said Mark.

"It is simply a matter of—"

"I'm willing to come to an accommodation."

"Sir?"

"Five hours, five hundred dollars."

"I'm not sure I understand."

"I'll leave and come back in five hours. I'll tell the embassy I got lost. That should give you the time you need to fix the records."

The deputy director of security stared first at Mark, then at Daria. "And why, sir, would I want to do that?"

"Listen, I don't give a shit what happens to Kirkuk or the cash that's been smuggled through this airport. It's an Iraqi problem as far as I'm concerned. But you want five hours, it'll cost you five hundred dollars. If you try to stall without paying me, I'll call the embassy myself and they'll have a peshmerga general in the airport within the hour. Those are your options."

The deputy director of security stuck out his jaw defiantly. "You have misjudged the situation here, sir. You have greatly misjudged both me and the situation, I can assure you."

Ten minutes later Mark and Daria were led to a back room. The deputy director of security unceremoniously dumped a huge stack of flight records on a metal fold-up table.

"The records you requested," he said. Then, with some indignation, he made a point of saying that the airport security force had nothing whatsoever to hide and would assist the Department of Border Enforcement however they could, as quickly as they could.

The flight records were in Kurdish. Daria was able to translate the headings of the different columns, explaining how one was for the date and time of each flight, one for the destination and point of origination, and another for the registration numbers of the individual planes.

It was a low-traffic airport, with usually no more than ten arrivals and departures per day. Knowing the size of the runway—it was nearly two miles long—and seeing how little use it actually got, made Mark think that the Kurds must be an awfully optimistic group of people.

Many of the registration codes popped up again and again, the same commercial planes making their biweekly runs to Dubai or Amman or Istanbul or Damascus. All Mark really cared about was a few days in July.

He soon came upon a charter plane that had departed on the morning of July 16, at 7:05 a.m., headed for Dubai. Its registration code—M-GBHN—corresponded to a Lockheed Jetstar.

It didn't take long for them to check the rest of the flights. The Jetstar was the only Lockheed plane on the list.

Daria, who was watching over his shoulder, said, "I don't have any contacts in Dubai."

"I do," said Mark.

53

New York City

Colonel Henry Amato was being driven down Forty-Second Street in a black Cadillac limousine, en route to the United Nations headquarters, when the call from Iraq came in. Lieutenant General David Obeir, a former protégé of Amato's who'd stayed in Army Intelligence and had risen quickly through the ranks, was on the line.

National Security Advisor James Ellis was also in the limo, reading a dossier on the Iranian ambassador to the United Nations—with whom he and Amato were about to meet. The meeting would be secret and pointless, Amato knew. The Iranian ambassador would pretend to be shocked at the US accusation that Iran was in the midst of a major military mobilization, and Ellis would pretend to be shocked at the Iranians' denial.

Speaking into his BlackBerry Amato said, "David, how are you?"

Amato had felt uncomfortable asking Obeir for such a big favor—they'd never been personally close and hadn't spoken in years—but Obeir had been decent about it.

"NSA got a hit on the names you gave me."

Amato tightened his grip on his BlackBerry.

"What's the word?"

"Mark Sava left Sulaimaniyah Airport three hours ago."

"*Left?*"

"Yeah."

Which meant, thought Amato, that every cent of the $30,000 he'd wired private contractors—to watch both Esfahan and Ashraf—was down the drain. The Ashraf team wasn't even supposed to arrive on site until later today.

Dammit. He hadn't thought it possible that Daria could have gotten so far so quickly. *Dammit to hell.*

"When did he come into the country?"

"We have no record of him entering, but he's definitely on the departure list."

"Alone?"

"No. He was traveling with a woman who checked in as Jennifer Tirani. But that's almost certainly not her real name. The passport number matches a diplomatic passport stolen from a State Department rep in Baku a year ago. They're both headed for Dubai, Iraqi Airways flight 180. They'll touch down any minute. You got access to assets in the Emirates?"

"Maybe."

Sure, he could get assets in place, but in time to make a difference? Amato didn't think so.

"Anyway, I just found out."

"I appreciate it, David."

After Amato hung up, Ellis said, "Who was that?"

The limousine was passing through Times Square. Amato stared out at the electric-blue Chase Bank logo and Madame Tussauds and McDonald's and the blinking NASDAQ tower with its LCD facade and streaming stock quotes…The intensity of the lights made him think, with something bordering on shame, of the Latin masses at Saint Mary, Mother of God, and of the mustiness of the old church, and he suddenly felt that those old ways, his old ways, didn't stand a chance in this new world. *He* wasn't even fighting for the old ways anymore. Somehow things had gotten all twisted up.

"A guy I know from Army Intelligence," said Amato. "He's holed up in the Green Zone monitoring a couple of Revolutionary Guard units in Iraq. I want to be clued in when the Iranians really start panicking."

"Smart move."

Amato forced himself to turn his gaze from a giant billboard—advertising some action movie that he'd never see—to the screen of his BlackBerry.

Ellis, who still hadn't looked up from the file he was reading, said, "Any sign of panic yet?"

"No. We're still good."

54

Dubai, United Arab Emirates

Nine years ago—the last time Mark had met up with Larry Bowlan—his old boss had still looked formidable. A bit grizzled perhaps, but with lines of experience that suggested a hard competence. They'd had a few too many drinks together.

Those lines of experience had since deepened into lines of old age, Bowlan's Adam's apple had grown more pronounced, the skin that covered it sagged, his salt-and-pepper hair had gone completely gray, and he'd shrunk a bit.

The Marlboro cigarettes he still chain-smoked used to seem like a cheerful poke in the eye to the young health nuts in the Agency, but now seemed more like a slow way to commit suicide.

His appearance certainly didn't suggest that this was a man who'd graduated from Yale with a degree in classical studies, although Bowlan had. He was old-school CIA, the white elite.

Mark and Daria sat down across from him at a table in the Take Five restaurant at the World Trade Center Tower in downtown Dubai. It was really just a run-of-the-mill self-serve cafeteria, located a few floors below the US consulate. The surrounding tables were empty but the cafeteria lines were long because the *Mahgrib salat*, the evening prayer coinciding with the setting of the sun, had just ended, marking the end of the day's fast.

Bowlan palmed a large cup of cardamom coffee and glanced with disgust at the food line. He shook his head. "I can't wait until this crap is over. Every restaurant closed from sunup to sundown and then it's a feeding frenzy. Christ, just look at them go."

"It's good to see you, Larry."

Bowlan smiled. "Good to see you too. An unexpected surprise."

"Kind of a spur-of-the-moment thing."

Mark introduced Daria. Bowlan shook her hand lightly and awkwardly, as though embarrassed by the huge gap between her youth and beauty and his current condition. He said it was a pleasure to meet her and asked whether her flight over was comfortable.

Daria started to reply when Mark interrupted. "We're in a bit of a time crunch, Larry. By the way, I've left the Agency."

"No kidding? On your terms?"

"Mostly. I wasn't pushed out."

"I don't blame you for leaving. Kaufman's a prick. I assume you heard that I came back."

"Yeah, I did hear that."

Five years ago, Larry Bowlan had been running his own station in Belarus. When Langley recalled him, instead of taking a figurehead position, he'd retired. A year later he'd begged to come back. Only he hadn't been rehired at his former GS-14 level. Instead he'd been offered a temporary contract analyzing suspicious visa applications in US consulates and embassies abroad. It was roughly the equivalent of an executive vice president at a major company retiring and then coming back to work in the mail room.

Mark said, "Dubai's the place to be—good for you."

"Don't patronize me, Sava."

Mark had no love for Dubai. The place was like Disneyland. The tallest building in the world! An island resort shaped like a palm tree! A mall with a ski resort inside of it! But it was also true that Iranian and American spies were all over the city—the Iranians to keep an eye on antiregime activity and to protect the flow of black market goods going from Dubai to Iran, and the Americans to keep an eye on their business interests and on the enormous port of Jebel Ali, which the US Navy used more than any other port outside the United States. The whole spy-versus-spy game that had developed as a result reminded Mark of the Cold War.

"It's a spy's paradise," he said.

"If you're actually in the game. Which I'm not. But I'll grant you that being a spectator is better than rotting away at home. Believe me, I tried rotting. A lot."

Mark tried to picture Bowlan gardening, or even just playing golf—ridiculous notions unless paired with booze and some duplicitous espionage-related scheme.

"The thing is," said Mark, "something's come up. I've come back temporarily on a contract basis."

"Well, I hope they're paying you better than they're paying me."

"Two thousand a day."

"What?" said Daria. "Are you kidding me?"

"You bastard," said Bowlan. "Well, good for you. What's the contract?"

"You heard Jack Campbell was assassinated?"

"Damn, they pulled you in for that?"

"They didn't have much choice."

"That's big time." Bowlan coughed.

People were beginning to sit down at the tables now. The noise of chairs being pulled out, silverware clinking, and conversation was growing louder. Mark glanced around to assure himself that he couldn't be overheard.

"Who hired you?" asked Bowlan.

"Kaufman. Larry, I could use your help."

Bowlan stared at him for a while. Mark noticed the thin spider veins around his nose, evidence that Larry still liked his cocktails.

"Shoot."

Mark took the coffee-stained napkin out from under Bowlan's coffee cup and scribbled down a series of numbers and letters. "This is the registration ID of a Lockheed Jetstar that flew from Sulaimaniyah, Iraq, to the airport here in Dubai on July sixteenth. I need to know where it went after it landed in Dubai, and who owns the plane."

Bowlan took the napkin and stared at it for a moment. "Why me? Why not go through Kaufman?"

"Because Kaufman will want to know more than I prefer to tell him at this point."

"Whereas you figure you can get by without telling me jack shit, is that it?"

"Pretty much. We have history, Larry."

Bowlan fingered the napkin. "I'm aware of that."

Mark had just been twenty-two years old when he'd first met Bowlan.

"Can you do it?" Mark pressed. "Do you still have your security clearances?"

"When do you need this?"

"Now."

"Is this going to come back to bite me in the ass?"

"I doubt it."

"Why don't I feel reassured?"

"Because you're not an idiot."

"Meet me back here in an hour. I'll see what I can do."

Bowlan returned to the restaurant at the appointed time and handed the napkin with the Jetstar's registration code back to Mark.

"The plane's been sold—by a company called Bede Limited to a company called the Doha Group. Bede is registered on the Isle of Man and the Doha Group is registered in the Seychelles, but the Doha Group also has an address here in Dubai. The transaction took place here the same day the plane flew in from Iraq."

"Private companies?"

"I think—couldn't find either listed on any exchanges. Couldn't find out who owns them either."

Bowlan handed Mark a few more sheets of paper. "This is everything I've got on the Doha Group. They're a small oil services company whose specialty is injecting carbon dioxide into aging fields to boost production. Dubai address actually looks legit. I checked—it's not just a mail drop."

Mark leafed through the information Bowlan had printed out. The Doha Group was operating in United Arab Emirates, and... "Says here they have a contract to develop the Maraj field in Iran?"

"Yeah," said Bowlan. "That's their biggest project as far as I can tell."

"I know that field," said Daria warily. Bowlan and Mark turned to her. "The Revolutionary Guard company that was supposed to redevelop it wound up backing out of the contract after getting paid for two years and doing nothing. A newspaper in Tehran made a stink about it, but the government killed the story."

Mark was reminded of how much Daria had taught him about Iran.

It was common knowledge that Iran's elite Revolutionary Guard troops were heavily invested in a variety of businesses throughout Iran. But Daria had dug deeper and found out the names of the life insurance companies and banks and shopping malls owned by the Guard—along with the names of the top generals who ran those businesses. And Daria had been the one who had given him a better sense of all the factions within the Guard: the professional soldiers truly dedicated to protecting the Islamic regime; the businessmen soldiers who only paid lip service to Islam; the politicians who only joined the Guard to advance their careers...It was a complicated organization, and no one knew it better than her.

She said, "So if this Doha Group is working on the Maraj field, it's because the Guard subcontracted the work. But I'm sure some general is getting a big cut out of whatever the Doha Group is getting paid."

Mark considered what Daria had told him. If anything he was more confused than ever.

The MEK had stolen highly enriched uranium, allegedly to give to the International Atomic Energy Agency. But instead of handing it over to the IAEA, it looked likely that they'd instead transferred it to the Doha Group, a company that was tight with Iran's Revolutionary Guard.

But why? The MEK wouldn't have stolen the uranium from the Iranians just to give it back to them.

Mark said, "So this Lockheed Jetstar plane that Daria and I are tracking flies from Iraq to Dubai, and right after it lands in Dubai it's sold to the Doha Group. Do we know what happened next? Is the plane still here?"

"I made some calls," said Bowlan. "The same day it was sold, it took off for Salalah, Oman. I know a Brit that works down at the embassy in Muscat. He talked to the Omanis. They have no record of the plane ever landing."

"So it just disappeared."

"It just disappeared."

"We could check other airports."

"There are a lot of airports out there. And half of them are private, or military."

With records that neither Bowlan nor the CIA would be able to get at, Mark knew. Bottom line was that if whoever was flying that plane had wanted to disappear, it wouldn't have been difficult.

"So we go after the Doha Group," said Daria. "They bought the plane. Someone in the company has to know what happened to it."

55

Mark bought a new pack of SIM cards for his cell phone and checked into a room at a Ramada Hotel. Larry Bowlan met him there after telling the consulate he was sick and needed to leave early.

"Just like old times," said Bowlan cheerfully.

"Something like that."

Bowlan called room service and ordered two Heinekens for Mark, two for himself, and a salad with fat-free dressing. He chain-smoked while he waited for the food and beer as Mark, who'd bummed a cigarette, kept an eye on a four-story limestone building just across the street.

They talked about how screwed up Langley was until around five in the evening when men in business suits—some Caucasian, some Arab—started to trickle out of the building across the street. Most were carrying briefcases. Some were picked up by taxis, others walked. Mark and Bowlan watched them all through binoculars.

As each one left, Bowlan would study the guy and then say, "No."

This went on for the better part of an hour.

Eventually Mark said, "Larry, you have to pick one. If you don't, I will."

Down on the street, Daria waited to be told which one to follow.

Another man left. "No," said Bowlan.

But then a long snow-white chauffeured Rolls Royce pulled up to the front of the building. A couple of minutes later a man in a dark suit strolled out to meet it.

"That's our mark," said Bowlan.

"Are you kidding me?"

Prey on the little guys—the weak, the young, the needy. That was the Larry Bowlan way. That was how Mark, when he'd only been a stupid and idealistic graduate student, had wound up a prisoner of the KGB in Soviet Georgia, forcibly addicted to heroin, sleeping in a deep ditch fouled with his own shit, and watching other prisoners get shot at point-blank range in front of him.

You used the little guys to learn about the big guys. You didn't start with the big guys.

"It's not his Rolls," said Bowlan dismissively.

"How can you tell?"

"Just by looking at it. It's a white Phantom. Belongs to the Burj."

"What's the Burj?"

"The Burj al Arab. It's a hotel, you've seen it."

"I don't think I have."

"Yeah, you have. Just drive to the coast. It's huge, shaped like a sail."

"Oh, that thing."

Mark hadn't known what it was called, but he'd seen pictures of it everywhere: on postcards, on advertising posters at the airport, even on the room service menu Bowlan had just ordered from. It was an enormous structure, shaped like the billowing spinnaker of an Arab dhow blowing in from the Persian Gulf. Dubai's version of the Eiffel Tower.

The chauffeur opened the rear door of the Rolls and their mark climbed inside.

"The Burj has got twelve of those cars, all white, just like this one. The Russian mafia-types and people who've never been to Dubai and don't know any better eat it up. You really know the city, you go to one of the classier places in Jumeirah. And did you see that dark suit he was wearing? No one who's spent any time here wears a suit like that on a hundred-and-ten-degree day. He's a fish out of water. Ten to one we can rattle him."

"If he's not local he might not even work for Doha. He could be a client."

"He just came out of their main office. He'll at least be able to tell us who the real players are."

"You getting this?" said Mark to Daria, speaking into his cell phone as the Rolls pulled away.

"Don't even bother tailing him," said Bowlan. "I can tell you how to get to the Burj. He'll show up there eventually."

"Haul ass to get there before him," said Mark. "And figure out his name and room number if you can."

56

Daria took a big sip of her cranberry cosmo and eyed her man.

He had short hair that was graying at the temples. Clean-shaven. Wore rimless eyeglasses and a gold wedding band. Probably in his fifties. A snifter of some brown liquor sat in front of him, but he rarely touched it. His motions as he switched between typing on his computer and eating his dinner were precise and quick.

He had a clear view of her—she was seated at the bar—but he was focused on his work, his eyes darting back and forth as he scanned his computer screen. This despite the fact that she knew she looked awfully good in the black cocktail dress she'd just bought for $600 in one of the ground-floor shops.

She took another big sip of her cosmo. The oversized glass was rimmed with red sugar and the sweet lime-scented booze inside tasted almost good enough to justify the thirty dollars she'd paid for it. And then there was the view—the restaurant occupied the top floor of the Burj and was ringed with panoramic windows. Outside, all of Dubai was lit up in rose by the waning sun: the towering skyscrapers, the palm-shaped island resort just down the coast, the white sands of the Persian Gulf…

In a corner of the room, under a ceiling dotted with primary-colored polka dots, a live band from Oman played a bad reggae version of "Karma Chameleon."

When a young Arab guy tried to hit on her, she turned him down but it got her thinking of Mark, and how pleasant it could be, in some alternate reality, to just enjoy a carnival like Dubai together. But that daydream soon made her feel guilty, so she forced herself to brood yet again on darker matters, like Astara, and the Trudeau House.

Eventually that line of thought led her to consider how much she hated the mullahs in Iran. Which in turn led her to wonder for the millionth time whether the mullah's Revolutionary Guard shock troops really had raped her mom, before they'd killed her, all those years ago. Her uncle, after too many glasses of wine, had told her of his fear that it had happened. Evidently rape was a common occurrence at that time because the beasts had believed that virgins couldn't go to hell, and they'd wanted to make damn sure that was where all their enemies ended up. The fact that her mother had already had a child probably wouldn't have mattered. They raped plenty of mothers just to make sure.

After swirling that around in her brain for a while, mixing it all up with the alcohol, Daria eyed the excess around her and decided she hated Dubai. Her mother had never known anything except Tehran—a dirty, crowded city ruled by the Shah and then the mullahs. The thought that her mother had never really been able to experience anything of the wider world made Daria want to hurl her frilly cosmo glass into the mirror behind the bar.

Mark's call interrupted her thoughts. She answered using the earpiece hidden beneath her hair.

"Status?"

"He's eating dinner. I'm watching him from the bar."

"Why didn't you call in?"

Daria checked her watch. The time was 6:47 pm. She'd said she'd call with an update by 6:45.

"I got distracted. Decided to have a drink."

"Jesus, Daria. Focus."

"I'm plenty focused."

"Do you need me?"

"No."

"Name and room number."

"I'll get it."

She finished her drink, ordered a bottle of Pellegrino water instead of the second cosmo she wanted, and observed the flow of the restaurant for the next half hour while Rolls Royce Guy slowly pecked away at his dinner. At some point she realized that the clientele was divided between hotel guests and people who were just there for drinks or dinner. The difference was clear because some paid for their drinks with cash or a credit card, while others were presented with a computer tablet that they signed.

When the waiter came by with a dessert tray, Rolls Royce Guy snapped his laptop shut and chose a crystal goblet filled with what looked like vanilla pudding.

Daria called for the bartender.

"Offer a drink to the gentleman in the restaurant seated by himself," she said. "Anything he likes."

Upon delivery of the message, Rolls Royce Guy flashed Daria a polite smile and shook his head awkwardly in what could only be interpreted as a gentle rebuff.

Which she'd expected. But it didn't matter. She'd made him uncomfortable. That was all that mattered. She took out her phone and switched it to camera mode.

A few minutes later Rolls Royce Guy finished his dessert and asked his waiter for the check. Daria palmed her phone and approached his table just as he was signing a computer tablet.

She lightly touched his shoulder, bent down far enough into his personal space so that she knew he'd be rattled, so that he could feel her breath on his cheek, and said, "I'm certain we've met before. It was London, wasn't it? The Grosvenor House?"

"I haven't been to London in five years, Miss." He smiled uneasily as he placed the computer tablet back on the table.

"If not London, then was it here?" In a low voice that she gauged was somewhere between seductive and pathetic, she said, "I wouldn't forget a face like yours."

Rolls Royce Guy stole a quick, embarrassed glance at her breasts and said, "Miss, ordinarily I'd love to talk, but the honest truth is that I am up to my eyeballs in work."

57

In the glass-walled panoramic elevator that led down from the restaurant atop the Burj al Arab, Mark watched as Daria pushed a few buttons on her phone and then showed him the display.

"His check," she said.

Mark squinted. "I can't read anything."

Daria cropped it so that only the relevant portion remained, and then she enlarged that section and clicked on a filter that sharpened all the lines in the image.

They were able to determine that Rolls Royce Guy had eaten a meal of assorted seafood canapés, followed by a Wagyu beef tenderloin. He'd indulged in one snifter of Lagavulin single-malt scotch, followed by a white chocolate mousse. The meal, with tip, had cost $227. At the bottom of the page was an indecipherable signature, beneath which it read:

Deluxe Suite, Room 302
Waltrop, Stewart R.

"Got him," said Mark, thinking that he'd show up at Waltrop's room later that night, flash his old CIA identification card and diplomatic passport, and start pressuring the guy.

Meanwhile, Daria was already Googling "Stewart Waltrop."

The search didn't return a single direct hit.

So she Googled "Waltrop" by itself and got over a million hits.

When she tried "S. Waltrop" five direct hits came back, but they were all obscure references to a German town.

"Try Stu Waltrop," said Mark.

Thirteen direct hits popped up. Five had something to do with the German town. The rest were related to an executive vice president who worked in the business development unit of an Oklahoma-based company called Richter, Inc.

That Stu Waltrop had attended an oil services industry conference in Houston the previous April. And he'd been quoted in *Oil and Gas Journal* as being optimistic that Richter's new line of roller-cone drill bits would soon turn a profit for the company. His e-mail was listed on a contact page associated with the company's website.

Daria followed the links to Richter's homepage. And it was there, at the top of the page, right under the flashy Richter banner, that Mark read the words *Partners in Progress*, followed by what he recognized as the logo for Holgan Industries.

"Well, would you look at that." Holgan Industries was the largest oil services company in the world, he knew. An American firm, but headquartered in Dubai.

Daria's eyes narrowed a bit.

She clicked on the *Partners in Progress* link and was taken to a page that explained that Richter, Inc. had recently become a valued member of the Holgan Industries family.

Since Holgan supplied tools and know-how to nations and companies that pumped oil out of the ground, it made sense to Mark that Holgan would be interested in a firm like Richter.

What didn't make sense to him was the connection—if there was any—between Holgan and the Doha Group. They were both oil services companies, so they should have been competitors.

"Go to the SEC's website. See if Holgan and the Doha Group have done any deals together."

Daria followed the links until she got to a page that allowed her to search all of Holgan Industries' filings with the US Securities and Exchange Commission. There were thousands. Starting with the most recent and working back, she searched each for the word *Doha*. It didn't take long to get a hit.

It was in an end-of-year 10-K report, under a heading listed as *Exhibit 21: Subsidiaries of the Registrant*.

"Goddamn," said Mark, as he squinted, trying to read the page that had loaded onto Daria's phone. The Doha Group was near the top of a list of over fifty companies, all owned by Holgan Industries. "Holgan's not just doing business with the Doha Group. They *own* them, just like they own Richter."

It made Mark's head spin to keep all the connections straight, but they were there. The uranium had been stolen from the Iranians and delivered to the MEK. The MEK had passed it on to the Doha Group. And the Doha Group was owned by Holgan Industries. Which made Holgan Industries, a huge American firm, the most likely recipient of the stolen uranium.

"Stu Waltrop, this is your lucky night," said Mark.

"I'm not following."

"We don't need him."

"Why not?"

"Because I already know who to go after next."

58

The receptionist at Holgan Industries was a young blond woman with a Texas accent. She wore a pink blouse and matching pink lipstick. Mark's question appeared to amuse her.

"And do you have an appointment?"

It was eight thirty in the morning. Mark hadn't slept more than an hour the night before.

"I don't."

A pair of thick-necked guards—expats from Oman or Saudi Arabia, Mark guessed—exchanged a look. Wondering whether they had a crazy on their hands.

Holgan Industries had been founded half a century ago by Jimmy Holgan Sr., a former Eagle Scout and graduate of the US Naval Academy. But recently Jimmy Sr. had turned the day-to-day operations of the business over to his son, Jimmy Jr., who had promptly shifted Holgan's headquarters from Houston to Dubai, to be closer to his customers.

And unless you were the head of a first-world nation, or a third-world despot with gobs of oil, you didn't just breeze into Jimmy Jr.'s office.

"Then I'm afraid you won't be able to see Mr. Holgan," said the receptionist cheerfully.

"My name is Mark Sava. I'm with the CIA." He produced his diplomatic passport and allowed her to examine it. "If you tell Mr. Holgan I'm here, I believe he'll want to speak with me."

"Mr. Holgan doesn't speak to anybody without an appointment, sir. There are no exceptions."

"I said he'll want to speak with me."

"And what, may I ask, is the nature of your business?"

"The nature of my business involves national security and it's between Mr. Holgan and myself."

She stared at him. Mark stared back.

Holgan Industries occupied the top twenty floors of the Iris Bay Tower, an enormous silver banana-shaped building that had sprung up on Sheikh Zayed Road, Dubai's main thoroughfare. But there were no public elevators to Holgan's upper floors. To even get near Jimmy Holgan Jr., Mark first had to make it past Holgan's ground-floor lobby.

And what a lobby it was, Mark thought, looking over the marble floor mosaics and gleaming brass doors and brilliant light shafts set off at an angle as though the ceiling had been pierced like a pincushion. The place was cavernous and smelled of disinfectant.

"If you know Mr. Holgan, why haven't you contacted him directly or arranged for an appointment?"

"I didn't say that I knew him. I said that he'd want to speak to me." Mark pointed to the ceiling-mounted security camera behind the receptionist. "He'll recognize me."

He gestured to a cluster of overstuffed wingback chairs that formed a conversation pit near the reception counter. "I'll wait. But not longer than a half hour. What I have to say to Mr. Holgan is time sensitive."

The receptionist gave him another stare then reluctantly put in a call and gave a professional account of the situation. When she was through, she said, "Your request has been delivered. Beyond that, I don't know what to tell you."

Exactly thirty minutes later, two more security guards showed up. Only these guys were Americans, with close-cropped hair and shoulders that barely fit inside their blue blazers. Each carried a Sig Sauer pistol, visible in shoulder holsters beneath their blazers.

Mark was escorted down a long hall to a locked steel door, which opened with an electronic key.

Three more guards, who looked as though they could have been brothers of the first two, stood in a room with a concrete floor, concrete walls, and a ceiling of exposed I-beams.

"We'll need to search you. Raise your hands above your head."

Mark did as instructed. First they used a metal detector. Then they did a pat-down.

"I thought that kind of thing was illegal in this country," said Mark as they worked beneath his belt. No one laughed. Finally he was told to walk through a backscatter machine. They didn't find any weapons because he wasn't armed.

One of the guards ushered him—using subtle pushes and pulls as though leading a horse—into a service elevator. After a fast ascent followed by ten minutes of twists and turns down a maze of hallways, they arrived at Jimmy Holgan Jr.'s private reception room.

What appeared to be original Frederick Remington paintings lined the walls and a bronze Remington statue of a cowboy riding a rearing horse dominated one corner of the room. Behind a desk sat a middle-aged secretary, her hair pulled back in a tight bun. She frowned when she saw Mark and the guard.

After quite a bit more silent frowning, she spoke quietly into her phone. Then she cast a disapproving glance at Mark and said, "Mr. Holgan will see you now." She got up and opened the oversized French doors behind her. The guard began to follow Mark, but the secretary shook her head. "You wait."

The inner sanctum was a corner office on the top floor and it came with the obligatory sweeping views. A lord in his seat of power looking out over the sea of humanity toiling below, thought Mark. It was diminished only by the fact that there were so many other seats of power, in so many other skyscrapers, visible across the horizon.

A few ten-foot-tall potted cacti had been placed by the panoramic windows. On one of the inner walls, set in a framed glass display box, lay a rolled horse whip, a bolo tie with a fancy turquoise clasp, and a sheriff's silver star.

"Nice office," said Mark, as he looked over the display box.

Between all the marble and artsy-fartsy light shafts in the ground-floor lobby, the original Remingtons, and now this office, Mark thought that if he'd been a client actually considering hiring Holgan he'd worry about how much effort was going into impressing people rather than just focusing on delivering a good product. Apparently his sentiment was not mirrored by actual clients, however, because business for Holgan was booming.

"The Arabs like this crap, Mr. Sava." Holgan was seated behind a vast desk into which a variety of horse-themed scenes—a herd drinking by a river, a lone horse galloping across a plain, another pulling a plow—had been painstakingly carved. "When they visit they want a show. They like to think they're doing business with a hard-headed cowboy."

"That would be you?"

Holgan laughed, but it wasn't a nice laugh. He was a big man, in both height and girth, with bags under his eyes. His teeth were straight and white but they seemed a little too small for his mouth. Mark remembered reading that he was worth around $30 billion.

He tried to wrap his head around that figure, to imagine what it must feel like to be Holgan. *Holy shit* that was a lot of money.

"I just canceled a meeting with the Emirates energy minister to accommodate you. So maybe you should sit down and tell me why you're here."

Mark felt swallowed up by the oversized leather chair in front of Holgan's desk. He wondered whether it had been designed to make people feel small. If so, it was working.

"I work for the CIA. I used to be the station chief in Baku, but now I'm on contract. You already knew that, though, or I wouldn't be here talking to you right now."

"I wouldn't make any assumptions about what I know and what I don't know."

"How about Jack Campbell. You know him?"

"Former deputy sec. def."

"Assassinated in Baku five days ago."

Jimmy Holgan Jr. fixed his unblinking eyes on Mark for a moment before saying, "So I'd heard."

"I won't bore you with all the details, but suffice it to say that Campbell wasn't the only American killed in Baku. A lot of CIA personnel were also hit. I was hired to figure out who did it. My investigation led me to an Iranian resistance group—the Mojahedin-e Khalq, or MEK as they're known in Washington. I believe you're familiar with them?"

His question was met with a tight smile and dull stare.

"Maybe not," said Mark. "Anyway, it came to my attention that an MEK cell in Azerbaijan had been attacked at the same time Campbell and the CIA were hit. I figured maybe there was a connection between all this killing. So I looked into it. And you know, I was kind of bummed because I really wasn't able to find any connection, at least not yet, but along the way I did learn that the MEK recently acquired a small amount of highly enriched uranium. Stole it from the Iranians, who got it from the Chinese. It's potentially weapons grade, dangerous stuff. Maybe, I thought, this uranium has something to do with all these deaths. So I tried to figure out what the MEK did with it after they stole it. Turns out they brought it to Iraq, where they have a big camp, and then here, to Dubai. Stroke of genius, really, the way they did it."

Mark explained how the highly enriched uranium had been stored in the tail ballast of a Jetstar business jet. As he did, he studied Holgan's face. The man betrayed nothing. But the fingernails of Holgan's hands, which he was steepling under his chin, had turned white from the pressure he was applying.

"The thing is, on the same day this plane lands in Dubai, it's sold—becomes the property of this company called the Doha Group. Naturally, I try to find out who owns the Doha Group. Imagine my surprise when I find out they're owned by Holgan. Or, if you prefer, by you."

"Get to your point."

"My point is that the MEK stole uranium from the Iranians and then sold it to Holgan Industries. And I know it." Mark got up out of the giant chair. "And my colleague Daria Buckingham also knows it. And we both think it has something to do with what happened to Campbell and the CIA in Baku. Daria Buckingham is here in Dubai, by the way. Waiting to hear how our meeting goes."

Jimmy Holgan shook his head. "Quite a story. What do your buddies at the CIA think of it?"

"Oh, I haven't told them about any of this yet. You see, I like to preserve a little operational flexibility."

"Operational flexibility."

"Means I don't like people breathing down my neck, telling me what to do. Or what not to do. Like, say, barging in to see you. I'm not sure Langley would have approved."

"I see."

"Which brings me to why I came here in the first place. You've got two choices. The first is that we play it straight. Meaning you tell me why you bought the uranium from the MEK and what you did with it. Eventually—after I've concluded my investigation—I'll report what you've told me, along with everything else I've learned, back to the CIA. At which point you can deal with Langley and all the questions they'll have."

"Seeing as I don't have the information you're looking for, I'm afraid that's not a viable option."

"I'd think about it."

"I have."

"The second choice is that both Daria Buckingham and I break off all contacts with the CIA and go to work for Holgan Industries. Of course, we would abide by whatever confidentiality agreement you should see fit to impose. Including one that forbids us from discussing the story I just told you." Mark looked past Jimmy Holgan Jr., out at the sea of construction cranes dotting the Dubai skyline. Eventually he said, "Naturally, Ms. Buckingham and I would expect to be compensated."

Jimmy Holgan Jr. was perfectly motionless as he stared down Mark. "How much?" he said after a time.

"Four million dollars. Cash will do. Dollars or the equivalent in euros." Holgan was about to respond when Mark said, "You don't have to answer now—I'll come back today at five o'clock. Send one of your representatives to the lobby downstairs to meet me."

He paused to let his words sink in before adding, "Of course, if anything were to happen to me in the meantime, Daria Buckingham will issue a preliminary report to both the CIA and appropriate media outlets detailing how Holgan wound up buying stolen uranium from the MEK." Mark checked his watch. "In fact, she's prepared to deliver such a report within a half hour if she doesn't hear from me."

"You insult me."

"Think it over."

Holgan stood up and pressed the intercom button on his desk. "Mr. Sava will be leaving now," he said, glowering at Mark as he spoke. "Please arrange for an escort."

59

Mark stepped out of the ground-floor lobby of the Iris Bay Tower and was blasted by heat so oppressive he felt as though he'd stepped into a steam room.

He turned right and began walking down a palm-lined side-walk, staring straight ahead and not even trying yet to get a make on the men he was certain were following him. After a hundred yards or so he hailed a taxi.

"Mall of the Emirates."

They pulled onto Sheikh Zayed Road and soon were speeding past gleaming new buildings and bleak plots of undeveloped land where foundations for even more new buildings had been laid but where construction had come to a halt. In between were a few construction sites teeming with Indian and Pakistani and Iranian workers, all covered in cement dust. The taxi driver played Arabic techno music and the air conditioner was going full blast. The cloudless sky was an angry gray-blue.

All over the road, cars darted in and out of crowded lanes. Mark used the rearview mirror to note the make of several behind him.

"Slow down a bit, would you?"

The driver shrugged and eased off on the accelerator.

"A bit more, if you could."

The car directly behind them honked and then veered to the side to pass. In the taxi's rearview mirror, a blue Mercedes sedan about a hundred yards behind them slowed down.

In front of the main entrance to the Mall of the Emirates were a few benches and a fountain that squirted blasts of water timed to the beat of a digitized version of the "Flight of the Bumblebee." Mark paid the taxi driver, sat down on one of the benches, and called Daria.

"At least two," he said.

"I've got a visual on you."

She was behind him, somewhere inside the mall, and he was relieved to be in her orbit. Working in the field with someone was a dance routine of sorts, part choreographed, part improvised, with an underlying rhythm that both partners needed to feel for it to work. The night before on their training run, they had both felt it.

"Can you see the blue Mercedes?"

"I have it," she said.

"That's our tail. Point was a gray Lexus that came in just before me."

"Was there a wing?"

"Don't know."

"They rotating positions?"

"Can't tell yet."

The blue Mercedes had pulled over to the curb not far from the turnoff that led to the mall parking lot. Two men still sat in the car. The gray Lexus had disappeared after rounding a corner on the north side of the building. Mark watched the footpath leading from that corner.

Soon a man in a blue pinstripe suit, wearing a maroon Sikh turban, appeared from that direction. He passed by Mark without even a glance and went into the mall.

"Our point," said Mark.

"Got him."

Mark snapped his cell phone shut. The domed entrance leading into the mall resembled that of a nineteenth-century European train station. He walked through it and toward the shops beyond.

Daria would be watching from one of the upper levels, wearing a sequined green Muslim robe, a green veil, and shoes with two-inch heels. In her purse would be a red veil, a light black silk robe, a spare pair of flat-heeled shoes, and a digital camera.

Mark took an escalator to the second floor and walked a quarter mile or so deeper into the mall. Just beyond an Adidas store he came to a public bathroom where he locked himself in one of the back stalls and called Daria again.

"There's a wing," she said. "The point stayed on the ground floor and the tail is a couple hundred yards behind you, but your wing, she surfaced and stuck."

"She?"

"High heels, blue blouse. Tan purse. Looks young and slutty. Waiting right outside the men's room."

"She reeling in the rest of the team?"

"Uncertain."

A little while later Daria said, "She just slipped on glasses."

"I'm coming out."

Mark walked quickly now, at a pace that stood out. He headed past a Chili's restaurant and on to the five-star Kempinski Hotel. A red-liveried doorman greeted him as he stepped into the second-floor lobby. He took an elevator to the fifth floor, then quickly descended a stairwell to the ground level where there were seven ways to exit the hotel; it would be impossible for his pursuers to know which one he was going to pick.

He left via a service exit, made his way back into the mall, and called Daria.

"I think you're clear," she said. "I'm on the wing right now, she's questioning the valet parking guy in front of the Kempinski. As for the tail and point, I had a visual on them a minute ago and I don't see how they could have picked you up. How do you feel?"

"Like I'm good. I'm gonna hole up for a while."

Daria's next call came ten minutes later. "Your tail is staking out the main entrance by the fountain. The point is at the hotel entrance, and the wing is between the car park entrance and the entrance to the indoor ski area, trying to do double duty."

Once they'd lost him, Holgan's surveillance team had spread out and covered the multiple exits as best they could. The way Mark had suspected they would.

As he exited the mall he intentionally passed within fifty feet of the point man, who was sitting at a bench near the musical fountain.

"He has you," said Daria.

Mark climbed into a taxi. "The Gold Souk Hotel," he said.

60

The Gold Souk Hotel stood adjacent to the gold souk itself—a massive shopping bazaar crammed with shops where people from all over the Middle East came to buy and sell gold jewelry. There was no doorman at the hotel, only a sullen-looking Indian guy at the front desk who didn't even glance up at Daria and Mark as they passed.

Inside the shabby room they'd taken the night before, everything was as they'd left it—the voice recorder, the timers, the cameras, their change of clothes…

Mark walked to the big front window, cracked it open, and pulled back the curtain. The sweet and fruity smell of hookah smoke drifted up from a nearby café. Car horns were honking. They were in an old part of Dubai where the streets were narrower, the sidewalks cracked, and the buildings less glitzy. It was a part of the city that had just evolved gradually over the years, instead of being planned out and built overnight by global construction firms.

Daria came to his side and for thirty seconds or so they pretended to have a real conversation, so that Holgan's men—who had followed them from the mall to the hotel—would report back to their boss that Daria Buckingham and Mark Sava were in hiding together, unprotected. They'd say, Sava thinks he's evaded us. He suspects nothing.

When Mark was reasonably certain he and Daria had been spotted together, he closed the curtains and donned a woman's black chador, headscarf, and veil. Daria put on tight black jeans, a sleeveless red blouse, Prada sunglasses, and a New York Yankees baseball cap.

They left via a store in the back of the hotel and individually made their way to another dumpy hotel across the street. In a room on the third floor, Daria sat down on a frayed easy chair and stared at the LCD screen of a digital camera. She had slipped the camera's long telephoto lens under the bottom left-hand corner of one of the closed window shades. Slipped underneath another window shade was a digital camcorder, held in place with a tripod.

"We got movement?" Mark asked, after she clicked a few photos.

"Just the team that followed us here. They have all the exits covered."

"Give it a half hour. They'll be replaced."

"We'll see."

"No way those clowns are breaking down doors."

Mark had pegged the team that had followed them to and from the mall as Holgan's regular security detail. But he was certain that once Holgan was told that Daria Buckingham had been found, and that she was with Mark Sava, Holgan would send a different team to execute a takedown—he wouldn't be able to resist trying to save himself $4 million and a potential headache. The new team would be an elite force, probably comprised of people already in the know about the uranium, people Holgan trusted to keep their mouths shut no matter what they heard.

Those were the guys Mark was after.

On a table in the center of the room, a laptop computer played live video and audio from a wireless webcam hidden in the corner of their room at the Gold Souk Hotel.

Over the laptop audio, Mark heard his own voice declare, "I'm going to take a shower."

The digital voice recorder they'd purchased the night before at a Radio Shack was set on playback. Anyone trying to listen to what was going on in the room would hear the occasional sound of Mark and Daria walking around, using the bathroom, or discussing the logistics of the $4 million cash transfer they believed would take place at five o'clock that evening.

<hr />

The attack came at half past two that afternoon. Mark almost missed the initial entry, it was so subtle—just a quick popping sound as the weak door was forced open with a crowbar, followed by the soundless entry of three men, each of whom held a silenced pistol.

An unshaven guy with an angular face and jet-black hair ordered the other two to search under the bed and in the bathroom. What struck Mark most was that the guy spoke in fluent Farsi.

All the men were professional, communicating with hand signals and holding their weapons like soldiers. Definitely not MEK, Mark judged. Instead they reminded him of Yaver.

"You fucker," he said, thinking of Holgan. He wondered whether Holgan had cut a deal with the Iranian regime.

After it became evident that the room was empty, one of the men noticed the hidden webcam on top of a curtain rod. The leader picked it up, turned it over in his hands, and then threw it into the wall.

But it was too late.

Daria replayed the video of the attack. Whenever she had a good view of one of the attackers' faces, she paused the recording, cropped and expanded the image, and then saved the file as a still photo.

Seeing how fast she worked made Mark feel old.

After she'd compiled decent head shots of all three, he said, "All right then, let's get these to Bowlan."

61

Mark slid the cash-stuffed briefcase to the side of Holgan's desk.

He'd shown up at Holgan Industries headquarters at five o'clock as though nothing had happened and he was just there to collect his money. Only instead of taking off with the cash, he'd demanded to see Holgan again. Jimmy Jr. wouldn't kill him now and risk exposure, he knew. Not with Daria at large again.

Where the briefcase had been, Mark placed a laptop computer, turned it so that the screen faced Holgan, and pushed Enter.

"I'd like you to take a look at this," he said, and then he methodically walked Holgan step by step through the evidence that he and Daria had accumulated related to the path of the stolen uranium. There were copies of the plans for the hollowed-out tail ballast, of the flight records at Sulaimaniyah Airport, of information about the Lockheed Jetstar that proved the Doha Group had bought the plane from a company controlled by the MEK…Finally there were photos from that afternoon that tied Holgan to a Revolutionary Guard hit squad that had shown up at the Gold Souk Hotel just a few hours ago.

Holgan, however, didn't appear particularly threatened, or even interested. He observed the presentation sitting far back in his chair, twirling a gold pen around in his hand and occasionally glancing at his watch. When Mark started explaining how the CIA had helped him identify the leader of the hit squad—evidently he was well-known on the streets of Dubai—Holgan, with little enthusiasm, said, "I guess I shouldn't be surprised. Lie with dogs you're gonna get fleas. You'd be one of the dogs, by the way. A mangy two-pound poodle. Just take the damn money and get the hell out of here, Sava. You've done all right for yourself considering you're dealing with shit you don't understand."

"It's not about the money."

"I've heard that one before."

"I won't take the money."

"Now you're breaking new ground."

"I want to know what happened to the stolen uranium. And if I don't get what I want, I'm going public with all I just showed you as soon as I walk out this door. Or Daria Buckingham will if I can't."

Holgan cradled his head in his hands for a moment. Sounding tired and a little annoyed, he said, "OK. You win. You want information, you got it. It's not my fault that the National Security Council didn't send the memo to the CIA."

"Meaning?"

"Meaning the only reason I came up with the cash that's in front of you now is that James Ellis—that would be the president's goddamned hand-picked national security advisor!—asked me to. Which is the same reason I bought that plane with the uranium on it—paying forty million for it when the plane itself is worth maybe a quarter of that. And I didn't even get to keep the damn plane! Furthermore, I didn't know there was uranium on the thing until you showed up. But I refuse to put Holgan Industries at risk anymore by playing the middle man between all you bumbling government idiots. I'm out—I'm not carrying Ellis's water anymore. It's just not worth it."

DAN MAYLAND

"You know, I'm gonna need more information than that. Because I don't have a clue as to what the fuck you're talking about."

"Three years ago I get a call from Ellis. He tells me he knows one of Holgan's subsidiaries—the Doha Group—is working with some top Revolutionary Guard generals in Iran. Which we were." Holgan jabbed a finger at Mark. "Iran's a big market. If in ten, twenty years the US and Iran ever put their differences behind them, I want Holgan positioned to do some real business. Of course we're not allowed to contract with the Iranians directly, but the Doha Group was a foreign subsidiary with no Americans on the payroll. I'll admit it's kind of a gray area, and I thought Ellis was going to pressure me to sell Doha, get the hell out of Iran and whatnot, but instead he asks if he can slip a couple of his men into Iran by having them pose as employees of Doha."

"To what end?"

"To build relationships with some of these generals in the Revolutionary Guard that the Doha Group was working with. To try to turn them against the mullahs. The request came straight from the president. So I agreed. One, because I'm a patriotic guy. And two, I've been doing business with the government long enough to know that you don't grow your business by turning down a direct request from the president of the United States.

"Anyway, that was all it was until a little over a month ago, when, like I said, Ellis called up and asked me to buy that plane. Said it had to do with developing ties with more Revolutionary Guard generals they were working on turning, which I took to mean they needed a way to funnel the Iranian generals some money in a way that didn't look like it was coming from the US government. Again, he says the request comes from the president. So I do it. I buy the damn plane."

"So you're telling me the MEK stole the uranium from the Iranians and instead of handing it over to the International Atomic Energy Agency, they sold it to the US National Security Council. And that you helped broker this deal."

"Something like that, assuming you got your facts straight on your end."

"What's the National Security Council planning to do with this uranium?"

"Hell if I know. All I do know is that I bought the plane like they asked and then you show up raising hell. So what do I do? I call Ellis, tell him what you told me, and ask him to straighten things out with the CIA and get you the hell off my back. None of this is *my* problem."

"If it wasn't your problem, why'd you have your men follow me when I left your office this morning?"

"Maybe I didn't like your attitude. Maybe I don't like my government barging in here and threatening me when I've just shelled out forty million as a personal favor to the president of the United States."

"I'm not your government."

"You were hired by the CIA. That's close enough. What I can tell you is that once Ellis's team took over this afternoon, my team backed off."

"Only Ellis's team turned out to be a hit squad from the Revolutionary Guard. Nice."

"Hey dipshit, in case you haven't figured it out yet, Ellis doesn't always play by the rules. And it's not my fucking problem if the CIA's on his bad side. What you got to do is have your people in Langley talk to the goddamn NSC. And while you're at it, you can leave me the hell out of it. The CIA and NSC can duke it out on their own and you can stuff your threats up your ass from now on, and the same goes for Ellis. You want to go public with what you know? Well, two can play at that game."

"Where'd that plane go after the Doha Group bought it?"

"I have no idea. You'd have to ask Ellis. I just bought the plane, he supplied the pilot. It took off the same day I bought it and I haven't seen it since. Guess I loaned it out."

"At this point I'm thinking Ellis might be less than forthcoming."

"What I will tell you is that two people met that plane when it landed in Dubai, and they were on it when it left Dubai. My security guys ID'd them. The first was Colonel Henry Amato, Ellis's top Iran advisor. Good luck getting anything out of him. The second was Maryam Minabi—the head of that MEK group you were talking about. She might know what happened to the plane, or, for that matter, why Ellis is sending Iranian Guard troops after you."

"You know where Minabi is?"

"Last I heard she was holed up at her place outside of Paris."

"Last I heard no one's been able to contact her in Paris."

"Then you know more than I do. Now get the hell out of here. And if you screw with my company any more than you already have, I'll come after you for spite no matter what you tell the public."

PART IV

Port of Jebel Ali, United Arab Emirates

Above the deck of what looked like an Emirates Coast Guard boat hung a ten-foot-long metal tube.

"OK, lower it," said the lead soldier to the crane operator. Then, "Slower! Slower!"

The tube needed to be inserted into a hole that had been cut into the deck of the boat. But only a few inches of clearance had been left on either side, so the descent had to be perfect.

The crane operator complied, but he did so too quickly, provoking cries of alarm from the other men in the warehouse as the tube jerked to a stop. A grinding sound echoed off the warehouse's steel walls.

There was no air-conditioning and the lead soldier was sweating as he stood on the deck of the boat. The metal tube hung four feet above his head gently swinging back and forth in a way that unnerved him.

62

Auvers-sur-Oise, France

Even with his lousy eyesight, Mark could tell who it was from a hundred yards away.

John Decker drove down the empty main street in a little compact Hyundai, looking ridiculous with his knees rising up on either side of the steering wheel and his head brushing the ceiling, as though he were in a toy car.

He had dirty-blond hair now and was wearing glasses that would have made him look studious were his neck not so thick. He slowed to a stop on the corner where Daria and Mark were waiting and gave each of them a rough pat on their shoulders after they'd squeezed into the car.

The little French village of Auvers-sur-Oise was an unlikely place for an Iranian resistance group to set up shop, thought Mark as they drove over the bridge that spanned the Oise River. The sun hadn't risen yet but the predawn sky was light enough that he could tell the banks framing the river were green and lush. The town itself, although only fifteen miles from Paris, was a world away from the poorer suburbs where bored and angry youths burned cars every night.

This was the France of old stone inns and narrow alleys with ivy-covered walls. It was where Pissarro, Cézanne, and Corot had come to paint, and where Vincent Van Gogh had spent his famous final weeks, working madly before killing himself. There were *boucheries* and *patisseries*, houses with terra cotta roofs, and little parks with bright flower beds and well-manicured plane trees.

But even though he couldn't see it, Mark knew there was also a compound, consisting of several houses bristling with satellite dishes, that had housed the political leadership of the MEK since the mid-1980s.

"It's good to see you," said Decker.

"Good to see you too," said Daria.

"After what went down outside of Astara, I wasn't sure—"

"Just take us to the compound," interrupted Mark.

He'd already explained over the phone the basics of what they'd learned in Dubai, and that they'd come to France to try to question Maryam Minabi. Decker had said he'd found the MEK compound, but hadn't been able to locate Daria's uncle yet. He hadn't seen anyone that matched the description of Minabi yet either.

"Well, that's the thing. Something's come up." Decker exhaled and focused on the road.

"I'm not going to like it, am I?" Mark was dead tired. He hadn't slept at all on the red-eye from Dubai to Paris.

"No, you won't. It's a freakin' complete clusterfuck."

"What happened?" asked Daria.

"So like I said, first day I was here I found the compound and started up surveillance from a barn loft a couple lots down. I didn't see a lot of activity, just a few guys who looked like guards patrolling the perimeter. Five guys total on the inside. None of them was your uncle. On the outside it's just a bunch of old French geezers riding by once in a while on bikes.

"Then just six hours ago, around an hour before midnight it was, I'm watching from the barn and a laundry-service van pulls up to the front gate. A few guys wheel out a couple canvas sacks and dump them in the truck. I'm talking big sacks, these guys can barely lift them. It doesn't take a genius to figure out that whatever's inside them, it sure as hell ain't somebody's dirty underpants. So I follow them.

"They drive to a field, ten clicks or so to the northwest, in farm country. I watch the two guys who'd been driving the van meet a couple more guys who are waiting for them there in the field. When they're all together, damn if they don't pull out two bodies from those laundry sacks and then set about burying them in the field.

"They dig one grave and put both bodies in it. There's a lot of other areas that had been dug up recently too. And I mean a lot— whole field's scattered with them. More graves probably, though I didn't try to dig them up because after these bodies get buried, I follow the two men that hadn't come from the main compound. They drive straight to this farmhouse a couple clicks away from the field and disappear inside. So I set up a surveillance post in an abandoned church not far away but didn't see shit and then I had to blow to pick you two up. How many people used to live inside the main MEK compound?"

"Probably a hundred or so, maybe more, maybe less," said Daria. Her voice was hard, but trembled.

"Fucking hell," said Decker. "I hate to say it, but I think they're toast. That compound is practically empty."

"Then ditch the compound. Take us to this farmhouse," said Mark coldly. If Minabi was dead, he'd learn what he could from her killers.

"Going there now, boss."

63

Decker pulled to a stop in front of a big stone church encircled by a six-foot-high chain-link fence on which notices had been posted, warning people away and proclaiming that the church had been slated for destruction. Down the street, a few old stone houses abutted the road.

"If you hop the fence, you can get inside through a door in the back that I popped open," said Decker. "Behind the altar to your left are steps to a lookout. The first twenty feet or so have been ripped down, but I pimped a ladder from a house down the street. Once you get to the top, look due south. You'll see the farmhouse in the middle of a field."

Decker got out and opened the trunk of the Hyundai, revealing two sets of high-powered binoculars, food supplies, a large brown canvas tarp, and a digital camera with a telephoto lens.

"Won't need the camera," said Mark brusquely. "Bought one in Dubai."

He eyed the church. It was made of stone similar in color to the surrounding houses, but unlike the old houses, the church walls had more of a smooth, polished look. Built just a hundred or so years ago, he guessed. Which meant no tourists would bother to visit it—not when there were gorgeous medieval cathedrals to look at all over France—and since hardly anyone in the country under the age of eighty bothered to go to church for religious reasons anymore, tearing it down had likely been deemed a more practical option than renovating it.

Evidence of neglect abounded. The roof had a few big holes in it where patches of slate tiles had fallen off, exposing the wood timbers beneath; the pavement surrounding the building was half-covered with weeds; and most of the varnish on the massive front entrance door had peeled off. Anything of value appeared to have been removed—a gaping circular hole hovered behind the altar where a rosary window had once stood, and what Decker had called a lookout Mark pegged as a former bell tower whose bell and roof had been salvaged, leaving just an open platform on top.

"Are workers going to be showing up this morning to take the rest of this thing down?" asked Mark.

"Maybe, but I'll be watching from the ground so I can call you if we get any surprises."

In the east the sky looked as though the sun would crack the horizon at any moment. Except for the sound of a distant owl, it was absolutely quiet. Mark concentrated on the silence, listening for a break in it, maybe the sound of an approaching car.

He heard nothing. "All right, let's do this."

64

Washington, DC

Colonel Henry Amato fumbled in the dark for his cell phone, finally locating it on the end table next to his bed. After pushing a few wrong buttons, he found the one that allowed him to answer.

"Amato, here," he half shouted, still disoriented from the several glasses of grappa he'd downed just a few hours ago. He was bare-chested, wearing only boxer shorts.

An antique brass lamp embossed with a Persian design stood on the end table. He turned it on as he sat up in bed.

"This is Martinez, sir."

Amato asked for a verification code. Upon receiving it, he said, "Confirmed."

"There's been activity in France. Two individuals are monitoring Minabi."

"Have they been identified?"

"No, sir."

"What's their present status?"

"Well, they're watching the house from a church tower."

Amato ran a hand through his disheveled hair. "A church tower?" he said skeptically.

"Yes, sir, it's about a half kilometer away from the compound where Minabi's being held. One of our NightEagle drones picked up a suspicious thermal image on top of it five hours ago."

"Human?"

"We thought. But the image was taken from a few miles up, so it wasn't conclusive. We continued to monitor the site from a better angle but didn't see anything else—until dawn that is, when we picked up two bodies. That'd be zero one thirty your time, just a half hour ago."

"You have the images?"

"I sent them to your account."

Amato slipped out of bed, being careful not to stand up too quickly because of his bad back, and made his way out to the spare bedroom where he kept his laptop computer.

He logged on to an anonymous, nongovernment e-mail account and typed in an additional security code to view the files. The first was a five-second infrared video clip shot five hours ago. The central image was a grainy blur of green, red, and yellow—indicating heat—against a background of deep indigo blue. The video had been shot from directly above the church, and the size approximation was in meters, so it was impossible to know whether he was looking at a large bird or a human being.

He played the second video clip, which had been recorded just a half hour ago. Here there were two blotches, each a mix of red, green, and yellow. This time the video had been taken at a forty-five-degree angle to the church, allowing for a size approximation down to the nearest centimeter.

In this clip each figure looked like a ghostly human being.

One was of average height, just under six feet tall. His thermal image was distinct and bright, with a hot red core. The other was shorter in stature and gave off a thermal image dominated by yellows and greens.

Amato felt a stab of pain in his gut and his chest tightened.

"Sir?" said Martinez.

"I have the images."

"I anticipate I'll be able to get you some decent conventional photos within the hour, assuming they stay up there and the clouds hold off."

Would they have had time to travel from Dubai to France? Barely. But how could they have known to go right to where Minabi was being held? It was insane. How could they possibly have figured that out?

Amato was both proud and appalled. "You've already alerted the Iranians, I take it?"

He needed time to think, but he didn't have time.

"It was the first thing I did, to confirm that they weren't just maintaining precautionary surveillance on their own compound."

"What was their response?"

"They're arranging for a takedown."

How could he have let it come to this?

Amato looked around his spare bedroom, as if searching for an answer. His eyes lit on a crucifix that he'd hung on the wall, a simple ceramic one that his wife had picked up on a trip they'd taken to Rome fifteen years ago, and then on a photo of his parents that he'd inherited when his father had died last year.

He stared at his father, gray-haired and stooped from years of laying brick, and for a fleeting moment remembered how his father used to sing to him at night before bed, then kiss him on the forehead. That small display of love had meant the world to him when he was a little boy.

He hadn't deserved a father like that.

"Do we even know that the subjects are still in position?"

"The Iranians sent a team over as soon as we alerted them and they haven't reported any movement. And the subjects were still showing up on our thermal images until a few minutes ago, when dawn hit."

"They need to be taken alive."

"Those were my instructions to the Iranians, sir. They agreed to wait until the subjects descend and then take them on the ground rather than storm the tower. It'll be safer that way, especially if the subjects are armed."

"The Iranians will still foul it up," said Amato sharply. There was a long silence. "It'll piss them off, but I want you and Davis there as an auxiliary force to ensure the capture goes as planned. The subjects have to be apprehended alive and interrogated. Is that understood?"

"Understood."

"Not shot through the head and half alive. I mean definitively alive."

"Wilco."

"In the meantime, tell the Iranians not to alter the daily routine for Minabi or do anything else that could send signals that they know they're being watched. Also..."

Amato's voice faltered. If he spoke the words that were in his throat, he would be crossing the Rubicon.

Of course he should never have let it get to this point. He should have acted sooner, years ago, when he'd first learned Daria had applied to the Agency. He should have used his connections to have her rejected, to steer her into a profession that didn't involve such terrible risk. At the very least he should have found a way to protect her after Minabi had told him that a CIA officer named Daria Buckingham had helped the MEK steal the uranium.

But he hadn't. At every stage of her life, he'd been absent. Because he'd been a coward. As a young man he hadn't wanted to admit it, but he was too old now to lie to himself.

"Also, I'll be joining you in France to assist with the interrogations. Inform the Iranians that immediately after the takedown you are to take possession of the detainees."

There was a long pause. Amato knew his announcement would come as an unwelcome shock—a case of a higher-up trying to micromanage a field operation. Martinez said, "What's your ETA, sir?"

"As soon as I can get there—figure ten hours tops. I'll contact you for coordinates when I'm close."

"If the subjects are set up for a long stakeout, it's possible the capture won't even have been executed by the time you get here, sir. Unless you want us to try to force them down, which again, I wouldn't recommend. Better to stay back a bit until this thing plays itself out."

"If I can be on the ground with you prior to capture, all the better."

Amato hung up, dialed another number, and gave orders for a C-37A jet—the military version of a Gulfstream—to meet him at Reagan National in an hour.

He did the calculations in his head—deal with Ellis quickly, make it to the airport on time, figure a six-hour flight, then an hour or so to get from the airport to the church…he could be there by late afternoon French time.

The last thing he did before getting dressed was to go online to his personal bank account and electronically wire every cent of what was left in it to an offshore account he'd set up yesterday, just in case.

65

The sunrise was stupendous, a pastel smear of red and yellow. Blackbirds, perched in trees around the church, were calling out. But all Daria could see was an image in her head of a muddy field with newly dug graves and all she could hear was the voice of her uncle.

He'd been panic stricken when she'd told him of her intention to help smuggle the uranium out of Iran.

You have given enough!

It will be enough when the mullahs are dead.

Don't talk like that. Don't do this.

I already told Minabi I would.

Minabi doesn't care about you—

I'm not doing this for her.

She and Mark sat forty feet off the ground, cross-legged and hunched under a brown canvas tarp atop a rickety half-rotted wood platform. A two-foot-high stone parapet, which had previously served as a base for the roof of the bell tower, encircled the platform. Directly behind the church stood a grove of apple trees, and a half kilometer or so farther away, amid a fallow field overgrown with weeds, lay the farmhouse.

"We'll take shifts," said Mark. "I'll watch the house first, you scan the surrounding fields and woods."

Daria recalled presents her uncle had given her on her birthday—a little Iranian jewelry box decorated with ivory inlay; a gift certificate to Macy's; a miniature watercolor, painted on camel bone, that depicted beautiful yellow irises. Her uncle had never wanted her to get involved with the MEK in the first place. The only thing he'd really pushed her to do was to study hard at Duke and get her degree.

"OK?" said Mark.

"Yeah, fine," she answered, but what she was thinking was that she didn't know whether she could do this anymore. Anger had sustained her for so long. But losing her uncle went beyond anger. The mullahs had now taken from her everything in this world that she'd loved. They had won. There was nothing left for her to be angry about.

"Switch every half hour?"

"That works."

At seven thirty in the morning two men with automatic rifles emerged from the rear of the house. The stone wall that enclosed the backyard blocked out their legs, but through the telephoto lens of her camera Daria could see them from the waist up. They could be Iranian, she thought—but they could also just as easily be French, given the mix of cultures in the country.

"Know any of those guys?" Mark asked.

Daria looked for markings on their olive-green shirts, searching for clues as to their identity.

"No."

She saw Mark squinting as he looked through his binoculars. It reminded her that, back in Baku, he'd sometimes worn glasses.

"Their rifles are Iranian-made AKMs," Mark said.

"How can you tell?"

"Black plastic stocks."

Her uncle had been right, Daria thought. This hadn't been worth it. She should have done something decent with her life. Her uncle should have done something decent with his life. Instead they'd both devoted their lives to a failed cause.

A couple of minutes later a woman wearing a red headscarf emerged. She was shorter than the armed men who'd preceded her, and wasn't carrying a weapon.

"Heads up," said Mark.

But Daria had already seen her. She stiffened as she focused the telephoto lens on the camera and leaned forward against the wall. The woman in the red headscarf began to walk back and forth across the small walled-in yard behind the farmhouse. Each time she reached the far end, her full body was visible.

For the first time since hearing Decker's story about the graves, Daria felt something approaching hope.

"That's Minabi!" she whispered.

"You're sure?"

"She walks a little duck-footed, often with her hands clasped in front of her. The way she's walking now. Besides, I can see her face well enough."

"You've met her in person?"

"A few times. If Minabi's alive, there's a chance…"

"A chance."

There was a chance her uncle was still alive too, she thought. If Minabi had been spared, her uncle and other top MEK leaders might have been too. She eyed the guards around Minabi, taking better stock of their weapons, feeling a little flicker of that old familiar anger return.

When Minabi finally went back inside the farmhouse, it was clear from the way the guards gestured with their guns that she'd been ordered to do so.

Mark said, "So it's the middle of the night, Minabi's locked up in a room, maybe sleeping maybe not, and suddenly you slip in and tell her to hightail it out of there with you while Deck and I deal with the guards. Does she trust you? Does she recognize you? Does she scream?"

"I'm not sure. Depends on how I approach it."

If her uncle was in there, she'd get him.

"Think about it. You got all day. Meanwhile we'll keep watching."

66

Washington, DC

From a pay phone on Twelfth and Madison, Amato called National Security Advisor James Ellis at his home in McLean, Virginia.

Ellis picked up after two rings, sounding alert but speaking softly. Trying not to wake up his wife, Amato assumed.

Amato often called at night, when Ellis was reading in bed—the man hardly slept at all—and it was always the same routine. In a moment Ellis would walk to his study.

"We need to meet," said Amato.

"Hold on."

Amato heard the sound of Ellis's footsteps as he padded from his bed to his study, then the sound of a door closing shut.

"What's going on?" said Ellis.

"Not over the phone."

Ellis was silent for a moment. "How soon can you get here?"

"Your guards will record it if I come."

"For Christ's sake, Henry, you're my assistant. Who cares if they record it?"

It occurred to Amato that in all the years he'd worked with Ellis, it had apparently never once occurred to his boss that taking the

Lord's name in vain, repeatedly and excessively, might somehow cause offense.

Ellis sighed. "Where, then?"

"The Vietnam Memorial. As soon as you can get there."

"Give me twenty minutes."

"There's a bench on the north side," said Amato.

"I'll be there."

The half moon that had hung in the sky earlier in the night had by now dipped below the horizon, but the weak starlight that remained illuminated the pale, dry grass in front of Amato. In the distance he could just make out the looming black shadow of the long stone wall.

Amato thought of all the names he recognized and wondered what the men who'd served under him would think of what he was about to do. Then he wondered whether Ellis recognized any of the names on the wall, or whether the multiple deferments that had allowed him to pursue a doctorate in international relations had completely insulated him from the madness of that era.

Amato checked his watch, feeling remarkably calm as he considered the situation. He'd tried to avoid having things get to this point, but he'd failed and now he had to act accordingly. There would be no second-guessing. His only real concern was timing.

In the distance, through a grove of trees, he saw the white glow of the Washington Monument, and beyond that the Capitol, its dome all lit up from below. He checked his watch again, and began to pray. *O my God, I am heartily sorry for having offended*

Thee, and I detest all my sins because I dread the loss of Heaven and the pains of Hell but most of all because they offend Thee, my God, who art all-good and deserving of all my love…

✵

Even at a distance, and in the dark, Amato was able to recognize the black silhouette of Ellis's narrow shoulders as his boss approached from the south.

"Thanks for coming," he said when Ellis reached the bench and sat down.

"For Christ's sake, Henry. What's this about?" Ellis wore a suit but no tie. On his head was a dark navy-blue Georgetown baseball cap, reminding Amato that Ellis's son played college ball.

Amato spoke quietly. "A surveillance team has been detected at Minabi's house outside of Auvers."

"Have the Iranians been notified?"

"Yes."

"We know who it is?"

"No. But from thermal profiles and process of elimination, I suspect it's Sava and Buckingham. The Iranians are planning the takedown. I don't trust them to do it right so I ordered our team to—"

"Call them off."

"The Iranians will need help. Buckingham and Sava aren't civilians, they won't be an easy grab."

"We're to avoid any type of engagement on French soil at all costs. That order, by the way, comes from the top. So don't go getting your ass in an uproar, Henry, or thinking you can convince me otherwise."

"And I'd like to go to France to help with the interrogations."

"What the hell is the matter with you, Henry?" When Amato didn't answer, Ellis said, "We agreed no foreign travel for either of us for three weeks prior to launch."

"That was before the complications. That was before Sava and Buckingham got involved."

"You're not even trained for interrogations."

"That's not entirely true."

"No, Henry. You're staying right here and the Iranians are going to handle it without our help. Is that all?"

Amato closed his eyes for a moment. He'd tried to give Ellis an out; that was all he could do.

His right hand rested in his coat pocket, and he could feel the cool metal chain against his palm. With his thumb and index finger he made his way, link by link, down to the end of it. The metal jingled a little, as if he were fiddling with change in his pocket.

He could still taste the stale grappa in his mouth. The stink of alcohol sweating out of his pores was mildly repulsive even to himself.

"No, James, there's one more thing we need to talk about," said Amato. "It's more of a personal matter, though."

"Be quick about it."

"Walk with me. I'll go in your direction." Amato stood up and waited for Ellis to do the same.

Ellis exhaled loudly through his nose as he pushed himself off the bench. "I'm parked on Twenty-First." He began walking.

For a moment, Amato fell in beside him, so that they were nearly shoulder to shoulder.

"After the conclusion of this operation, I'd like to put in for a—"

As Amato spoke he pulled the metal chain out of his pocket, gripped each end of it tightly, and swung it over Ellis's neck.

Ellis sensed something was wrong and at the last second managed to slip a few fingers between the chain and his neck. He fought like a rodeo bull, kicking his legs back violently and trying to smash the back of his skull into Amato's face.

The ferocity of Ellis's counterattack surprised Amato, but he held tight with every ounce of strength he possessed, squeezing so hard that his arms shook. Ellis still struggled, kicking his legs wildly. Eventually he tried to throw Amato off balance by suddenly dropping to the ground like deadweight.

But Amato had been a soldier. And even though he was old and out of shape, with a bad back and aches that made waking up in the morning painful, his raw strength hadn't lessened much over the years. When Ellis tried to drop down, Amato held fast and Ellis wound up just hanging there, making little spitting sounds.

In two minutes it was over. Amato dropped the chain and made sure the job was complete by breaking Ellis's neck with the heel of his shoe. When he collapsed on the ground next to his dead boss, his chest was heaving and he felt lightheaded, as though he might pass out.

When he'd caught his breath, he pressed a button on his wristwatch, illuminating the faceplate. It was nearly three o'clock. If he was going to be at Reagan National in under a half hour, he had to be quick about it.

He dragged Ellis into the center of a cluster of bushes, stripped him of his wallet, and covered him with dead branches and old leaves. The longer it took for Ellis to be discovered and identified, he thought, the better.

67

At three thirty in the afternoon, Mark's cell phone vibrated. It was Decker, sounding agitated.

"I don't know how they did it, sir, I don't know how they did it..."

Mark and Daria had been detected. "I only got a partial visual but I'm almost certain they're the same guys I followed last night."

"How many total?" Mark was still beneath the brown tarp atop the bell tower, fixated on the farmhouse with only his eyes poking up above the stone wall. He didn't see how anyone could have noticed them—which made him wonder what else he wasn't seeing.

"Two. They pulled up in a van a couple hundred yards down the street from the church and—"

"When?"

"Just a minute ago. I was going to check it out when two guys climbed out and hopped the fence outside the church."

"They see you?"

"No."

"Are they armed?"

"Couldn't tell but you have to figure pistols at least. Shit, if they're coming for you now—I just lost a visual, they went around to the south side."

"It'd be two on two with us on the high ground and they can't be sure we're not armed ourselves."

"So maybe they'll wait it out."

"What do you have in the way of weapons?"

"A knife. I couldn't risk smuggling anything into the country."

Mark clicked off his phone and eyed the low parapet in front of him. Some of the wide, flat stones had been dislodged in the process of taking off the top of the bell tower. He pulled five down, sat on two just in case anyone started shooting up the stairwell, gave two to Daria to sit on, and then held one in his hand so that he could crack open the skull of anyone who might try to ascend the tower.

"We need a better plan than this," said Daria, as she took another rock for herself.

It was sunny out, a gorgeous day. The deep green of the forest to their left contrasted with the blue of the sky and the white of the few lingering clouds. Mark wondered for a moment whether it was as magnificent a day back in Baku, and he imagined it was. He thought of what it would be like to be sitting out on his balcony. For a moment he grew irrationally nostalgic for the smell of petroleum.

"This is our plan. We've already drawn two of them away from the house."

"That's not a plan. That's putting the best face on a disaster."

"There's a difference?"

"I still don't trust Decker."

"I do."

"We can't rely on him. The two of us need to think our way out of this."

"I am thinking. I'm thinking all we have to do is hold these idiots off until dark and stick with the plan we already agreed on. End of story."

"That's four hours from now."

"We'll make it."

68

At first Amato didn't pay much attention to little ribbon of black smoke he saw snaking its way up into the gray, twilit sky. He figured it was probably a farmer, burning brush in a nearby field.

It was nine o'clock at night and he was driving through the French countryside. The trip from Washington had taken longer than he'd hoped. But he'd make it in time. The takedown wasn't scheduled to go down until ten.

Then he rounded a corner.

Good God, that trail of smoke is coming from a church.

He checked the coordinates on his GPS unit as he sped up, hurtling past a wheat field at top speed. And that wasn't just any church, it had to be *the* church, where Daria was.

When he looked up, he could see the first tiny flickers of flame creeping up through a giant hole in the roof. *No. NO. I am not seeing this. Those heathen beasts.*

Amato called Martinez. "Captured alive! Those were my orders! What the hell do the Iranians think they're doing! Burning a church! In the middle of France! Are they fucking insane!"

"They didn't have anything to do with it, sir. The targets set the fire themselves a couple of minutes ago."

"If that whole roof goes up—"

"Stay back and let us handle it, sir."

"Who's going in for Buckingham and—"

"Sir! Please! Stay back and let us handle it!"

69

First there'd been just a hissing sound as the lithium from Mark's camera battery, which he'd cut up and thrown down one of the holes in the church roof, reacted with the water he'd poured over it. Next came a tiny orange glow and the faint hint of a burning smell as the flaming battery parts ignited both the hundred-year-old insulation in the church attic and the gothic vaulting just below it, vaulting that Mark—on his way in—had noticed was constructed of wood instead of the more costly stone that an older church would have used.

When flames had begun to creep out of the hole, Mark had flipped open his phone and dialed the international number for emergency.

Now, having been transferred to a local police dispatcher, he said he wanted to report a fire coming from the roof of a church on Route D928. "It's the Eglise Saint-Martin. And if someone doesn't get here quick, it's going to take down the whole roof."

Minutes later, the fire was roaring loudly and, despite being twenty feet above it in the stone bell tower, Mark could feel its heat. He imagined what the Iranians inside the church must be thinking. They must be getting a little frantic by now, unsure of whether to stay where they were or to wait outside, potentially exposing themselves. It didn't really matter, he decided—when the cops and firemen arrived they'd have to leave.

Soon after a portion of the roof collapsed into the church, Mark heard sirens in the distance.

A police car pulled up and the gendarme got out and ordered a few locals who'd gathered in front of the church to step back. A minute later a fire truck pulled up, sirens blaring. Four firemen jumped out. Mark stood up.

"I'll go first," he said to Daria.

"I'll be right on your heels."

Below he hoped Decker was already on the move, either disarming the Iranians if they were still in the church, or hightailing it to the farmhouse if the coast was clear.

He descended the circular steps as quietly as he could, silently choking on the smoke that was making its way up the tower. When he reached the last step he grabbed the ladder that he'd pulled up through the stairway's central chute, quickly lowered it to the floor, and slid down it as if it were a fireman's pole. When he hit the ground he rolled into the church then sprinted to a marble pillar halfway between the altar and the rear exit. He flattened himself against it. A second later Daria was at his side.

If Decker had managed to take out the two guys inside the church, Mark figured he and Daria could be at the farmhouse within a couple minutes. The men guarding Minabi would be distracted by the fire and vulnerable.

In front of him a few piles of collapsed ceiling timbers were burning, while thirty feet above them the fire continued to rage, sucking so much air into the church now that Mark felt a strong breeze on the back of his neck. Soon the whole ceiling would collapse.

He peered out from behind the marble pillar, searching for Decker, but he couldn't see any sign of him. The rear exit was a fifty-foot sprint away, underneath a crucifix-shaped collection of bolts in the wall.

He stepped out from behind the pillar and began to run. Then he felt his head snap to the side. As his legs collapsed, he was overwhelmed by the sensation that he'd stumbled into a bottomless pit.

70

Through the flickering smoke-filled gloom, Daria saw a black shadow slam Mark's head into a stone wall.

On the opposite side of the church, the side that faced the road, police lights flashed wildly and a gendarme pushed people back from the chain-link fence. Daria figured she could be out on the street in a matter of seconds. The police might try to detain her, but she'd figure out a way to ditch them.

She clenched her fists, poised to run to safety.

Dammit, Mark!

Screw him, she thought. She'd told him not to get involved. She'd warned him. He'd pushed himself on her anyway, for $2,000 a day.

She turned toward the flashing police lights. Firemen were rolling out a hose. In the confusion, she might even be able to blend into the crowd.

This was your fault, Mark! Your plan!

At Daria's feet lay a narrow four-foot-long board smoldering among the ceiling debris. She grasped the end that had gone untouched by the fire. It was heavy, made of oak she guessed. The blackened end had a cluster of rusty old nails sticking out of it.

She eyed the potential safety of the street one last time. Then she turned toward where she'd last seen Mark and began to run after him.

71

Mark regained consciousness as he was being dragged through a gap in the chain-link fence outside the church. He heard voices, one of them a woman's—Daria, he thought—and cries of pain.

He tried to flip on his stomach and grab his attacker's legs, but as soon as he landed a hand on the man's thigh, a knee rammed him in the temple. When he came to again, his hands were being bound behind his back with plastic FlexiCuffs and he lay at the edge of a forest.

He heard distant shouting coming from the church, which was now just a tiny glow barely visible through the trees.

"Martinez?" called a voice from the darkness.

"Yes, sir."

The guy named Martinez was maybe six feet tall with a goatee. His thick forehead was covered with blood that was dripping out from a knot of puncture wounds above his right eye. He wore loose brown pants, a long-sleeved black shirt, a radio headset, and a night-vision monocle. His right hand gripped a pistol and he was breathing heavily.

"What happened? I heard shooting."

"I've apprehended one of the subjects."

A tall barrel-chested man, with a partially bald head and silver temple hair that stood out in the darkness, emerged from behind the black shape of a car. He wasn't wearing night-vision equipment and he held only a small hand radio. He looked at Mark and grimaced.

To Martinez he said, "Where's Daria Buckingham?"

"Someone else was in the church that we didn't know about. He's fucking with everything. One of the Iranians is down, his weapon's been taken."

"Answer my question."

"The bitch came after me. I took her down—"

"She wasn't supposed to be harmed!"

"I had to defend myself, sir. She'll live."

"Davis was supposed to stay on her!"

"He got ambushed and lost his weapon. One of the Iranians might have also got hit. Whoever's out there knows what they're doing."

Mark's head was suddenly yanked back so hard he thought his neck was going to snap.

"Who are we dealing with?" asked Martinez.

Mark didn't answer.

The older man said, "I'll watch this punk. You've got to go back for Buckingham! Now!"

"There are firefighters and cops out there. I can try to avoid them, but I'm telling you, before I go after Buckingham I need to take out the guy who—"

A shot rang out. Martinez clutched his thigh, fell to the ground, and fired into the trees.

A second later, Decker came up from behind and smashed the butt of his pistol into Martinez's face five times, rapid-fire. Then he tackled the old guy into a tree, knocking the wind out of him.

Decker cut Mark's hands free with a knife and handed him Martinez's pistol. "Cover them," he whispered, then he retrieved a couple of plastic FlexiCuffs from Martinez's back pocket and used them to secure both of his prisoners' hands.

Martinez was unconscious. The older man was groaning.

Mark's head was wobbly on his neck and throbbing so much it felt as though his skull were going to split open. He didn't know if he could stand. "You gotta go back for Daria."

"The Iranians just bagged her. I was going for you, I couldn't stop them."

"Is she alive?"

"I think." He added, "I took down one of the guys who was on you—he's tied up just outside the church, the cops have probably found him by now—and I was going for the second when I realized there were more people out there. I don't know how many. It's a cluster, man."

"Get Daria back," said Mark.

The older man struggled to pull himself up to his knees. With great urgency he said, "My name is Henry Amato. I work for the National Security Council."

Mark stumbled a bit as he stood up. He recognized the name.

"It's a rebel Iranian unit that has Daria," said Amato. "If you want to get her back, you'll release me."

"Keep your voice down."

"Your name is Mark Sava," said Amato, frantic but whispering. "You work for the CIA. I know why you're here."

Decker bent down and removed Martinez's night-vision monocle. He bound Martinez's ankles with FlexiCuffs and secured his hands, which were already bound behind his back, to his ankles. "I'm going for her," Decker said to Mark.

"I'll go with you."

"Screw that. There's a downed tree about a hundred yards south of here." Decker pointed with his finger. "Near the base of it is a hole where the roots got ripped up. I hid up there today. Wait for me there."

Decker ran off. Mark heard some voices shouting in the distance, but they were speaking French. More firefighters he determined. He took a deep breath, trying to get a handle on the pounding in his head, then yanked Amato to a standing position. The air smelled of smoke.

"Get your hands off me," said Amato.

"I said keep your voice down." Mark wasn't sure if his vision was blurry because of the darkness or because of the pounding he'd taken. He looked at Martinez. The man was still unconscious, or maybe dead. Mark decided to leave him.

"I need my radio," said Amato. "I can help get Daria back."

Mark took his pistol, which he'd been pointing at Amato's back, and jabbed the barrel into the base of Amato's skull. "Start walking."

"Did you hear me? I can help secure her release! The Iranians will listen to me."

"This rebel unit, they the same group of guys who tried to take me and Daria out in Dubai?"

"It's a complicated situation."

"I'll bet."

"The Iranians were trying to capture you and Daria tonight and then take you both to the house where Minabi's being held—to be interrogated. So help me God, I was trying to stop them."

"So help me God I think you're full of shit."

"Then you're a fool. And there isn't a chance they'll bring Daria to the house now. We have to find out where they're taking her before it's too late."

"A fool?"

"We're wasting time!"

"Who all is out there?"

"Four Iranians and the two men I brought." Amato added, "My guys were here to help you and Daria. Under my orders. Your friend ruined everything. He attacked the good guys."

Mark wasn't buying it. The pounding in his head stood as a testament to the fact that Amato's men hadn't been there just to mount a rescue. But if Amato had a connection to the Iranians, he'd find out what that connection was.

"Get your radio."

Amato hunted on the ground until he found it.

Mark raised his gun. "Any talk of our location and you're dead."

Amato fiddled with the channels and then depressed the send button. "This is Partner, do you copy?" He waited a moment. When there was no response he tried again, and again there was no response.

He switched to another channel, and then another.

They were in an open, unprotected area of the forest. Eventually Mark took the radio back and turned it off. "Walk," he said.

72

Amato went where he was told to go, but he was half tempted to turn around and fight so that he could start searching the woods for Daria on his own. Mark Sava was a slight, unimpressive man and Amato had little doubt that, despite being nearly twenty years older, he could wring Sava's neck if he had to.

"Let me try the radio again," he said.

"Keep walking."

"Do you believe in God, Sava?" Amato could see the church burning through the trees. Part of him wondered whether he'd already descended into hell and just didn't know it yet.

"Faster."

"I'll take that as a no. I know your type."

Sava was a weasel of a man who was used to lying and sneaking and living off his guile, thought Amato. Which is to say he was typical Agency and not to be trusted with Daria's life. He had to get Sava out of the way.

"You can take that as an order to walk faster."

"Well, I believe in God. And I believe that my God will send me to hell if I don't do everything I can to save Daria. Let me try the radio again."

"Not yet."

Nearly shouting, Amato said, "I refuse to—"

Amato felt a pain shoot from the top of his head, down into his neck, and then hit his legs so hard that they crumpled underneath him. Then Sava struck him again, just below his ear, in the sensitive area where his skull connected to his neck. He slumped to the ground.

"This is the last time I'm going to tell you, old man—"

The feel of Sava's chin stubble scratching his neck, and Sava's hot breath in his ear, was absolutely revolting.

"—keep your fucking voice down."

73

Mark found Decker's hole up on a little ridge and pushed Amato down into it. The massive root ball of a downed oak tree formed a natural earthen wall in back of the hole and Decker had arranged a screen of downed branches in front. Mark imagined that Decker would have had a view of both the church, which was still visible as it burned, and the farmhouse, which was now swallowed by the night.

His head still throbbed but his eyes had adjusted to the darkness. He handed the radio to Amato and for the next minute Amato switched from channel to channel, looking increasingly panicked as he tried to get the Iranians to respond.

Eventually Mark said, "You're wearing a suit." Amato looked completely out of place in the middle of the woods. And he hadn't shaved in a long time.

"I left in a hurry."

"From the States?"

"Direct from Washington."

"So you could be here when we were captured?"

"Or soon after."

"Why?"

"That's also complicated. For the love of God," said Amato, trying the radio again. There was still no response.

"Want to tell me what the National Security Council is doing running black ops in France, in partnership with a bunch of Iranian thugs?"

Instead of answering, Amato asked, "Will your man find Daria?"

"I have no idea."

Mark peered above the fallen tree. Fire trucks were dousing the church with jets of water that arced high into the sky. A malevolent black plume of smoke twisted up from the bell tower. He listened but he couldn't hear any gunshots. He couldn't decide if that was a good or bad thing.

Pointing his gun at Amato, he said, "Listen, I've had it with this shit. Either you tell me what's going on or I'm gonna decide you're useless to me and shoot you right here. I've dealt with too many lies over the past few days. I'm done with it."

"After we find Daria."

"Now."

Amato stared at Mark for a moment, as though trying to gauge whether he was bluffing. "The National Security Council's trying to take down the regime in Iran."

"How?"

"By supporting a coup by the Revolutionary Guard."

"And how the hell did the NSC and Revolutionary Guard wind up in bed together? No, don't tell me. The Doha Group."

"We offered the generals some big money deals. Pretty soon the top guy wanted in."

"Aryanpur?"

"Yeah."

Mark was genuinely surprised. And a little impressed. General Ali Aryanpur was the head of the Revolutionary Guard, the number-two man in Iran.

"He know he was dealing with the NSC?"

"Not until his hands were already plenty dirty. Understand, this is happening at the same time we're collecting some disturbing intel from the MEK."

"Minabi told you about the pipeline to China."

"And the defense agreement with China," added Amato.

"And the enriched uranium."

"She said she'd stolen some of it and did we want to buy it."

"Which you did. For forty million bucks, the price Holgan paid for the Jetstar plane that flew into Dubai."

"The deal was we'd give the uranium to the IAEA when we got done analyzing its provenance, but the problem was we still had to figure out how to deal with China. We couldn't let all the deals they'd cut with Iran stand, but with Khorasani in power..."

"I don't know that I want to hear this," said Mark. There were way too many moving pieces here. Far too many to control. It was crazy for Amato or anyone else to have tried.

"Everyone had been hoping the Green movement would topple the regime from within, but it's clear they're done. They have no leader, no real power. The only realistic alternative to Khorasani is Aryanpur. He was in a power struggle with Khorasani before we even approached him, he was with Khomeini in the revolution, and he's had some religious training, enough to be accepted as Supreme Leader at least..."

Amato paused again. Mark looked at his watch. Three minutes had passed. He could still hear the distant shouts of firemen.

"We made a deal with Aryanpur. If he seized power, we agreed to drop all trade restrictions and invest heavily in an oil pipeline, to be built by the Revolutionary Guard, from the Caspian Sea, across Iran, to the Persian Gulf. It's the shortest way, it's the way that always made sense.

"In return Aryanpur agreed to get rid of Iran's nuclear program and drop the China pipeline and defense agreement. Stopping the pipeline was a no-brainer. That was why he'd agreed to meet with us in the first place, because Khorasani had sold the construction rights to the Chinese, cutting him out.

"Anyway, the deal was the easy part. The hard part was figuring out how to get rid of Khorasani. And that's where the enriched uranium came in."

Mark just shook his head as Amato revealed that an American Intelligence Support Activities team was about to stage a bungled nuclear attack on a US aircraft carrier and that an elite Qods Force unit, controlled by Khorasani, was being set up to take the blame.

"Three days ago, Aryanpur leaked that Khorasani had this rogue nuclear unit on his hands. The army has been going ballistic ever since because they're terrified of a retaliatory attack."

"This bomb," said Mark. "Don't tell me you actually built it?"

"It's just a big tube, gun-style detonator. We jury-rigged it with Iranian penetrator bombs, stuff that's easy to trace. It won't work, but when it becomes clear that the Iranians tried to nuke one of our aircraft carriers, there'll be a cry for war.

"That's when Aryanpur will act. The Revolutionary Guard was set up to guard the Islamic Revolution itself. Aryanpur will declare that Khorasani's reckless command of Qods Force has threatened the revolution. He thinks the Assembly of Experts will accept his leadership.

"Once Aryanpur's been installed as Supreme Leader, he'll probably be as faithful to the Islamic Revolution as the Chinese are to communism. It'll be a new Iran. Not perfect, but a country we can do business with."

Mark was all for seeing Ayatollah Khorasani tossed out on his ass, but it occurred to him that the one constant in Iranian–American relations was that whenever Washington came up with a plan to gain the upper hand—whether it was installing the Shah, or backing Saddam Hussein in the Iran–Iraq war, or selling the mullahs arms in 1986—it somehow always wound up making things worse.

74

Decker vaulted into the surveillance hole.

"Daria's gone. I did a complete perimeter sweep. There was a car outside the farmhouse. It's gone too."

Amato cradled his head in his hands.

Mark said, "We need to double back, pick up the Iranian who's down, and interrogate him."

"Firemen already grabbed him," said Decker.

"You're sure the second guy on my team doesn't have her?" asked Amato.

"Your second guy was trying to track me, not Daria."

Mark turned to Amato. "Why do you care so much what happens with Daria?"

"None of your damn business." But then Amato appeared to think better of it and said, "I know her parents in Washington, they both work for the State Department."

"So you're just a good Samaritan, a guy who's had a change of heart?"

"A man like you wouldn't understand."

"You're right. I don't."

"She was never supposed to have been a target. No one in the MEK or CIA was. That was all Aryanpur, trying to cover his ass so that when he assumed power no one but Ellis and me would know how he did it. He started killing everyone."

"Not Minabi."

"Ellis insisted she be spared, but he'll kill her soon too. I tried to help Daria by sending Campbell to warn her, by the way, and I tried to get someone to help her in Esfahan."

"And you did this because she was the daughter of friends."

"Believe what you want."

Mark stared at Amato for a moment. Showing that kind of sympathy was the way a normal person might act. But Amato hadn't gotten to where he was in life by thinking like a normal person.

"You're full of shit, dude, but whatever."

"I want to help find her."

"That much I believe."

"Aryanpur will have her killed, but probably not before his men interrogate her, to find out who else she's told about the stolen uranium. We still have time. I've severed all my ties to Ellis and the Security Council but Aryanpur doesn't know that. There's a chance he'll tell me where his men are taking her."

"You're telling me you could pick up a phone and talk to General Aryanpur? Like now?"

"It would take more than a single call."

Mark thought about that for a moment.

Amato said, "Sooner or later—probably sooner—people in Washington are going to figure out that I'm not playing their game anymore. When that happens, those two ISA soldiers working for me out there are going to be ordered to take me into custody. Let me call Aryanpur before everything goes to hell."

"You're not using a cell phone until we're in a car, moving fast enough that we'll be hard to intercept even if we're tracked," said Mark.

Decker had the Hyundai stashed nearby. Mark got in the driver's seat, Decker sat right behind him, and Amato sat across from Decker.

Mark turned right when he got to the main road. After a mile he handed his cell phone back to Amato. "You're up."

Amato fumbled the phone because his hands were still cuffed, but he eventually managed to dial the right number. Following a long wait, he spoke in Farsi for a minute and then hung up. "Someone will call back."

They were hurtling east, on a dark road that led through farmland. Both of Mark's hands were tight on the steering wheel. "You speak Farsi well," he said, as a thought suddenly occurred to him. "Ever been to Iran?"

Amato took a long time to answer. "A long time ago. Before the revolution."

"Not during?"

"I saw some of it."

"You deal with the hostage situation?"

"I got out just when that hit."

"What were you doing there in the first place?"

"It's really not relevant."

It was dark outside and even darker in the car. Mark glanced in the rearview mirror. Amato's face was little more than a sinister black shadow.

"Daria had an uncle—Reza Tehrani, he was Minabi's advisor. I believe you know him."

Amato didn't respond. Deep in thought, Mark let the car drift toward the shoulder.

"Watch the road," said Decker.

"Just for the record, I know why you're here," said Mark. "I know who you are."

Mark glanced in the rearview mirror just as Amato flashed him a nasty look.

"Daria's uncle is dead," said Amato. "Aryanpur had him killed two days ago."

75

Mark's cell phone rang and Amato answered it. After five minutes of heated conversation in Farsi, he clicked the phone shut and announced that he'd been talking to Aryanpur. "Daria's being flown out of the country."

Mark took his phone back and shut it off. "Can you stop them?"

"I said we had a team here that could interrogate her. But Aryanpur doesn't trust us when it comes to interrogations. He's having her taken to an offshore base in the Caspian, on Neft Dashlari."

Oil Rocks, thought Mark. That was the literal translation. It was a huge Azeri oil-production outpost in the Caspian Sea, a byzantine maze of stilt roads, leaky pipes, bleak communist dormitories built on landfills, and endless oil derricks. Fifty years ago it had been the pride of the Soviet Union. Now the place was a decaying and rusted embarrassment, and much of the infrastructure had succumbed to the rising sea waters. It was still pumping out oil in places, but the BTC pipeline had overshadowed it.

"I know it," said Mark.

"The Azeris have been leasing out some of the derricks."

"So I've heard." Mark had also heard that the big players hadn't been interested. It was too much of a hassle, dealing with the Soviet's god-awful mess, for too little oil.

"An Iranian oil company Aryanpur controls is leasing extraction rights near the southern end. Aryanpur's been using it as a military base."

"Can we intercept them before they get there?"

"No. Aryanpur's men are going through a rapid extraction contingency plan. Aryanpur hasn't even talked to them and won't until they're off French soil. He just knows where he'll order Daria taken once his team contacts him."

"And you think Aryanpur was being straight with you?"

"I gave him an incentive to tell the truth."

Mark waited for Amato to elaborate.

"I told him my men had captured you. Because I knew he'd want to interrogate you and Daria together, so your stories could be matched against each other."

"So you offered—"

"To bring you to him."

"To Neft Dashlari. To be interrogated."

"I don't expect you to actually come," said Amato sharply. "I don't expect a damn thing out of you, Sava. I told Aryanpur what I had to so he'd tell me where he was taking her."

"But you'd go if I let you? With or without me?"

"Of course."

"How would you get there?"

At Le Bourget Airport, Amato said, just outside Paris, a government plane was waiting—assuming Washington hadn't figured out what he was up to yet. If Mark were to drop him off there, he'd arrive in Baku around the same time as Daria.

As he drove, Mark thought about Neft Dashlari. It was a wretched place. The rotting detritus of an old empire.

He wondered how Nika would react if he were killed there. Would she mourn him? At this point, given all she'd been through on his account, she might be relieved.

He considered the rest of his ties to the world. His students at Western University could easily be taught by someone else. His mother had committed suicide over twenty years ago and he hadn't spoken to his father since, so ties to parents weren't an issue. He was on good terms with his two younger brothers and older sister, there was real love there, but he hadn't seen much of them since joining the Agency.

It really didn't say great things about his social abilities, he thought, that the only person in this world who had any real need of him was Daria.

"I'll go with you to Neft Dashlari," he said to Amato. "But going in is pointless if we don't have a decent plan to get her out."

76

As the C-37A circled over Heydar Aliyev International Airport, Mark had the sense that he was coming home. From up high the polluted Absheron Peninsula didn't look so dreary, and there were even wide patches of deep green interspersed among the ribbons of road and gray blocks of industry.

Flashes of white reflected off the sea in the Bay of Baku. The long promenade that ran along the sea was clearly visible and, using the promenade as a landmark, Mark was able to pinpoint where his apartment building must be. As the plane descended, he saw cars moving along the highway and it suddenly struck him that none of what had happened since the night he was brought to Gobustan Prison was really relevant to the lives of the vast majority of the people below. If the United States and Iran wanted to claw each other to death, what did they care? Even if the Azeri's crown jewel, the BTC pipeline, were to be rendered obsolete, the average person wouldn't be affected much. Despite a state oil fund that had been set up to combat corruption, most of the money was going to the government elite anyway.

Two black Mercedes were waiting for Mark on the tarmac when the plane touched down, the result of a series of calls he'd made while airborne.

He was driven through downtown Baku, with Amato and Decker trailing in the second car, and then up through the Yasamal Slopes section of town, past modest apartment buildings and houses that predated the Soviet period. Just past the green-domed Taza Pir Mosque, in the shadow of one of its minarets, the car stopped.

The streets were crowded with worshippers who had just finished the morning *Fajr* prayer.

A long black Jeep Commander with dark windows pulled up next to the Mercedes.

"Get out," said Mark's driver.

Mark did so and then looked behind him. The car that was supposed to have followed with Amato and Decker was nowhere to be seen. A rear door opened on the Jeep Commander. Mark climbed inside.

Orkhan Gambar wore a dark blue suit with pinstripes and smelled of aftershave. The air conditioner was going full blast and it was excessively cold. "Welcome back to Baku," Orkhan said, frowning, in a tone that Mark sensed was faintly hostile.

"I know who killed Campbell."

He told Orkhan everything, or nearly so.

Orkhan never questioned the truth of the story. Nor did he seem particularly surprised. Violent plots, gross deception…that was just the way the world worked.

"Of course, even if this coup in Iran was to succeed, Aryanpur would never give up Iran's nuclear weapons, any more than Khorasani will," said Orkhan.

"Of course not. Ellis and everyone else at the NSC are deluding themselves."

Iran was sitting on the world's fourth-largest reserves of oil in an unfriendly locale. The United States was at their door in Iraq and Afghanistan, and Russia to the north was always a worry. Aryanpur would want the weapons for the same reason Khorasani and the Iranian people did—for protection, pride, and power. To really get rid of the weapons you had to address those issues. Which deposing Khorasani wouldn't do.

Eventually Mark came around to explaining what had happened to Daria, and that she was being held prisoner in Azeri waters.

Orkhan said, "If what you say is true, then we will evict the Iranians. They have no right to station armed forces at Neft Dashlari. As for your compatriot, I grieve for her."

"I didn't come to you looking for sympathy. I came for help."

"Then I fear you will leave disappointed."

"I was hired by the CIA to find out who killed Campbell and took out our station in Baku. I found out. And on the flight from Paris, I told my former division chief what I just told you. Bottom line is that the CIA got slaughtered because of something our National Security Council cooked up with Aryanpur. The CIA won't take that lying down. They certainly won't let Aryanpur seize power. He's toast."

"Toast?"

"Finished. As good as dead. I guarantee you the Agency will try to shut down the phony attack on the USS *Reagan*. But even if it goes off you can be damn sure they'll find a way to fix it so that Aryanpur never gets his chance to rule Iran. They'll expose his ties to the National Security Council and once that happens, the Iranians will kill him themselves. There's nothing either you or I can do about it. But meanwhile, Aryanpur's still operating in Azerbaijan, right under your nose. Which means you're backing the loser in this game and it will come back to bite you."

"We are backing no one."

"Aryanpur is running his operation from somewhere on Neft Dashlari. In Azeri waters. People will conclude that you are backing him whether you are or not. I'm doing you a favor by helping you to pinpoint his base. Instead of having an international incident explode under your nose, you can get ahead of the game, take out Aryanpur's men yourself, and then sell all the intel you collect back to the Americans. Not a bad deal for you."

"And you expect what, in return for this…favor?" A mean, but not entirely unfriendly, smile formed on Orkhan's face.

Mark told him.

Orkhan appeared deep in thought. After a time he said, "Go back to your car. I need to speak with Aliyev."

77

The aging Russian Mi-2 charter helicopter that transported Mark and Amato to Neft Dashlari was piloted by an Azeri Air Force captain who wore Levi's jeans and a T-shirt that said *San Francisco Sucks.*

The two Azeris crewing the helicopter were also dressed like Americans; both were armed with M16 rifles.

Amato was wearing the same suit he'd had on since leaving Washington. He'd combed his wild gray hair, but his five o'clock shadow had grown into a stubbly beard. Around his waist he'd strapped a military belt with a large Glock semiautomatic pistol. He was a big man, and the juxtaposition of the gun and the business suit and the unshaven face made him look more than a little unhinged—and dangerous.

They flew east, screaming along the coast to the end of the Absheron Peninsula, and then over open water for another thirty miles until Neft Dashlari came into view. From the air it looked like a giant mutant spider, with a central mass of buildings surrounded by a vast snarl of stilt roads that led to oil derricks. Even from the air, Mark couldn't see the eastern end of it.

The helicopter banked right and for five minutes followed a derelict stilt road that occasionally dipped below the shallow water. They shot past a few dilapidated industrial buildings, some on stilts, some on small landfill islands. But then they hit a section where the road had been repaired and there were a few bright new buildings clad in yellow-painted steel and emblazoned with the names of oil companies Mark didn't recognize.

The sky was overcast and threatening rain.

Amato held a GPS locater in his hand. "We're close!" He had to shout to be heard above the roar of the rotors.

Mark turned his back to Amato and allowed himself to be handcuffed.

Minutes later, a floating helipad came into view. A large white circle surrounding a yellow bull's-eye had been painted on the black rubber surface.

Mark reminded the pilot not to even touch down and the pilot flashed him a thumbs-up. A small guard shack sat in one corner of the landing pad. A man emerged from it and shot off a single flair.

"Good to go!" said Amato.

As the helicopter hovered a few feet above the landing platform, Amato grabbed Mark by his shirt collar, raised him to a standing position, and shoved him out the bay door. With his hands secured behind his back, Mark couldn't steady himself. So when he stumbled onto the landing pad he fell on his face.

For a moment the roar of the helicopter was deafening and the wind intense. But soon the noise died down to a point where Mark could hear the lonely sound of the sea lapping up against the floating platform. He felt the butt of Amato's gun on the back of his neck.

A second man emerged from the guard shack. Both he and the first carried AK-47s and were dressed like soldiers, but with no indentifying marks on their uniforms.

Amato spoke to them sharply in Farsi. One of them raised what appeared to be a digital camcorder. He focused on Amato's face, and then Mark's. Not long after, the soldier with the camera received a call on his radio. Mark understood enough to realize that he and Amato had been positively identified.

He was led to the little guard shack where they stripped him naked, cutting away his shirt because of the handcuffs. They searched every pocket and inch of fabric. Then one of the men cold-cocked him on the side of his head. Mark thought he blacked out for a moment.

"Open your mouth!" ordered one of the soldiers.

His body was searched. When they were satisfied that he wasn't hiding any physical paraphernalia, they dragged him back out onto the helipad.

Blood from Mark's nose ran in small rivulets down his chest. His nakedness, and the rough wet rubber of the helipad beneath his bare feet, made him feel vulnerable and defenseless.

The Iranians spoke to Amato in Farsi and pointed to a flat-bottomed inflatable boat that was tied to the edge of the helipad.

"Get in," said Amato. He gave Mark a push. At that point the Iranian soldiers stepped up, grabbed Mark by each of his arms, dragged him to the boat, then shoved him forward so that once again he fell flat on his face. Someone threw a blanket over him. The two Iranians climbed in the boat.

"Stay down," said Amato.

Mark turned his head so that his left eye could see through a slit in the blanket. They motored quickly along a route that took them under several stilt roads and then followed a newer road along which men were working and derricks were actually pumping. Little patches of oil floated all over the water. He saw a white van driving along one of the stilt roads.

After a while one of the Iranians kicked him in the gut and pulled the blanket completely over his head so that he couldn't see anything. When the boat finally came to a stop, and the blanket was pulled away again, Mark found himself looking at a dismal concrete-block Soviet-era building that measured about a hundred feet long and was surrounded by water. The small scrap of landfill on which it sat had been reclaimed by the rising Caspian, leaving the ground floor about two feet under water. The stilt road which used to provide access to the building had fallen into the sea, leaving behind only a few rotting posts.

In the distance, maybe a quarter mile away, Mark saw the vague shape of a newer lime-green building with a shiny silver roof.

One of the Iranian soldiers tied the boat to a rusted metal stanchion, then waded in knee-deep water to a door. A new soldier emerged from inside the building and a frantic conversation about where to take Mark ensued.

"Stand up." Amato jammed the butt of his pistol into the back of Mark's neck. "Get out of the boat."

Mark stepped into the water. It was warm and smelled of oil. Beneath his bare feet lay an algae-covered concrete staircase. He slipped a bit before righting himself.

Upon entering the building he saw two Iranian soldiers, one of whom punched him in the gut before dragging him down a hallway.

He imagined he was back in Baku, in his apartment, on his balcony. The sun was setting. It was warm. Pain was just an illusory sensation that his mind could shut down if it needed to, he told himself. Put it aside.

The soldiers took him to a cramped room—an old dorm, Mark thought—with a bare minimum of space for the two Soviet laborers who would have been crammed into it back in the day. After hitting him again, the Iranians secured his hands to a bolt on the floor. Because his hands were cuffed behind his back it was a struggle to keep his head above the two feet of water sloshing about in the room. Eventually he realized that if he just took a deep breath, and then relaxed and let himself slip fully under until he needed to take another breath, he'd be better off.

Oily water slipped into his ears. The muffled sounds echoing throughout the building had an unreal and distorted quality to them. He heard a door slamming and what could have been more yelling. But no sounds of motorboats or gunfire, which is what he was hoping to hear. He wondered whether he'd pushed his luck too far this time, and whether Amato had even activated the GPS signaling device on his phone.

He wondered whether he'd been foolish to have trusted Amato.

78

After a while, Mark was brought to a larger room, the old cafeteria he guessed. In it were four soldiers, an older-looking Iranian, and Amato. Everyone stood in knee-deep water.

Amato looked crazy.

His jaw was closed, his chin was jutting out, his nostrils were flared like a bull's, and he seemed to have grown a few inches taller. This wasn't a man feigning anger, thought Mark. This was a man on the verge of exploding.

A second later, he saw why.

Mark had been prepared to see Daria in a bad way. And he'd thought that his own brushes over the years with intense brutality had dulled his ability to be deeply affected by such depths of depravity.

But he'd been wrong.

Seeing her there, tucked away in a corner, drug-addled and shivering, stripped and beaten and broken, abandoned like a piece of garbage that had floated in with the sea, cut him more that he had thought he was capable of being cut.

He forced himself to stare at her for a moment. Her eyes were glassy and fixed on the motion of the water below her. She gave no acknowledgment that she'd seen him.

"Daria!" he said.

Someone hit him and he fell to his knees. She still didn't look up. "Daria!" he called again.

This time one of the Iranians jammed his head under the water until he began to choke. When he was released, he heard Amato talking to the older Iranian, the interrogator, a man of average height with an angular face, a bony nose, and a trim black beard. They were arguing in Farsi about how to conduct the interrogation. It was just Amato stalling for time, Mark knew.

After a little more back-and-forth the Iranian interrogator shrugged and ordered that Mark be tied flat on his back to a bench, the top of which rested an inch below the surface of the water. He ordered that Daria be similarly restrained on an identical bench.

"Hold on, Daria. You're going to be OK," Mark called out as they strapped him down. He had no idea whether this was true, or whether, given the state she was in, it would be possible for her to ever be OK again.

After his outburst, one of the Iranians kicked Mark in the side. A few of his ribs cracked. If Daria had heard his words of encouragement, she gave no indication.

Amato appeared above him and demanded to know who he'd told about the stolen uranium.

Mark detected a note of hesitation in Amato's voice. And asking about the uranium straight away pegged him as someone unfamiliar with interrogation techniques.

"What you tell me will be matched against what she's already—" Amato turned away from Mark. "What the hell are you doing!"

Mark raised his head. The bench to which Daria had been strapped had been turned on its side by one of the soldiers. Daria's legs were kicking underwater.

"Answer the question." The Iranian interrogator spoke to Mark in clear, calm British-accented English. "When you do, we'll let her breathe."

"One person," said Mark. "John Decker is his name. For Christ's sake, let her up."

"Tell me about this John Decker."

"He's a former SEAL, I worked with him in Baku."

"Where is he now?"

"He's dead, killed in France."

"I'll need to know more than that."

"He's an independent contractor, I hired him to help me. Let her up! I'm not telling you anything else until you let her breathe."

"She's no good to us if you kill her!" bellowed Amato.

The interrogator gave Amato a questioning look. "Very well," he said.

The bench to which Daria was strapped was righted. She coughed up water and gasped for air. Mark listened to her desperately trying to breathe. At least she was still trying, he thought.

Directly above him, Mark saw Amato's face and was afraid the man might do something rash. Four armed soldiers stood in the room. There was no way Amato could take them all on at once. But he clearly wasn't capable of completely concealing his concern for Daria.

Next it was Daria's turn to be questioned and Mark's turn to be held underwater. He couldn't hear what she said, which was the point. It was a violent twist on the classic interrogation tactic of going back and forth between two people in separate rooms, playing one off the other and comparing information. He was under for a long time, but instead of struggling he tried to distance himself from the pain by envisioning his raging need for oxygen as something that was a removable part of himself, a desire that he could calmly exhale out and let float away on the water.

After a couple of minutes he pissed himself, and then he passed out. He woke up to one of the Iranian soldiers punching his stomach.

Amato said, "You shared information about the uranium with people you trusted in Dubai, as a backup in case one of you was ever captured. What are their names?"

Mark tried to think the way Daria was thinking, but it was hard for him to think at all given the intense, mind-numbing pain he felt in his gut and chest. He wondered whether one of his broken ribs had punctured a lung.

Had she given them Bowlan's name? Or had she just made up names? Mark didn't want to mention Bowlan.

He made up two names.

"Wrong answer," said the Iranian interrogator.

Daria was held under for a long, long time. And then, after Mark gave them Bowlan's name, it was his turn again. And then Daria's...

Mark was beginning to lose hope when he heard the sound of gunshots coming from outside the building.

79

One of the soldiers in the interrogation room received a call on his radio. As he held the handset to his ear the staccato bursts of gunfire outside grew louder. After a moment he clipped the radio back to his belt and ran out with two other soldiers following on his heels. One soldier stayed behind with the Iranian interrogator. Daria and Mark were left strapped to the benches.

Amato faced the interrogator. "What's happening?"

The dispassionate calm the interrogator had projected during the interrogation was gone. Now he looked a little frightened. "I don't know."

Amato pulled out his pistol and turned to face the hallway, as though preparing to fend off an armed assault. The interrogator had drawn a pistol as well. "How many men do we have in the building?" Amato asked.

The interrogator looked unsure of whether to answer. "Eight, I think, maybe ten more nearby."

Amato gestured to the remaining Iranian soldier, who was pointing his assault rifle at Daria and Mark. "Tell him to cover the back hall. You guard the prisoners. I'll cover the front exit."

The interrogator hesitated but then issued the order. As soon as the soldier with the assault rifle turned his back, Amato raised his gun and shot him in the head. A half second later, he shot the interrogator in the face.

Amato bound over to the interrogator and fired one more shot, at close range, directly into the man's forehead. He did the same to the downed Iranian soldier and then holstered his pistol and raced over to Daria. Without saying a word he worked frantically to release her restraints.

Some of the buckles were under the bench and hard to release. Amato briefly ducked his head beneath the water.

Mark heard more shots from outside, and screams. He kept one eye on the two exits leading out from the room and one eye on Daria.

Amato finally got her free. His suit was sagging on his bulky frame and the fat around his gut was visible where his dress shirt was plastered to his skin. "Follow me," he said to her.

She just lay there, so he began to raise her up.

What happened next flashed by so quickly that Mark, who was still trying to watch the exits, barely saw it from the corner of his eye.

One second Daria was deadweight, and the next she'd slammed her knee into Amato's crotch and was going for his gun. Amato barely caught her hand as she tried to yank the gun out of its holster.

"For the love of God, girl, I'm—"

At that moment an Iranian soldier with an AK-47 appeared. The compound was under assault, he roared, and orders had been given to execute the prisoners and evacuate. With the butt of his AK-47 pressed to his shoulder and his finger on the trigger, he ordered Amato to step back.

Instead Amato wrenched his pistol from Daria's hands and placed his body between her and the Iranian.

Three bullets ripped through Amato's chest. He kept standing long enough, however, to fire off a single shot in return.

80

As he slumped to his knees, Colonel Henry Amato's mind flashed back to a moment in time over thirty years ago, in downtown Tehran. He was on Taleqani Avenue, just outside the US embassy. A black Volkswagen Beetle with a dented fender screeched to a stop a few feet in front of him. An old woman in a black chador slipped out. She had leathery, sunbaked skin and a dowager's hump.

"Mr. Simpson! Mr. Simpson!"

He kept walking at a fast clip, as though he hadn't heard, but the old woman was nimble and managed to glide directly in front of him on the crowded street. As she walked backward, keeping step with him, she opened her robe to reveal a little girl swaddled tightly in a green blanket.

The image in Amato's mind was clearer now than it had been that day.

He'd only glanced at the baby for a moment, just long enough to look into her miniature brown eyes and notice the little wisps of dark hair poking out from underneath a white knitted cap trimmed in pink. But in the decades that followed he'd tried to re-create those eyes and every other detail of that day, as if by doing so he could somehow go back and change what had happened.

Because not taking his daughter in his arms that day, not caring for her and loving her when she'd needed him most, had been the biggest mistake of his life.

"You know who she is!" called the old woman. "You must take her, take her to America!"

She followed him all the way down the street, calling out to him again and again, trying to thrust the child into his arms, until he ducked into a cab and slammed the door in her face.

With one hand the woman held the baby girl and with the other she banged on the back window of the cab. "Cursed are those who hold back the small kindness! If you cannot care for her, find her a home! Take her I say! Her mother is dead!"

Cursed are those who hold back the small kindness…

It was as if the old neighbor woman was still yelling those words in his ear.

Minutes later she'd dropped the baby girl into the hands of a dumbfounded embassy worker, insisting that he—that the American government!—force Derek Simpson to take responsibility for the life he'd helped create.

He never had.

Amato opened his eyes and saw bleak concrete walls and dirty water. He suddenly realized he was going to die in this hellhole, within seconds. To have even a chance at salvation he needed to ask God for forgiveness. Now, for what he had done to his daughter—it was a mortal sin—and across all these long years it had gone unconfessed.

Then he looked at Daria standing above him. Her eyes were glassy and unfocused. But they were the same eyes he had seen all those years ago.

"Save her!" he called out, pleading to his God not for his own salvation but for hers.

His voice came out as a gurgled, inaudible whisper.

"Save her!"

81

Amato wobbled on his knees in front of Daria, looking old and sad and beaten. The Iranian soldier he'd shot in the chest collapsed against the far wall.

Daria was shaking, a thin reed, looking as though the energy she'd just expended fighting Amato was the last ounce she'd had in her. Her eyes, heavy-lidded, slowly scanned the room.

More gunshots erupted from another part of the building. Amato crumpled into himself and then his head dipped underwater.

"Daria," said Mark. "I'm over here."

She turned and made eye contact with him for the first time.

"We're getting out of here," he said.

Daria approached. She was shaky on her feet and her right arm was deformed. Mark had the sense that a light breeze would blow her away. Her face, and the damage that had been done to it, filled him with a sense of blinding despair.

"Can you untie me?" he asked.

Daria nodded, but then she didn't move. Whether it was drugs or trauma or some combination of the two, she was hanging onto consciousness by a thread.

"You can do this," he said.

Daria looked at him again and Mark nodded at her. "We're almost home."

She walked a few steps, knelt down in the water next to him, and then tried to release the straps that bound him. But she was incapable of loosening the buckles with her left hand alone and when she tried to use her right, her face contorted into a look that was part anguish, part exhaustion. Her fingers wouldn't move, the arm was too broken.

"I can't," she whispered, "I can't…"

Mark felt her good hand brush up next to his bound wrists, beneath the bench. He took her hand between his palms and said, "Stop trying."

Daria let her head rest on his chest. He could feel the warmth of her cheek on his bare skin.

A minute passed. In the hallway gunshots rang out and then a voice. "Mark! Are you there! Mark!"

"I've got her!"

Seconds later John Decker appeared, dressed in full battle gear and gripping a machine gun.

"Oh man," he said as soon as he saw them. At first Mark thought Decker was reacting to what had been done to Daria, but then he realized that Daria's face was turned and that Decker was really looking at him.

"I'm OK," said Mark. "She's not."

Daria didn't move while Decker untied him. Her head was still on his chest, her eyes closed. Decker was about to lift her to his shoulder but Mark said, "I'll take her. You guide us out. Give me your pistol."

Decker unholstered the 9mm Glock at his waist and handed it over butt-first. Mark sat up with Daria and fired twice into the chest of the Iranian soldier that Amato had shot, having noticed the man was still breathing.

"Let's blow, boss, we got a boat outside."

Mark carried Daria in his arms as he slogged through the water after Decker. Near the exit they passed the bodies of several fallen Iranians who were bleeding into the dirty water, tinting it red.

Outside it had started to rain. Mark blinked for a moment before he saw the seven unmarked Soviet-era landing craft—the same kind of old boats that regularly delivered supplies to the outposts on Neft Dashlari. Azeri soldiers were wading in the water and standing on the boats and guarding the nearby stilt roads.

Mark staggered toward the closest boat, still carrying Daria, and collapsed in the back.

EPILOGUE
Baku, Two Weeks Later

Mark glanced into his spare bedroom. Daria lay sleeping beneath yellow cotton sheets. On a table next to the bed, in a clear vase, stood a tall bouquet of white gladioli. It was eight in the morning. Rays of bright sunlight slipped through gaps in the window curtains.

They'd arrived at his apartment the day before, after having spent the past week in hiding at a house north of Baku, guarded round the clock by Orkhan's men. Western-educated doctors had tended to Daria's recovery, including a plastic surgeon and orthopedist that Mark had arranged to have secretly flown in from Paris. Which, to his dismay, had taken care of the rest of his CIA money and then some.

As she healed, Mark had focused on confirming his theory that Colonel Henry Amato had been Daria's birth father.

His first step had been to threaten to go public with what he knew about what Amato and Ellis had been up to. In exchange for keeping his mouth shut, the director of national intelligence had allowed him access to all of Colonel Amato's records.

Whereupon Mark learned that Amato had never even been CIA.

He'd started his career as an infantry grunt in Vietnam, had switched over to Army Intelligence after the war, and in the late 1970s had been assigned to an intelligence unit in Tehran commanded by Jack Campbell. His mission had been to infiltrate a prominent Iranian family with ties to the National Front, a group opposed to Khomeini's Islamic revolution. Evidently the way Amato had tried to infiltrate this family had been by developing a relationship with the twenty-five-year-old daughter of the family patriarch.

The same file had revealed that many years later, while Amato had been working on a sensitive project for the Defense Department, he'd been questioned by internal investigators about large sums of money that had been transferred out of his personal account. He'd quickly been cleared, however, when he'd provided proof that the money had been used to pay for multiple, but ultimately unsuccessful, in vitro fertilization attempts for his wife.

⬡

Mark's cell phone rang. He walked out to his balcony before answering and sat down on the plastic lounge chair in front of his dead tomato plants.

"Hey," said Decker. "She good?"

"Yeah. Still sleeping."

The CIA now knew about Daria's relationship to the MEK. Records recovered at Neft Dashlari had incriminated her, as had files on Ellis's computer. She wouldn't be prosecuted—Mark still had enough leverage with the Agency to prevent that from happening—but she'd be recalled and fired as soon as she recovered.

Mark wasn't looking forward to telling her the news. Nor was he looking forward to telling her the truth about her father. He'd have to come clean about everything soon, though. Last night she'd started asking questions.

"You?"

"Never better," said Mark, which wasn't a complete lie.

He was alive. Daria was alive. And Nika was safely back in Baku as of yesterday, although Mark doubted she'd ever want to see him again.

As for the rest of it, there'd been no bungled attack on the USS *Ronald Reagan*, and no coup in Iran. Two days ago Mark had read that Aryanpur had suffered a massive heart attack and had died peacefully in his sleep.

Which told him that the CIA had delivered evidence of Aryanpur's treason to the right people in Iran.

"By the way," said Mark. "I got your general discharge upgraded to honorable."

"No shit!"

"Funny how quick things can happen when you threaten to go public with intel the government wants to keep secret."

"Thanks, boss."

"No worries."

"Really, I mean it. That's awesome."

"Will you go back to the States?"

"No can do. I've got a job coming up next week. Actually, that's why I'm calling. Thought you might be interested in teaming up again."

"I already got a job, Deck."

"This one's in Uzbekistan."

"You got your discharge upgraded. What do you need another contractor job for? You can get a real job."

"We'd be working for CAIN, it's a—"

"Spies-for-hire outfit. I know the guy who runs it."

"I figured you did."

"He's an asshole."

"Didn't you used to work with him?"

"Yeah, that's how I know he's an asshole."

"He'd just be subbing the work to us. The real job would be a security detail for some dudes from Oklahoma with cash to burn. They're checking out a couple spots for oil platforms in the Aral Sea. One week, in and out."

Mark had been surprised at first at how well Decker had handled the aftermath of the assault on Neft Dashlari. The act of killing five men hadn't seemed to bother him—Decker had said he'd followed his own rules of engagement, and that was what was important. He was fired at and he fired back. End of story.

Mark, by contrast, had been having nightmares. He'd been fine when moving at light speed, just trying to survive. But when he stopped to think, everything came at him. He kept telling himself that it was pointless to dwell too much on it, but he did anyway.

"No thanks."

"It'll be a cake walk, and good cash."

"Classes at the university start in three weeks. And I told Orkhan I'd start helping his kid with the SAT." And on top of that he was going to make himself finish his book on Soviet influence in Azerbaijan...It was time to get on with the business of building a life outside of the CIA or he'd just slip back into his old ways.

"I'll go fifty-fifty with you. We don't have to be there for two weeks."

For a fleeting second Mark considered it. He was close to broke, teaching paid squat, and nightmares or not Uzbekistan probably would be a cake walk because the place was dirt poor and unbelievably corrupt—even more corrupt than Azerbaijan, which was saying something. A few dollars placed in the right hands could buy a lot of information in Uzbekistan.

He saw himself getting plastered on rounds of vodka shots in a seedy bar in Tashkent, making bad toasts to the health of some Soviet-era bureaucrat he'd bribe by the end of the night. In and out in a week could work, he thought. For ten, no, fifteen grand—he wouldn't take a dime less. He'd spent over twenty years slumming around grimy underworlds, and yes, there was a meanness to them that was corrupting to him and everyone else who set foot inside, but what was one more week?

Then he pictured Daria. Her right arm had been snapped in two. Her jaw was still wired shut. The cuts on her face were still raw. That woman had been beat to hell inside and out.

"I've got other plans," he said.

ACKNOWLEDGMENTS

I am indebted to the people in Azerbaijan and Iran who treated me with such hospitality and kindness; to Richard Curtis, my outstanding agent; to Christina Henry de Tessan for her skill as an editor; to Andy Bartlett at Amazon for reading my book the way I was hoping it would be read; to my wife, Corinne, and my children, Kirsten and William, for all the love and good times; and to my friends and extended family for their unfailing encouragement.

I would also like to thank the many reporters, scholars, and ex-CIA officers who, through their books, lent insight to this novel. An annotated bibliography can be found at DanMayland. com.

ABOUT THE Author

Dan Mayland spent years exploring the outer limits of Western civilization and beyond. He has slept on the streets of Europe, summited mountains in Colombia and Bolivia, trekked through Bhutan and Nepal, visited remote Buddhist monasteries in India, and explored Shiite mosques in Iran and Azerbaijan. An international news and foreign policy junkie, Mayland is an avid reader of Stratfor.com, AlJazeera.com, ForeignPolicy.com, Ettelaat. com, and Rferl.com, and he has written articles for Iranian.com. Mayland's first book, *The Colonel's Mistake*, is the inaugural novel of the Mark Sava series.

Made in the USA
Charleston, SC
16 September 2012